DANGEROUS THREADS

DANGEROUS THREADS

A Virginia Davies Quilt Mystery
Book One

By
David Ciambrone

Names, characters, businesses, places, events, and incidents are either the products of the author's imagination or used in a fictitious manner. Any resemblance to actual persons, living or dead, or actual events, is purely coincidental.

No part of this publication may be reproduced, stored in a retrieval system, or transmitted in any form or by any means, electronic, mechanical, photocopying, recording, or otherwise, without the written permission of the publisher.

Text Copyright © 2022 David Ciambrone

All rights reserved.
Published 2022 by Progressive Rising Phoenix Press, LLC
www.progressiverisingphoenix.com

ISBN: 978-1-958640-07-4

Printed in the U.S.A.

Book and Cover design by William Speir
Visit: http://www.williamspeir.com

This title was originally published by
White Bird Publications
ISBN: 978-1-63363-009-3
LCCN: 2014946990

ACKNOWLEDGMENTS

It is said that writing is a solitary affair. This statement is mostly true. But any author will tell you their writing depends on a host of others who have provided needed information, ideas, inspiration, critiques and just plain support when we needed it. To this end, I'd like to thank the following people and groups for their support in bringing this book to life.

The Williamson County Coroners critique group for their sound critiques and support.

The Smithsonian National Museum of American History Textile Collection in the Division of Home and Community Life, for answering a multitude of questions.

My publisher, Amanda M. Thrasher, at Progressive Rising Phoenix Press, LLC.

My wife Kathy for her support and, as a quilter, it was her idea to use the 1933 World's Fair Quilt as the basis for this book.

Mrs. Joan Howes of the Chisholm Trail Quilt Guild for telling my wife about the mystery quilt, The Unknown Star.

The nice members of the Chisholm Trail Quilt Guild who made me an honorary member.

The U.S. Marshal Service for information about their authority and activities.

Roland Waits, Assistant Chief of Police of Georgetown, Texas for his support and information on police procedures. Even though I took a lot of liberties, they are not his fault, but mine.

CHAPTER 1

Virginia Davies-Clark tucked a strand of blonde hair behind her ear as she bounded down a carpeted, yellow-walled hallway with various pictures of geologic formations, Native American baskets, a cork bulletin board with various flyers from museums and universities, toward her office at the San Gabriel Museum in Georgetown, Texas. The budget meeting was hell and she was glad it was over. She smiled and nodded a greeting at a high school intern as she walked.

Virginia opened her door, strolled to her desk, and tossed the pile of documents on the top. Some papers slid off onto the floor. *Damn budget meetings. Those blasted accountants are going to drive me to drink. Where the hell am I going to get ten thousand dollars for the new quilt exhibit? Maybe I'll feed the accountants to the scientists and taxidermists. That would make an interesting exhibit—accountantosaurus.* She chuckled at her joke.

Virginia took off her red jacket and hung it on a hanger behind her office door. She picked up the papers from the floor and put them on the table. She crossed her office and sat in her high-backed leather chair behind her large wooden desk jumbled with papers, notepads, books, and pictures. Leaning back and placing her hands behind her head, she looked around the office at the photographs of places she had been scuba diving, awards, certificates, and a small quilt she had made hanging on her walls. A cluttered bookcase sat next to the door. Held in place by small magnets on her whiteboard was a target, with her name on the bottom. It had bullet holes in a tight cluster in the center.

She lowered her arms, smoothed her short blue skirt, and looked at the photograph of her and her husband Andy at a manor house in Scotland a couple years ago when they were engaged. She smiled. *It seems like yesterday. I was a twenty-six-year-old grad student when I met Andy at UCI. Now, six years later we're married, even though he usually catches the brunt of my escapades.*

A bright pink Post-it® note on her computer monitor from her secretary caught her attention. She leaned forward and looked at it.

> Dr. John Montgomery of the U.S. Government needs to see you on a matter of national security. Or so he says. Phone number (512) 555-2185.

A matter of national security? What does that have to do with the museum? Who's John Montgomery and which agency is he with? She was staring at the note when the phone rang. *Now what?*

"Hello?" Virginia answered.

"Mrs. Davies-Clark?" a man's deep voice asked.

"Yes, this is Virginia. How may I help you?"

"Mrs. Clark, my name is Dr. John Montgomery. I'm with the Textile Collection in the Division of Home and Community Life, National Museum of American History in Washington, D.C., and I need to see you as quickly as possible."

Virginia looked at the phone. "The National Museum of American History? I just got a note that you called. What can I do for you? I take it you're in the area."

"Yes, Ma'am, I could be at your office in ten minutes or at a later time if that would be more convenient, and I'd like your museum director to be there, too. That's Dr. Fred Doverspike, isn't it?"

"Yes, it is. May I ask what this is about?"

"A lost quilt that has become a national security issue."

Virginia frowned. *Is this a crank call? What do national security issues have to do with the Smithsonian? A quilt? This better be good.* "Yeah, ten minutes. I'll see if Dr. Doverspike is available on such short notice. Do you want me to call you back in case he isn't?"

"Among other things, I will be discussing some sizable grants to your museum for your help. Will that help get his immediate attention?"

Does the sun rise in the east? "Do you need directions?"

"No. I'm at the Georgetown police station, just a few blocks from you. I'll see you then. Thank you and Dr. Doverspike for seeing me on such short notice. Your museum will be well compensated for your time." He hung up.

Well compensated for my time? This is getting interesting. Virginia called her boss.

"Dr. Fred Doverspike's office," said his secretary into the phone.

"Hi Sue. This is Virginia. I need to talk to Fred right away. It's important. He's in his office, isn't he?"

"Hello, Virginia. Yes, he's in. He said not to disturb him after that budget meeting this morning. He isn't in a good mood."

"I guessed that from our meeting. This has to do with possibly more funding."

"I'll get him." Virginia heard elevator music as she waited.

"Virginia." Fred Doverspike's voice was tense. "I hope that meeting didn't upset you too much."

"No. Not any more than the others." She relaxed. He treated her like a daughter, and everyone at the museum knew it. He kept a scrapbook-journal of her adventures, a copy of the one Dr. Smithe, her old boss in California, started. "But that's not why I called. I got a call from someone from the Smithsonian, and he wants to talk to both of us in ten minutes. Something about national security and providing us some grants. Can you be available in the main conference room in ten?"

"He mentioned possible funding?"

Virginia silently chuckled. *Hint about a grant or money and I can get his attention in a nanosecond.* "Yes, that's what he said."

"Well, when he gets here, let's not keep him waiting. Any idea what he wants?"

"No. But it did sound both interesting and confusing."

"Yes, well, let's give the gentleman a chance to talk. I'll see you shortly."

In precisely ten minutes, the receptionist called and escorted Dr. John Montgomery to the brightly painted main conference room.

Virginia looked at the tall, lanky man. She judged him to be about six feet five and in his late forties. His brown sport coat had the requisite elbow patches, and his old leather briefcase had years of scars. His black hair needed a trim. He removed his coat and draped it over a chair against the wall.

After some pleasant introductions, Montgomery handed Dr. Doverspike and Virginia his card. "The Smithsonian Institute and the government need your help." He pulled out a chair and sat at the polished, wooden conference table that was surrounded by eight leather chairs that sat in the middle of the room. He placed his briefcase on the chair next to him. A smaller table was on the far wall with a phone and phone book. To the side was a table with a computer interface panel. Suspended from the ceiling was a projector. On the wall at the end of the table was a viewing screen.

Virginia and Dr. Doverspike sat across from him. She leaned forward. "You said this was a matter of national security. If that's the case, why are you here? Why not Homeland Security or the FBI, or CIA, or some other alphabet soup organization? And museums are not usually involved in national security issues."

"I'll get to that. But let me say, for now, that the United States Government needs your help and you are uniquely qualified to assist us."

"Just how is Virginia uniquely qualified and how does this… whatever this is… affect our museum?" Doverspike asked.

Virginia watched Dr. Doverspike as he folded his hands in front of him on the table. His charcoal suit, crisp white shirt and red and blue regimental tie were impeccable, and his gray hair was styled. *Mention money and he really gets in the business mode.*

She turned her attention to Montgomery. "And, how is the Smithsonian involved with national security?"

"Virginia... may I call you Virginia?" She nodded.

"Well, first let me answer Dr. Doverspike's question. As I'm sure you know, Virginia is already a trained special consultant and reserve field agent with the Smithsonian Central Security Service. That, coupled with the fact she is a historian and a good quilter. The quilter part of her background makes her uniquely qualified for this mission. I believe you're a member of a couple of quilt guilds as well."

"Yeah. I'm a member of the Chisholm Trail Quilt Guild and the Main Street Quilt Guild." Virginia looked at Dr. Doverspike then at Montgomery. "I get the part about being a special agent... kinda... I'm a special consultant for when they need me. But how does being a historian and a quilter play into this? Don't forget, I have a job here at the museum I'm supposed to be doing. And again, why is the Smithsonian involved with national security?"

Montgomery nodded. "Yes. Well, let's talk first about your museum's benefit for you help us."

Fred sat up straighter. Virginia frowned.

"The government will pay all your salary, insurance, and overhead costs, plus give the museum ten thousand dollars a week while you are working for us. We'll cover all expenses you incur, like the last time, and pay you a tax-free stipend of four hundred dollars a day while you are helping us."

There goes my accountantosaurus exhibit. Virginia raised an eyebrow. "What exactly would I have to do for all this good will? There is no such thing as a free lunch."

"Let me answer that in a minute."

Virginia started to speak when Montgomery reached into his briefcase and withdrew a file, opened it, and set it on the table. "Do you know anything about the 1933 World's Fair in Chicago?"

Dr. Doverspike took a breath. "A little. During the height of our country's worst economic depression, the city leaders of Chicago decided to host an exhibition called the Century of Progress. During the fair, Sears Roebuck and Company® sponsored the largest quilt contest in history. Almost twenty-five thousand women jumped at the chance to win over one thousand dollars in prize money."

Virginia wet her lips. "A lot of quilters know about that quilt. The thousand dollar prize was in nineteen-thirty-three dollars—that's equivalent to about twenty thousand dollars today. The winning quilt was called *The Un-*

known Star and was entered by Margaret Rogers Caden of Kentucky. There is some controversy about that. It was later presented to the wife of the President of the United States, Mrs. Roosevelt. I believe the quilt was lost after that."

Fred Doverspike took out his pipe, giving Virginia a forlorn look. Virginia's frowning face made him put it back in his coat pocket. He looked at Montgomery and lifted one shoulder in a semblance of a shrug, then asked, "What does that have to do with us? How has this quilt, after almost seventy years, become a national security problem?"

"Well, it looks like I've got the right people for the job. But to answer your question, I'll first ask another. Have you ever heard of the unified field theory?"

Virginia fidgeted in her chair. "What does that have to do with the missing quilt?"

"I'm getting there. Please... just a couple minutes and everything will be clear," Montgomery said.

Dr. Doverspike shook his head.

"Yes." Virginia nodded as she straightened up. "My husband is an engineering professor at the University of Texas and he mentioned it. It is the theory in physics that ties all the other theories like relativity, quantum mechanics, and gravity together into an overall uniform theory of time, matter, and energy. Only they can't seem to find it. There is, at present, no one theory that explains everything. Even Einstein couldn't do it."

Montgomery nodded. "Very good. But that now appears to be slightly wrong. We recently discovered some old documents that imply Dr. Einstein did find the uniform field theory. But, since his relativity theory was, at that time, leading to the development of the atom bomb, he was worried that this new theory and equations could lead to something much worse. Einstein, it seems, made wire recordings of it and destroyed all the files. In nineteen thirty-nine, on a visit to the White house to see the President, he managed to get the lengths of recording wire, which is about the thickness of a human hair, woven into the World's Fair quilt. The quilt was later lost in history. But, now that we know what may be in the quilt, the government wants it and we need you to find it. Your cover, while you're working to recover the world's fair quilt, is as a special consultant to the Smithsonian. Being a consultant and a quilter is all true. Only the real reason for wanting it is secret."

Virginia's eyes narrowed. She leaned back in her chair and crossed her arms. "Okay, who do you really work for? It sure as hell isn't the Smithsonian. They don't have the kind of money you're throwing around, and they're usually not involved in things like this. Quilts yes, unified field theory maybe, but national security issues, no way."

"They said you were good. Now I *really* believe them." Montgomery turned to the chair holding his jacket, reached into a pocket, and pulled out an ID case. He looked at both of Dr. Doverspike and Virginia. "This will not leave this room. Under United States Code, what I'm about to tell you is secret. Agreed?"

They nodded.

"I am Under-Secretary for Intelligence with the Department of Defense. I'm assigned to obtain the quilt and the material it may contain. I'm using working as an employee of the Smithsonian as my cover." He produced his badge and credentials for them to see. "We need to locate that quilt and what may be in it before any other nation or rogue group gets it. If it falls into the wrong hands, it could be disastrous. Your background fits perfectly with someone who could find it and take care of herself while doing it."

"Take care of myself?"

"Well… yeah… there seems to be others, one or more other countries, and some terrorists, have found out what that quilt may contain and they want it, too."

CHAPTER 2

Two hours later Virginia walked into Dr. Doverspike's well-appointed office, closed the door, and leaned against the wall. "Well, from the big grin on your face I take it all the paperwork is complete. You signed the contracts, and I get to play Sherlock Holmes."

He beamed at her. "Yep. All signed and sealed. We have the first installment of ten grand in the bank. There is also an extra two grand in your bank account for this week, even though there are only two days left. I think the museum can make more money loaning you out to the government than we can with exhibits and research."

"Very funny." She rubbed her eyes. "You know finding that quilt will be almost impossible."

Doverspike nodded. "Probably. But they are paying us handsomely for you to try."

"So, when do I start?"

"You already started. Dr. Montgomery left a file for you and a contact number. He also said not to forget your gun."

"Great. A pistol-packing quilter." She shook her head. "What am I going to tell Andy?"

"Oh yeah." Doverspike rummaged through the papers on his desk. "Oh, here it is." He held up a yellow Post-it note. "Your husband called while you were showing our esteemed guest around." He turned the message and looked at it. "Looks like he may already know." He handed the paper to Virginia. "Keep me posted of your adventures, okay? And good luck explaining this to Andy."

Virginia straightened, smiled, and gave him a left-handed salute. "Yes, Sir. Keep my office plant watered."

Doverspike grinned. "I'll take care of your cat for you while you are gone. Leo and I have become quite good friends, especially when I bring him kitty treats."

"I know. You spoil him rotten. Thanks." She took the yellow note, turned, and headed back down the carpeted hall. She walked into her office, closed the door behind her, then plopped into her chair. She leaned forward and dialed Andy's number at the University of Texas.

He answered on the second ring. "Hello, Beautiful. Guess what?"

Virginia wrinkled her nose. "You've been asked to help the Smithsonian finding something of scientific importance that is involved with national security, and you'll get the details from the government agent you will be assisting."

"Yes. How… how'd you know? It sounds exciting, especially since they said you would be working with me, too. Do you know what, exactly, we and the agent are going to be doing?"

"Well, Andy Dear, *I'm* the special agent you will be working with. I'll fill you in at home tonight. What did they do to get you released from the university to help?"

"They gave the college of engineering a very substantial grant, and they are subsidizing my pay and benefits while I'm on sabbatical. Also, they are paying me a stipend and funding my research for the next five years. How about that?"

"I get it. They bought us."

"I guess you could put it that way." He sounded dejected. His voice returned to its excited state. "Did you say you are the special agent in charge of whatever it is we're going to be doing?"

"They didn't tell you?"

"No. I just saw the dean and the president of the university. They told me what they knew and gave me a sealed envelope with some government credentials to use while I'm doing the job. The credentials say I'm an engineering consultant to the Smithsonian. What's up?"

"You'll have to wait until tonight, and I'll brief you. By the way, do you still have that .38 Special revolver?"

"Yes. It's in my den. Why?"

"You're going to need it, and you'd better buy more bullets and a few speed loaders."

Andy's voice strained. "Why? What are we looking for?"

"I'll tell you toni… it's a quilt with something important in it. The rest will have to wait for tonight."

"A quilt? Why would we need guns to look for a quilt?"

"Because it may have something in it so big even Einstein was afraid of it."

"Oh, shit."

"I've got a lot of work transferring what I was doing to my assistant curator and reading the files they gave me. I'll see you tonight. Love you." She hung up and called her assistant curator.

In her pajamas and fuzzy slippers, Virginia shuffled into the living room carrying a red plastic bowl of popcorn and sat on the floor, her back against an overstuffed chair. Andy, with his glasses perched on the end of his nose and in mismatched pajamas, lay prone on the carpet shuffling papers. Virginia looked at the clock on the bookcase, and then at her thirty-six-year-old husband. "It's after eleven. Let's go through this once more, then call it a night."

Andy ran his hand over his balding head, then grabbed a handful of popcorn. "That's got my vote. I'm seeing double as is. Are you sure this quilt is findable? It's been over seventy years since anyone was interested in it or even saw it. It's a very cold case at best. I'm not sure where to start."

"Remember, there are others looking for it. We need to work faster than them."

"Who's looking for it besides us?" he asked, his cheeks full of popcorn.

Virginia poked through some papers and pulled out a yellow legal size piece. "Dr. Montgomery said the Saudis, Al Mukhabarat Al A'amah or General Intelligence Directorate, and some other Arab factions. I think he said one was called the Golden Crescent. Not exactly lightweights. The Golden Crescent may be a bunch of religious fruitcakes, but they are determined, trained, and possibly ruthless. There could even be others we don't know about yet."

Andy sat up and munched on popcorn. "You've got to be kidding." He pushed his glasses up on his nose. "These people are professionals and we're… we're amateurs at best. We could get killed."

"What's new? That's why we go out armed. Plus we have our brains and a few other advantages."

"Like what?"

"We're Americans, and they aren't. They may stand out, and we won't."

Andy stroked her hair. "You'd stand out anywhere."

"Thank you. But I'd stand out as an American woman, not someone from the Far East. And I'm a quilter and speak the quilting language. I'm not sure how many of our opponents, especially Arabs, are quilters." She watched him eat another handful of popcorn. "You're going to have a stomach ache, eating all that popcorn so late."

"I'll suffer. Let's look at the information again and figure out where to start."

"I know where I'd start."

"Where?"

"In Virginia." She flipped through some pages in a spiral notebook. "There is a man who served as a military liaison of sorts, or aide-de-camp, at the White House from nineteen thirty-nine to nineteen forty-three. He now lives in Warrenton, Virginia. I looked the place up. It's the Fauquier County seat and has been around since our country was in diapers. They even have a quilt store and a cemetery where some Confederate soldiers are buried."

"If he worked in the White House during the early days of World War II, the guy has to be in his early nineties. Think he'll remember anything?"

"We won't know until we go and ask him. In the morning, you make our travel reservations and I'll do some hunting on the internet to see what the government didn't give us."

He chuckled. "You already know they have a quilt store in Warrenton?"

"Yes, they have a quilt store. Warrenton's civilized."

Andy smiled. "I'd like to see that cemetery, too. Confederate soldiers are buried there? Wow."

"We're on an investigation, not a holiday."

Andy gave her his little-boy look. "I'd still like to see the cemetery."

"Okay. We'll see the cemetery."

Andy pointed to another paper. "It looks like there might be someone else in Middleburg, Virginia we can talk to. It isn't too far from Warrenton, is it?"

"No, it isn't. Who is it?"

"A woman who was a cook in the White House from nineteen thirty-seven to nineteen forty-seven. She may not have seen the quilt, but the help usually talks to each other, and she may have heard something."

"Good point." Virginia yawned. "How old is she?"

"Ninety-two."

"Okay, get our reservations. I'll organize our notes and finish up on the internet search."

"Oh, do you know what the weather will be like there in August? What should we pack?"

"From what I remember from a trip years ago, it can be hot, like in the nineties, and can be humid. I'm thinking we dress like tourists for this investigation."

"I'll get the reservations, but have you got any idea how to get our guns to Virginia?"

Virginia grinned. "Of course."

Andy, with Virginia checking her GPS and providing directions, drove the black Honda Pilot SUV out of the Dulles International Airport car rental lot and headed for Interstate 66 west toward Warrenton, Virginia.

"It says here that Warrenton is southwest of here," Virginia said. "When we get to Gainesville, we need to get off the freeway and go onto

US 29 then take that into Warrenton. The Hampton Inn is just off 29."

"Okay."

Virginia glanced behind them and watched for any cars that might be following them. "No one is tailing us, I think."

"Do you really think anyone would be? I didn't know where we were going until last night. No one but the government, your museum, and my university know we are even working on this project."

"I know. That's what's got me nervous. I've learned to expect the unexpected." They drove onto Interstate 66 and continued west.

Twenty minutes later, Andy took an off ramp. "Okay, we're on US 29. Now what?" Andy looked at the scenery as they drove. "This is really pretty. Lots of elm, oak, and maple trees."

Andy followed her directions as Virginia consulted her GPS. They drove up and down rises and small hills on the divided highway. "Okay, now take the first right onto Walker Drive for two miles, and the hotel is on the right."

Andy followed her directions and found the hotel. They entered and registered. Andy placed their bags on a luggage trolly. Virginia leaned over the counter and smiled at the young deskman. "Do you have a package for us? It was supposed to be delivered before we got here?"

"I'll check, Ma'am." He went in the back office and returned in a minute lugging a medium-sized wooden box with metal straps around it. "This is addressed to you. It arrived about an hour ago. Be careful, it's heavy." He set it on the counter. "Is there anything else I can do for you?"

"Yes. Where is a good place for dinner?"

"I'd recommend the Black Bear Bistro on Main Street."

"Thank you."

Andy put his hand on her back. "Let's go to our room and see what your uncle sent us." She placed the box on the luggage trolly and followed Andy. They went to their room and unpacked.

Andy borrowed some metal snips from the hotel maintenance man and returned to their room. He cut the straps on the box and opened it. Inside were two Walther PPK .380 semiautomatic handguns and six spare magazines, two hundred rounds of ammunition, holsters, two federal concealed carry permits and two iPhones. He also removed a Taurus 850 CIA .38 caliber revolver and two hundred rounds of ammunition and three speed loaders. There was a pocket-sized canister of bear strength pepper spray. "Hey, they sent a revolver like I requested along with the autos." Andy shook his head. "Man, six hundred rounds of ammunition. This is enough to start our own private war. How much did you request?"

"Two hundred rounds. Why they sent six hundred, I don't know. Maybe they got a price break when they bought them."

He picked up a note inside the box and unfolded it. "What's the note

Dangerous Threads

say, Andy?"

Andy read the paper to himself.

> Dr. and Mrs. Clark,
> Here is the equipment you requested and the permits. We included a revolver like Dr. Clark asked for. We have word from the CIA that the Golden Crescent -has stepped up activity in the Washington area asking about quilts. No word on the Saudis.
> Use the secure cell phones for any communications.
> Good luck, Montgomery

He folded it and looked at her. "We have good news and bad news."

"Tell me the good news."

"We've got our guns and permits as you requested."

"I gathered that. The bad news?"

"The Golden Crescent has people in the Washington area asking about quilts. Montgomery doesn't know about the Saudis or others yet."

"Well, we'd better get to work then. I'll call the gentleman here in Warrenton and set up an appointment."

Andy returned the note to the box and removed one of the Walther PPKs, inserted the loaded magazine, racked the slide, and handed it to Virginia. He did the same to the other gun. He put it into a holster and tucked it into his belt inside his pants. He loaded the revolver and speed loaders, put them in a pocket holster and stuck it in his pants pocket.

Virginia set the gun on the desk while dialing the phone. After a brief conversation, she hung up and turned to Andy. "Okay, we have an appointment with Mr. John Carver at eight tonight at his house. I have the address." She tore off a piece of notepaper from the small tablet on the desktop. "Now, let's go get something to eat."

At eight o'clock, Andy pulled into Mr. Carver's gravel driveway on Waterloo Street and parked his rental car next to a sprawling Weeping Willow. Shadows from the dusky light that weaved through the trees added a sense of mystery to the two-story white house with black trim.

Andy looked at the house. "It may have been built around the mid-eighteen hundreds, but it's been renovated. I love all these real old houses and huge oak trees lining the street. Seems like a good place for a mystery."

Virginia nodded. "Yeah. I agree." She peered out through the windshield. The old trees overhanging the street and the dense, dark green hedges added to the eerie scene. "The house looks freshly painted. The old boy takes good care of it. Feels spooky though, like from an old black-and-white horror movie." She stepped out of the car, slung her backpack over one shoulder, and smoothed out her tan slacks. She joined Andy on the walkway and headed for the front entrance.

As they approached the front steps, Andy turned to Virginia. "This guy's name is Carver, right?"

"Yes. John Carver. He was a First Lieutenant when he served in the White House during World War II. I think the paperwork said he was a Lt. Colonel when he got out sometime after the war."

"I hope he remembers his days at the White House."

"He sounded very astute when I talked to him on the phone. He was excited that someone wanted to talk to him about it."

Andy rang the doorbell. He heard a noise inside, then the deadbolt turn and the door opened. A short man with dense white hair and wire glasses answered. "Hello. Are you Mrs. Clark? Dr. Clark?"

"Yes, Sir. Mr. Carver?" Virginia extended her hand.

"Yes." He shook her hand, then stepped back, allowing them to enter. "Please come in. We can go to the right, into the sitting room. It's more comfortable there."

Virginia and Andy entered the long hallway. The walls were painted a soft light brown with pictures of horse ranches and pastoral scenes. One large photograph showed a group of soldiers in front of a building. On the bottom it said Third Battalion, Army Engineers. Virginia studied the picture. On the side of the group was a young version of their host. "You were in the Engineer Corp, Sir?"

"Yes. I was an ROTC grad from Clarkson College of Engineering at Potsdam, in upstate New York. Majored in mechanical engineering. I graduated and was commissioned, then was called to active duty right away." He led them into the comfortable sitting room.

As she entered, Virginia noticed a red brick fireplace flanked by floor-to-ceiling bookcases. Overstuffed chairs and a couch with massive wooden coffee and end tables were strategically placed. Two well-used red leather high-backed chairs that looked like they came from an English gentlemen's club sat facing the fireplace. A couple of oil paintings of Paris scenes adorned the walls. The hardwood floor had a large Persian carpet in the middle. Another smaller hooked rug rested before the fireplace. She strolled toward the fireplace and looked at the pictures of a woman on the dark oaken fireplace mantel. "Is this your wife?"

Carver nodded. "Yes. She passed away a couple years ago. I still tend to her garden and keep it as she would want it." He motioned for them to sit. "I've been curious why the Smithsonian wanted to talk to an old man like me. I'm not old enough to be in the museum yet." He chuckled at his joke while he sat in a plaid wing backed chair.

Virginia smiled. "Well, Sir, we wanted to ask you about something that may have happened at the White House while you were serving there. That was from nineteen thirty-nine to nineteen forty-two, wasn't it?"

"Yes." He looked at her for a second. "Oh, my. Where are my manners? Would you or Dr. Clark care for something to drink?"

Andy shook his head. "No, Sir. We just ate, and please call me Andy."

"Oh. Okay. What do you want to know about the White House? It was pretty hectic in those days, and I was just a lieutenant."

Virginia leaned forward. "Do you remember the quilt that was given to Mrs. Roosevelt from the 1933 World's Fair in Chicago?"

"Hmm." Carver leaned back in his chair, eyes half-closed, staring toward the window, deep in thought. "Yes. I remember it. I think it was called *The Unknown Star*, or something like that. I wasn't there when she received it, but I remember seeing it when she showed it to some people."

"Good. Do you remember Albert Einstein visiting the White house in nineteen thirty-nine?"

"Yes, only it was nineteen forty when he visited." Carver grinned. "Dr. Einstein made a number of visits to see the president and the secretary of war. He was a nice man. Funny, too. He liked practical jokes. Drove the Secret Service and the Army guards bananas. He even stopped to talk to me."

Andy pushed his glasses up. "Do you know if Dr. Einstein ever saw the quilt?"

"I'm not sure." Carver rubbed his chin. "He may have... yes, as a matter of fact, he did. I remember now. One day, Mrs. Roosevelt, Dr. Einstein, and an assistant of his were in the Lincoln bedroom with it for some time. I remember because I thought it was strange that a scientist would spend so much time with a quilt, even an award-winning one. It was strange, too, that there was a Secret Service man outside the door to the bedroom while they were in there. Dr. Einstein and his assistant then had a meeting with the president and left. Mrs. Roosevelt kept the quilt in the bedroom for a few days, then had it moved by the Secret Service."

Andy took notes. "Do you know or have any idea where it went?"

"No, I don't. I thought it unusual that the Secret Service moved it. But, as I said, things were hectic then, with the war and all, so I didn't really pay much attention to a quilt. It wasn't part of my duties to watch it. There were war preparation activities to attend to, and generals, admirals, and congressmen and the Secretary of War visiting all the time."

He looked off into space for a second. "You know they didn't log things in and out of the White House in those days. At least not officially, so I'm guessing your next question would be if there were a record of it being there, and where it went."

Virginia raised her eyebrows.

"I think the answer would be no."

"I understand." Virginia smiled at him. "You've been very helpful. Is there anything else you can remember about it?"

"No. It was a long time ago."

Virginia rose and stood in front of the fireplace looking at the photos of Carver's wife then turned toward him. "She was very pretty. I'm sorry for your loss."

"Thank you." Carver frowned. "There is one thing, though. Another man called after you did, and he wanted to see me tomorrow about the same quilt."

Virginia leaned against the mantel. "Did the caller say why, or who he represented?"

"No, not really. Just wanted to ask me about the quilt, same as you. Only you told me you were with the Smithsonian. I asked him if he was part of your group and he said no, he represented a collector and was looking for it for his client."

"Hmm. Did he leave his name?"

"Yes." Carver pushed himself up and stepped to a desk on the wall under a window overlooking the street with sheer window coverings draped across, and sorted through some papers. "Here it is. His name was Abdu Hammad."

Virginia mumbled as she walked to the desk. "Not very subtle." She looked at Carver. "What time is his appointment, if you don't mind me asking?"

"No, I don't mind. It's for ten-thirty."

Andy watched him. "Did you tell him we were coming?"

"Let me think... I think so... yes. I said some people from the Smithsonian were coming, but I didn't know what you wanted to talk about, except my time in the White House. He wasn't happy about that."

As Carver turned and started back to his chair, Virginia glanced out the window at the street. A bright red Honda four-door Civic low-rider was parked near a streetlight across the road in front of the house. She noticed exhaust streaming out of the tail pipe. Through the shadows from the trees, she saw two young-looking men seated in the front looking at the house. A third man, partially hidden sat in the back seat.

They drove past here when we pulled into the driveway. It's an unusual car for this type of town, especially in Virginia. Southern California or Miami I would understand, but not here. "Well, I think we've taken a lot of your time, Sir, and we should be leaving. Thank you so much for your help." She stepped to him and shook hands.

Andy closed his notebook and shook hands with Carver. He followed Virginia and Carver to the front door. As he walked next to Virginia to their car, he asked, "What happened back there? All of a sudden you wanted to leave?"

Virginia nodded toward the low-rider red Honda across the street in front of a three-story house. "That car was behind us when we left the Black Bear Grill and has been parked there since we got here. I don't believe in coincidences."

"I see them. Three guys inside. Let's leave and see if they follow."

"If they don't and they go for Carver, we have to intervene. I like that old guy."

Andy nodded as he unlocked their vehicle. "Get in, and let's see what happens."

While Andy backed out of the driveway, Virginia pulled her semiautomatic and racked the slide, loading a bullet into the chamber. "Showtime."

Andy headed down Waterloo Street toward Shirley Highway.

Virginia watched the side mirror as the red Honda pulled out and followed. "We've got company."

CHAPTER 3

Virginia looked again in the car's rearview mirror. "They are closing on us."

"Good. They're leaving Mr. Carver alone." Andy sped up, causing the car to lean as he navigated some bends in the road at higher speeds. Virginia watched the Honda following them in the mirror. "Oh boy, here they come."

As the low-rider sped past, a rear window came down, and the barrel of a gun was thrust out. The man holding it waved for them to stop.

"Go ahead and stop. We'll surprise them." Virginia released the safety on her pistol.

Andy pulled to the curb and stopped. He pulled his revolver and started to get out as Virginia slid out of the passenger side, her gun held close to her side. They stood behind the doors.

Dressed in jeans and long black T-shirts, the two young Middle-Eastern-looking men in the front seats of the Honda jumped out with semi-automatics by their sides and strutted back toward Virginia and Andy. The black man in the back seat, dressed in tan chinos and a red sport shirt, emerged and followed them. They froze when Virginia raised her gun.

"That's close enough," yelled Virginia. "Put down your guns, NOW! Who are you, and what do you want?" In her peripheral vision, she noticed Andy holding his gun on them as well.

With a look of surprise in their eyes, the first two men bent down, placed their guns on the ground, and straightened up. The third man came forward a few steps. "What did you want with the old man?"

Virginia's lips turned up slightly. "None of your business. What's it to you?"

"None of your business," he responded.

Andy cleared his throat. "Look. We can waste time standing here antagonizing each other or you can be cooperative. Your choice."

The man glared at Andy. "Why are people from the Smithsonian carrying weapons?"

"I bet you don't have permits, so knock off the bullshit, and answer the questions." Virginia continued in a sarcastic tone, "In case you didn't notice, we're the ones holding weapons on you."

The black man flexed his fingers, tension obvious from the tightness of the muscles in his arms. "Stay out of our way, and we won't have any problems."

"Exactly what does that mean? Stay out of your way? What are you after?"

"The quilt. We know you were after information about a certain quilt. Stop, and you won't get hurt."

She walked from behind the door toward the men. "You know something? If this weren't so ridiculous, I might be scared. But I'm the one with a gun. Now, here's how it is. You go back to your boss or whoever is behind this farce and tell him the Smithsonian wants that quilt, and if he or you get in my way, you will be very, very sorry. Now go."

The three men stood. The black man suddenly dropped onto one knee pulling a pistol from the small of his back. As he brought the gun around, Virginia fired. The report echoed off the buildings. Red burst from his right shoulder as he swung back toward the ground.

Andy aimed at the other two men. "Don't even think about picking up those guns."

The black man held his shoulder and cringed as he lay on the asphalt.

Virginia walked to him. "Not like the movies, is it? In real life, it hurts, a lot." She stuck her gun in her waistband and walked back to the car and called Montgomery on her cell phone. She could hear sirens approaching.

After hanging up, she said to Andy, "Montgomery's people will handle the police. When the cops get here, call Montgomery back and see if he can trace that call from Abdu Hammad to Carver's house. I forgot when I talked to him. Maybe we'll get lucky and get another lead." Andy nodded.

Within a minute, two white Warrenton Police cars screeched to a stop, their blue beacons illuminating the now-darkening street. The officers jumped out of their cars, guns out. "Put down your gun NOW!"

Virginia held up her gold badge. "Federal officers."

After checking her credentials and verifying everything over the radio, the cops handcuffed the two men from the car and called for paramedics.

One of the uniformed officers pulled Virginia aside. "What happened, exactly?"

"They ran us off the road at gunpoint, interfered with our investigation, and that guy with the hole in him tried to shoot me."

"Oh." The cop called for a detective.

Five minutes later, a short man in a wrinkled gray suit stepped from his unmarked car and walked to Andy and Virginia. He identified himself as Detective John Stark. "I've been told this is a federal matter, that you're a federal agent of some type, and more of the same will soon be around to take charge."

Virginia nodded. "That's about the size of it, Detective. Sorry, I can't tell you more, but at this point, I... well, I can't." She displayed her credentials and gave him a business card.

Stark frowned. "Smithsonian Central Security Service? Hmm, never heard of it. But hell, we didn't know about the NRO—National Reconnaissance Office—or NSA for years either. Why'd they stop you, and what's with the firearms?"

The paramedics arrived and started to work on the black man's shoulder.

"They wanted to tell us to stop what we're doing and tried to be intimidating and when that didn't work..." she pointed to the fellow on the ground, "...he tried to shoot me. I don't think they're professionals. From the looks of it, they're cheap hoods."

Stark looked at the men. "I think you're right. We'll get an ID on them and let your agency know who they are, if that's any help." He motioned to one of the uniformed officers and pointed to the man the medics were loading on a gurney. "Handcuff him to the stretcher and watch him until I get to the hospital. We'll keep him under guard until the feds arrive."

The ambulance and police cars roared off toward Fauquier Hospital.

Stark sighed. "Looks like you're in charge. I get it. Federal matter; hush-hush and all. I'm not happy about it, but I get it. Saves me a lot of paperwork, though. Does this have anything to do with the Army base on the edge of town?"

"No, Sir." Virginia shook her head. "There's an Army base here?"

"Yeah. No one seems to want to talk about it either. Not on any official maps."

"We're not with them, Sir."

"Can I ask what this is about?"

Virginia smiled "You can ask, but I can't really go into the details except it's about an old quilt."

"You don't say. A quilt? That guy got shot at over an old quilt?"

"Yep."

"Had to ask." Stark shook his head. "I'd love to know what they really do at that base and what a quilt has to do with all this. After it's all over, maybe you can tell me." He said goodbye and left.

Andy ambled over . "Local cop not happy being left out?"

"Yeah."

"I guess I wouldn't be either if I were him."

"He's not happy, but not too sad either. Poor guy is more confused than we are. I bet being close to Washington D.C. can have its share of problems for the local cops. Got that phone number?"

Dangerous Threads

With a flourish, he waved a piece of paper. "I have Abdu Hammad's phone number and an address. I'm not sure I believe it. Also, Montgomery said we could tap into the Smithsonian Central Security Service for help. They've been briefed."

"Okay, where is the location? It isn't a cell phone, is it?"

"No. The call came from a National Archives' office in Alexandria, Virginia."

CHAPTER 4

Virginia walked into the hotel room ahead of Andy, and after turning on the lights she glanced at the clock radio. "It's eleven o'clock. I think we should hit the sack. We've got a lot to do tomorrow." She headed to the bathroom.

Before Andy could respond, the phone rang. He answered. "Hello?"

"Dr. Clark, this is Detective Stark, Town of Warrenton Police. We spoke at the little confrontation you had this evening."

"Of course, I remember you. I'm sorry we have to be this secretive. Oh, and thanks for the support and help."

"No problem. I'm used to it. I wanted to tell you and Mrs. Clark that the two men we booked into jail got a lawyer who shut them up, and he was screaming that he wants access to you."

Andy's grip on the phone tightened. "That's not good."

"No. But it isn't all bad, either."

"How so?"

"We've charged them with felons in possession of firearms, a felony. And, in spite of what his clients tell him, I'm acting like you don't exist. We caught them, not you."

"That's good, isn't it?"

"Well, yes and no." Stark cleared his throat. "That's why I called at this late hour. While their lawyer was making his demands and telling his clients to shut up, something happened. Some very big guys with no necks, black suits, and crew-cuts with U.S. Marshal's badges came in with a federal writ and took them. They left the lawyer for us. The guy in the hospital, your wife shot, is in surgery and is now under the care of more federal marshals. He's being held under some sort of federal court order blocking anyone but his doctor from seeing him. His lawyer can't even go near him. He's to be moved to an undisclosed location as soon as possible. One of the marshals mentioned something about them being terrorists. His lawyer is frantic and pissed."

"Do you know who the men who attacked us are?"

"Yeah. That part was easy. Your wife was right. The two she didn't shoot are real losers. Their arrest and conviction records fill five tote boxes, and that's just in Virginia. This little stunt tonight could get them well over fifty years. That's if we still had them. Their names are Maloff Rafi and Ali Ahmad. Before you ask, they were born here in Virginia so they are U.S. citizens. The one your wife put a hole in is Jean Dumelle, a French national, here in the U.S. on an expired work visa."

Andy wrote their names on the little pad of paper by the phone. "You moved pretty fast."

Virginia came out of the bathroom wrapped in a towel. She crossed the room to Andy, and he handed her the paper.

"That's what I get paid for," Stark continued. "I'd just like my suspects back. Any idea who I need to contact tomorrow? I seriously don't think it's going to be the Smithsonian and the marshals will probably make the men disappear. The men's lawyer wants to know as well, and he wants to talk to you and your wife. He knows you exist and are federal officers of some type, but we haven't told him which agency yet. I'm not sure he'd believe the Smithsonian if I told him. He is one unhappy puppy."

Andy rubbed his eyes. "I'm afraid this has to do with—"

"I know, national security."

"Yep. And this time it isn't just hype."

"You're serious. Your wife wasn't kidding? This is for real? No wonder the marshals were here so fast."

"Yes."

"Oh. Oh shit." Stark took a breath. "I suppose I don't know where you are either when he asks again?"

"Right. Like your suspects, we've disappeared."

"Okay then, I've never met you."

"Right, and thanks." Andy hung up and looked at Virginia. "You look good in a towel."

"Thanks." She sat next to him on the bed and looked at the note with the names of their assailants. "Maloff Rafi, Ali Ahmad, and Jean Dumelle. Two Arab-sounding names and one Frenchman. What does that tell us?"

"Whoever hired them is Islamic or French, or hires whoever he can find locally, and he's cheap, doesn't like paying for quality help?"

"Maybe. I'll call Montgomery tomorrow and see what the gentlemen have told him. That may give us more to go on. I wonder if Maloff Rafi and Ali Ahmad are Islamic and belong to a mosque and if so, which one?"

"Trust me, Virginia, if they do belong to a mosque, the people there won't talk to us or the feds."

"Andy, Dear, we're feds." Virginia rose, walked to the dresser, pulled out some pajamas and slipped them on.

Andy pulled the bed covers down, then looked at her. "How'd they spot us and know what we're doing?"

"Good question." She yawned. "They started following us after we left the restaurant. The traffic was sparse by then, and only Carver and Abdu Hammad knew we were going to Carver's place. So Abdu Hammad had to sic them on us. When we went to Carver's they parked and watched. Then they wanted to find out what we did. Seems kind of stupid, since Abdu Hammad knew we would be there and why. That French guy," she looked at the paper, "Jean Dumelle knew what we were talking to Carver about, so I'm guessing Abdu Hammad sent them, but why?"

Andy climbed into bed. "And how'd they know we were eating at that particular restaurant?"

"Let's hope Montgomery will have some answers tomorrow. Let's get some sleep. Remind me in the morning, I need to clean my gun before we go to breakfast."

Virginia and Andy finished their IHOP breakfast. Then, over coffee, she called Montgomery. "Did you get a chance to interrogate our friends from last night?"

"Yeah. We talked to them all night." Montgomery sounded sleepy. "They kept saying they wanted their lawyer and were told by their mouthpiece at the jail to be quiet and not talk without him. But they saw the light about four this morning."

Virginia cracked a smile. "What did you do?"

"We told them we were going to charge them with assault on federal agents, interfering with a federal investigation, possession of a firearm by felons, and as terrorists, send them to Guantanamo, Cuba for who knows how long without a lawyer. And we took their holy books away from them, and had drug-and explosive-sniffing dogs go over them."

"Dogs? Isn't that against their religion or something?"

"Yeah. They got emotional about that. I'm supposed to be tolerant and all, but they're not? How many of our churches—or Jewish synagogues for that matter—do you see in Mecca? Not on my watch."

"Isn't that stretching the Constitution a little?"

Montgomery chuckled. "From what I've heard about your interrogation methods, mine seem benign."

"Okay, I'll give you that one. What did they say? Anything useful?"

"Not really. They're hired thugs who sell out to anyone who'll hire them. They were to stop you, find out what Carver said, and then rough you up some so you'd stop whatever you're doing. They thought it would be easy. You were supposed to be just two geeks from a museum. They hadn't counted on your being armed."

Virginia switched the phone to her left ear. "I bet. Who hired them?"

"The third guy, Jean Dumelle."

Dangerous Threads

"Did he say anything?"

"No. He won't talk and wants his embassy notified. And, he wants a lawyer. The Immigration folks put a hold on him as well. He's still on painkillers and isn't thinking straight yet either. I'm going to work on him more. I'm going to describe the accommodations and weather at Guantanamo, Cuba while I'm at it."

"Want me to talk to him?"

"No, thank you. I'd like him alive and in one piece. You already put a big hole in him. Right now he and his henchmen don't officially exist anywhere, they're nonpersons, and we'll keep it that way for a while. We can hold him on the same charges as the other two if need be, but that will mean bringing you and your husband into it and we don't want to do that, at least not yet. So, if push comes to shove, we'll hold them all as terrorists in Guantanamo. Because of what you are looking for and who we think the players are in all this, we can get away with it, at least for a while."

"You guys need to visit the National Archives in Washington more. There's a document there, you really should read. It's called the Constitution."

"Neither Congress nor the present President seems to care about it, and they took oaths to uphold it, so we're taking their approach at this juncture. Who knows, maybe they'll get their lawyers down the road. I'll let you know if Dumelle says anything useful. Good hunting. Oh, just so you know, we have Carver being watched by government agents so nothing happens to the gentleman."

Virginia hung up and looked across the table at Andy. "Our friends from last night are off the grid for a while, so they won't be a problem, but they haven't talked much to Montgomery's people yet."

"So, where to next? Middleburg?"

"Yep. Let's pay the bill and go. When we're finished interviewing the cook, we can look into how Abdu Hammad called Carver from the National Archives."

Following Virginia's directions, Andy drove east on US 29, Lee Highway, to US 15 north, James Madison Highway. He continued down the elm and oak-forested road with old stone and wood-sided houses, well set back from the road north, through Haymarket. He continued to U.S. 50, John Mosby Highway, and turned west, past big stately equestrian homes set back behind well-kept fences and horse pastures. They drove through the green rolling hills spotted with trees and barns, toward Middleburg and the wine and fox-hunting country.

They slowed as they entered the historic village and continued down the tree-lined main street with buildings from the eighteenth and nineteenth centuries, to the center of town. Andy parked on North Madison Street next to the brick Red Fox Inn. Virginia called the woman, Mrs. Vanessa Franklyn, who was a cook in the Roosevelt White House. The woman's daughter answered the phone.

"Hello, my name is Virginia Davies-Clark, and I'm with the Smithsonian Institution. I would like to talk to Mrs. Vanessa Franklyn, please."

A woman with a deep southern accent responded. "I'm her daughter, and she's not home at the moment. Can I be of assistance?"

"It is a matter that I think only she can help me with. Would it be possible to set up a meeting with her at a time when it would be convenient for her?"

"You said the Smithsonian, like the museums in Washington?"

"Yes. That's right."

"My mother loves them, especially the Museum of American History. I'm sure she'd love to talk to you. How's two this afternoon?"

"That would be wonderful."

"May I ask what this is about?"

"I have some questions about the White House when she worked there."

"Oh. I hope she can remember that far back. Do you have the address?"

"Yes. I'll be by at two this afternoon to see her. Thank you." Virginia hung up and turned to Andy. "You heard?"

"Yeah. And, since we have some time, let's look around town. It is really quaint." He pointed to the brick building they were parked next to. "We can eat lunch in there. The Red Fox Inn. Talk about historic. According to the internet search I just did on my iPhone, it was established in 1728. The inn is steeped in the lore of both the Revolutionary and the Civil Wars. During the Civil War, it was used as a Confederate headquarters and hospital. Now, it is still a restaurant and inn." He looked at her and grinned. "It has four stars for the food."

Virginia put her phone in her backpack. "My travel agent. What else does your toy tell you?"

"We are in farming country along with wineries and this area is famous for fox hunting." He looked at Virginia. "Do you think the fox ever wins?"

"I think so. Where to first?"

"Let's just walk up and down the main drag. Washington Street. Most of the shops are there. We can get a feel of the area. Look at the buildings, mostly brick and from the seventeen-hundreds. There's a bookstore, Books and Crannies, down the street."

"Okay. We can also watch for someone following us. I'll feel better talking to Mrs. Franklyn knowing no one else is watching."

They wandered around the main part of town, exploring the various shops, including the bookstore, where Andy bought two books. Virginia kept stopping and looking into windows as they progressed down the street.

Andy stood next to her in front of a Christmas shop as she bent slightly, apparently looking at the wares inside. "See anyone tailing us?"

"Yes. I've spotted only one person who seems to be more interested in us than anyone else."

"Do you mean the man with the gray slacks, dark blue sport coat, and blond hair about fifty yards down the block who's trying to look interested in that woman's store?"

"That's him."

Andy pretended he was pointing to an object in the window. "How do we go about losing him?"

"We don't. At least not yet. Let's go to Liberty Street and turn. That'll take us to the cemetery. If he follows, then we'll have a chat with him. One more thing, whatever I do, go along with it. Act cool. Any sign of fear or nervousness can be used to his advantage. Just stay with me on this."

"Okay. Knowing you, the cemetery might be an appropriate place to do whatever you're going to do." Keeping an eye on the man, they casually walked to Liberty Street, turned, and strolled toward Federal Street and the cemetery. The man followed. Virginia ducked into an alleyway, pressed her back to a wall, and waited.

The man turned the corner and took a few steps, then stopped. Andy stood facing him. Virginia stepped out and held her semiautomatic to the man's side. "Let's step in here. Nice and quiet-like, okay?"

The man slowly looked down at the gun poking him in the side and gave her a snide expression. "If you shoot, everyone will hear it, and the police will be here in no time."

"If I press this into your side and fire this close to you, your jacket and body should act as a sound suppressor. Want to test my theory?"

He swallowed. "No."

"Good. Frisk him, Andy."

Andy approached and ran his hands down the sides of the man's jacket. He opened the front and pulled a nine-millimeter automatic from a shoulder holster. He felt the man's back and down his legs. He removed the ceramic knife strapped to the man's right leg above his ankle. Andy studied the knife, then said, "Step into the space where she is."

Virginia moved back into the narrow walkway, holding her gun on the man. He slowly followed with Andy behind him. They stopped about six feet into the opening.

Virginia watched as Andy pushed the man against the wall. "Who are you and why are you following us?"

The man stiffened. "I do not have to answer your questions. You can't shoot me, I'm not armed."

Virginia shook her head. "You know, you can talk to us with or without pain. It really doesn't make any difference to me. And I'm getting pretty pissed at being followed, especially by people carrying guns."

"You two don't scare me."

Virginia noticed his lower lip twitch as she pointed the gun at the man's right side. She looked at Andy. "Andy, what lives here?"

Andy peered around the man where her gun was pointed. "I think his liver. That'll bleed pretty bad, especially with a hollow-point bullet ripping through it. It'll be painful as hell to boot. He'll probably bleed to death before any help comes." Andy backed up.

Virginia then kicked the man's feet out from under him. He fell back against the brick wall, banging his head, and slid to the ground. He rubbed the back of his skull. "What the hell did you do that for?" He started to get up.

"Stay where you are." Virginia knelt and pressed her gun against his kneecap. "I don't want to kill you, just talk and get some answers, quick. My friend Donna loves to blow guy's knees off while interrogating them. They usually became quite cooperative. I think I'll see how much luck I have with that technique."

He looked at her gun and then at her stern, unsmiling face. He swallowed. "Torture is illegal."

"So what?"

"You work for the government, you can't do that."

"Sugar," she said with a sweet voice. "When I'm done, you'll be in no shape to file charges. You won't be in shape to do much at all. If you live. Who are you, and what makes you think we work for the government?"

He looked at Andy.

Andy leaned close. "I'd cooperate if I were you. We have an appointment and need to eat lunch first, so you're a real inconvenience. She gets grumpy when her blood sugar gets low, and I think it's getting low now."

Andy straightened, took a few steps to the street, and looked both ways. "No one around. I think this is a good time to start your persuasion techniques." He returned, picked up two dirty rags from the alleyway then grabbed a handful of hair, pulled the man's head back, and stuffed one in his mouth. "This way, when she pulls the trigger, no one will hear you scream." He handed her the second rag. "Put this over the gun so you don't get any blood splattered on you when you shoot. Wouldn't look good at the restaurant."

Virginia nodded, took the rag, released the safety, and put the rag over the gun. "Thank you, Dear."

The man's eyes bulged. Perspiration beaded on his forehead. He pulled the rag out. "Okay, okay, I didn't get paid enough for this. My name is Andrew Bleeker."

Andy squatted. "Why do you think we work for the government?"

"I… I was told you work for the Smithsonian and wouldn't be armed. Just a couple of academics."

Virginia rotated the gun against his knee. "Good so far. Now, who do you work for?"

"I'm a private detective. Or I was one until the state pulled my license. Now I get what work I can."

"So, who hired you, and what were your instructions?" Virginia pressed the barrel of her gun to his right knee.

Bleeker looked at the automatic pressed against his knee. "I was to follow you and see where you went and who you talked to. That's it. I wasn't supposed to talk to you or try and stop you or anything." He wet his lips. "I was to just follow you, that's all."

Virginia smiled. "You're doing fine. Now, again, who hired you? This time I want an answer or you crawl out of this alley."

"A man. A man in Washington. He was in a gray Mercedes limo with diplomatic plates. He was dressed in an expensive-looking suit. Looked Middle Eastern. He gave me your picture, an envelope with a lot of money, and told me to follow you then report back. He gave me a number to call. I was not to interfere with you in any way, just follow, and report."

"What's the number?"

"This is what he gave me." Bleeker's hand shaking, he slowly reached into his shirt pocket, pulled out a small piece of paper with a phone number on it, and handed it to Andy.

Virginia smiled. "Good. See, that wasn't hard, was it?"

"What am I going to tell him? He paid me to watch you."

"You lost us, and you're still looking for us."

Bleeker rubbed his hands together. "Okay."

Virginia tossed the rag aside, then she and Andy stood. "You look kind of funny sitting on the dirty concrete like that. Why don't you get up?" She slid her gun into a pouch on her backpack. She watched his face as he got up, then pulled out a shiny red spray canister and held it to her side. "You can go now and don't try to follow us. If you do, I'll make sure you'll have to navigate with crutches, or a wheelchair, depending on my mood. Got it? Oh, one other thing. Remember, you lost us. You have no idea where we went."

Bleeker looked at Andy. "My gun and knife?"

Andy pulled the magazine out of the pistol and unloaded the round in the chamber and handed the empty gun back. He emptied the magazine into his hand and handed it back. "I'll keep the bullets." Andy handed back the knife.

Bleeker took them, tucked the gun in his belt, then spun toward Virginia with his knife in his hands. "You don't have your gun now!"

Andy hit him in the back of his head with the butt of his gun as Virginia fired a burst of pepper spray straight into his face. At a distance of four feet, she couldn't miss.

Bleeker dropped the knife, grabbed his eyes, and screamed. He banged against the sides of the buildings as he writhed in pain, then fell to the ground and rolled around, holding his face and swearing.

Virginia stepped over him. "That was stupid. We were getting along so nicely, too. Just so you know, that spray can bring down a grizzly bear. If you want to see again, you'd better visit an eye doctor, fast."

She stepped to Andy's side and gave him a quick kiss. "That's for hitting him. It gave me time to spray him."

Andy led Virginia out of the alley and back to Washington Street where they walked hand in hand to the Red Fox Inn for lunch.

Seated at an old dark wooden table near the fireplace, they ordered lunch. While they waited for lunch, Virginia sipped an ice tea. "From what our new friend said, it looks like the Saudis have arrived in all this."

Andy took a sip of his tea. "For a secret mission, it seems everyone knows who we are, but we don't know who they are. Doesn't seem fair somehow."

"Well, we have a pretty good idea who hired the thugs last night. Maybe that was the Golden Crescent. Now the people with the diplomatic license plates—that's most likely the Saudis. I wonder how many others are involved?"

"Are you going to give that number the fellow gave us to Dr. Montgomery?"

"After I call it." She pulled out her secure cell phone and dialed the number.

After three rings, a man answered. "Yes?"

"Next time, hire competent help."

"Who is this?"

Virginia hung up. The display said Saudi Embassy. She showed the display to Andy as their food arrived. "That may upset their applecart." She called Montgomery and gave him an update along with the phone number to the Saudi Embassy the detective had provided.

Andy nodded, unfolded his napkin, placed it on his lap, and watched the server set their food on the table. "How's our new friend going to explain that he lost two academics?"

"I really don't care, but they'll know they are up against more than a couple of geeks. Shall we eat and go see Vanessa Franklyn, and then visit the Alexandria National Archives office? I'm pretty sure there won't be any more problems today."

CHAPTER 5

At two in the afternoon, Andy parked the car in front of a square two-story stone house belonging to the old White House cook. The diminutive front had a lawn and well-tended roses planted across the front of the building, under large windows with green shutters. A giant old oak tree stood sentry on the right of the cobblestone sidewalk. Pine trees were clustered on the left of the walkway. Virginia and Andy walked up stone steps and knocked on the bright red door.

The door swung open, and a middle-aged black woman stood squinting against the light. Then, in a thick southern accent, she asked, "Are you Dr. and Mrs. Clark?"

Virginia nodded. "Yes." She presented her credentials. "We're from the Smithsonian."

The woman looked at the photo ID and the gold badge. "You're with security? I thought you were a curator or something."

"I'm both. Is Mrs. Vanessa Franklyn at home?"

The woman moved aside. "I'm Melissa Franklyn, her daughter. I spoke with you this morning. Please step inside." She pointed to their right. "You can use the parlor. I'll call Mama."

Virginia and Andy went into the parlor. Virginia took in the room. The walls were paneled with dark wood, leather chairs flanked a fireplace big enough to roast a whole pig, and there was a set of side tables and an old drop leaf secretary desk. The center of the floor had a worn hook rug over dark hardwood flooring. Andy stood by the window watching the street in front of the house.

A stooped, black woman with gray hair done up in a bun, entered and shuffled to a well-used leather chair. She sat and looked at Virginia. "Hello. I'm Mrs. Vanessa Franklyn. You wanted to see me? My daughter said you're from the Smithsonian."

"Yes, Ma'am. I'm Virginia Davies-Clark, and this is my husband, Dr. Andy Clark."

Mrs. Franklyn nodded. "Nice to meet you all.

"We're special agents of the Smithsonian Central Security Service and we need your help, Mrs. Franklyn."

"Oh my. First, why don't you call me Vanessa? I'm curious to know how I can help the Smithsonian." She pointed to some well-used overstuffed chairs. "Please sit."

Virginia sat in an orange and green plaid chair and cleared her throat. "You worked in the White House under President Roosevelt, correct?"

"Yes, I did." Mrs. Franklyn wet her lips. "Those were trying times. I was young then. I was just a cook, though. I don't know a lot about what went on there, other than what everyone ate."

"Well, Vanessa, sometimes people who work in places hear things that others don't think they heard. Does that make sense?

"Yes. It's like we'd walk around there, but go unnoticed, like the furniture."

"That's what we are hoping for."

Mrs. Franklyn leaned forward. "What do you want to know?"

"Some time during nineteen thirty-nine to nineteen forty or forty-one, Dr. Albert Einstein visited the White House. He spent some time with Mrs. Roosevelt. They were with a quilt. Did you ever hear about that?"

"The World's Fair quilt? I remember it. It was *The Unknown Star*. We all got to look at it." She raised her hand showing her twisted fingers. "When my arthritis wasn't so bad, I used to quilt. That's why I remembered it. Are you a quilter?"

"Yes, Ma'am, I am." Virginia's eyes widened. "That's the quilt. It was taken out of the White House a few days later by the Secret Service. Do you remember that?"

Mrs. Franklyn leaned back in her chair and stared at the fireplace for a minute. "Yes. I remember. I recall Dr. Einstein being a nice man and funny. Such a joker. The Secret Service agents really liked him, but were always nervous around him. He liked to pull jokes on them."

"Do you remember them removing the quilt?"

"Sure I do. They took it out through the kitchen. I remember because that was highly unusual. The agent carrying it stopped in the kitchen to get a big, waterproof, canvas bag to put the quilt in. It was raining that day. Two other agents, along with the one carrying the quilt were fidgety and one had a shotgun. I gave them the bag they wanted and asked where they were going with it."

Virginia's heart raced. "Did they say where they were going?"

"They said someplace safe."

"Safer than the White House? Did they say where it would be safe?"

"No, not exactly. But they were headed for the train and would be back in two weeks."

Andy turned from the window. "Did they say anything else or do you

Dangerous Threads

remember seeing them after their trip?"

Mrs. Franklyn sat quietly for a minute. "One of them came back in three days. I remember now, he liked my peanut butter cookies and knew I made them on Thursdays. He brought the bag back, too. It was empty."

"Did he say where he'd been?"

"No, and I don't think I asked. He was with the Secret Service, and they don't say much." Mrs. Franklyn rubbed her chin. "I do recall that some pattern makers sold patterns for that quilt under other names soon after that." She shook her head. "I'm sorry I can't remember anything else. It was so long ago, and it was a hectic place. My memory isn't all that it used to be anymore."

Virginia smiled. "All that happened over seventy years ago, so I'd say your memory is doing great. I can't remember what I ate last Friday."

Mrs. Franklyn nodded. "I hope I was able to help you some."

"More than you know. Thank you, Vanessa, you've been a big help."

Mrs. Franklyn's daughter escorted them out.

After getting into the car, Andy pulled into the street. "Where to? Alexandria?"

"Yeah. I think that should be our next stop. I noticed you watching the road from the house. See anyone of interest?"

"Nope. I think our path is clear for now."

Andy pulled up in front of the narrow red brick building in Alexandria, Virginia on North Washington Street and parked. He bent forward to look at it through the windshield. Virginia peered out the side door. He consulted the map. "This is the address, but I don't see any government agencies here."

Virginia glanced at the paper with the phone number and address and looked at the number on the front of the building. "We've got the address that was given to us, but something is wrong."

"Think we should go and see who's here?"

Virginia watched the building. In an upstairs window, the curtain opened slightly, a quick look by someone inside, then it closed. She held her hand to her throat. "Andy, start the car. Get ready to get us out of here fast."

He looked over his shoulder at the street. "Not with this traffic."

"Then go now. I don't like the set-up here. If we go inside, we could be in trouble. We may have just given our position away. Now they have a fix on us they'll be able to follow us. Go!"

"They? Who are they? Saudis or the Golden Crescent?" Andy started the car and eased into the traffic. "Traffic gets rough around here in the afternoon. Look at the tourists." He drove down the street then turned and headed west on King Street. The traffic thinned as they moved away from the old town area. "Where to?"

"I'm not sure which group, but I just got a bad feeling back there." Virginia looked around, then consulted her map. "Okay, keep going until we get to the freeway, that's I-395. Take that north into Washington, but get off on US 1 there and go to Constitution. Then left to 17th. Make a right and head for F Street."

"What's there?"

"If we can avoid a tail, I know a place near George Washington University we can hole up in for now and get our bearings."

"How do you know about this place?"

"A friend, Dr. Ciambrone, stayed there when teaching seminars at the university. He told me about it."

"Oh."

Andy followed her directions and found a parking place a block from the hotel Virginia pointed out. It was a refurbished four-story brownstone. They settled into their second floor suite facing the street.

Virginia plopped on the bed. "Okay, we'd better figure out what we've got, so tomorrow we have a plan."

Andy sat at the small desk and took out a pad and pen. "Let's first see what we know about the quilt so far."

"We've got the dates narrowed down for the quilt being seen in the White House." Virginia lay back on the bed and stared at the ceiling. "We know Einstein saw it with Mrs. Roosevelt under guard. It left with the Secret Service and went someplace for safe keeping that is either a one-and-a-half day to one-week distance away by train."

"Right. We'll need some idea as to where in a radius that big they could have taken it. But there is something that has bothered me about all this."

She rose onto one arm and looked at him. "What?"

"If this Einstein found the unified field theory—or the theory of everything, as it is sometimes referred to—why was he with Mrs. Roosevelt and not the president?"

Virginia raised an eyebrow. "I never gave that much thought. Maybe it was because the good doctor didn't want the president or the government having it. He was concerned about them making the A-bomb from his theory of relativity. Maybe she was a co-conspirator with him to hide it. As the first lady, she could ask the Secret Service to do things for her, and she liked Einstein."

"Okay," Andy nodded. "I'll buy that. Now where would they take the quilt?"

"Probably not to a military installation near either coast."

"Good guess. Maybe not any place near either coast. Some place where it would be safe."

Dangerous Threads

"Fort Knox, Fort Leavenworth?" Virginia sat up. "A federal reserve bank... hell, I don't know... West Point?"

"How about someone's home? Someone the First Lady knew who loved quilts, or made them, and was asked to keep it safe?"

"That's a lot of people." Virginia shook her head. "This is our needle in the haystack."

"You know, Mrs. Roosevelt had friends in Hollywood. Hell, so did the president. Could she have given it to someone there?"

Virginia's eyes narrowed. "That's on the west coast. You didn't think she would send it to anyone at either side of the country, did you?"

"I don't think we can just dismiss the idea. Some of the Hollywood stars in those days were friends of the president and the first lady and supported their positions on things. A lot of them actually went into the services during the war. So, we really should consider that, too."

"Fort Knox, Fort Leavenworth, and federal reserve banks are probably at the bottom of our list." Virginia fell back onto the bed. "If it were at one of them, by now the quilt would have turned up, or been seen and that fact leaked."

The phone rang. Andy answered. "Hello?"

"Sir, this is James from the front desk. You asked that I notify you if I saw anything out of the ordinary happen while you are our guest."

"Right." He stood up. "What happened?"

CHAPTER 6

Andy stood next to the desk chair. "Okay, James, what happened?"

"There has been a gray limo parked across the street in a no-parking zone, and a police car drove by and didn't do anything. That was suspicious. Probably had diplomatic plates. But a tall, dark-skinned gentlemen from the car, in a Brooks Brothers suit, came in a second ago and asked about you."

"What did you say?"

"Nothing. He knew you were here. He's on his way up to your room now. What should I do?"

"Don't do anything, we'll handle it."

"I'm sorry, Dr. Clark. I didn't mention this first, but just before he came in, the two men without necks who came in are now sitting over to the side of the lobby with newspapers. I spotted guns under their sport coats."

"What are they doing?"

"Nothing. They're just sitting and watching everyone who goes in and out. They aren't disturbing anyone. What should I do?"

"In that case, be nice to them. Offer them coffee or something. We'll handle the gentleman in the suit, James. Thanks." Andy hung up and looked at Virginia. "We're getting company, and he may be armed. And there are two more armed goons downstairs."

Virginia nodded. "Not the Fuller Brush Man, I bet."

"Tall, dark-skinned gentleman in a nice suit. Could be the guy at the Saudi embassy you stirred up."

"Either the other two are with our nicely dressed visitor, or they're Golden Crescent." Virginia moved to the window and looked out. "Nice car. Diplomatic plates. I bet it's the Saudis' Al Mukhabarat Al A'amah or General Intelligence Directorate guy." Virginia grabbed her semiautomatic and tucked it under a pillow she propped up against the headboard. She hopped on the bed and leaned against the pillow. There was a knock on the door.

Andy opened the door and stared at the man standing in the hall. "Can I help you?"

The man bowed slightly. "Yes, Dr. Clark, I am Haddad Abdel A'hsam. I am the cultural attaché from the Saudi Embassy. May I have a few words with you and your wife?"

Andy stood aside. "Come in. I'm sure this will be interesting."

He entered the room and glanced at Virginia on the bed, propped up against the headboard. He bowed again. "Mrs. Clark. It is a pleasure to meet you and your husband."

Virginia smiled. "Mr. Abdel Ahsam. Please have a seat. What can we do for an officer in the Al Mukhabarat Al A'amah?"

He sat in an armchair and smiled. "Please call me Ahsam. I am but a lowly attaché."

She shook her head. "And I have a bridge to sell you."

He frowned. "Pardon? A bridge to sell?"

"It means I know you're no lowly attaché. The cultural attaché is usually the head of station for the spies working out of an embassy. Now, like my husband said, how can we help you?"

He sat back and unbuttoned his jacket. "Yes, sometimes all is not as it seems, like in my case. I understand you are looking for an old quilt. One from your 1933 World's Fair, to be specific."

"Yes. For the Smithsonian. Why would that particular quilt interest the Saudi government or their intelligence organization? I didn't think quilts were all that big a thing in that part of the world."

"I'll come to the point. There is an Islamic fundamentalist group, the—"

"The Golden Crescent," said Andy as he sat at the desk.

Ahsam nodded. "You've heard of them?"

"Yeah." Andy twisted in the chair. "Nasty bunch. We've met."

"Our concern is that the Golden Crescent, a radical Islamic fundamentalist group, is looking for that old quilt from the 1933 World's Fair. Why would they be all that interested in it? As you so rightly put it, quilts are not exactly big sellers in our part of the world. And they are after the same one the Smithsonian is also searching for. Coincidence?"

Virginia pushed herself further up against the headboard. "Why is your government concerned? I heard that you were looking for it as well."

Ahsam took a breath. "We are also interested in the quilt, should it still exist, mainly because the Golden Crescent is after it. That, and it is rumored to contain the secret of the universe. This could mean the one who possesses it would have unlimited energy. We cannot let the Golden Crescent have it if it still exists, under any circumstances. And controlling that kind of power would be a big advantage for us as oil becomes increasingly scarce."

"Well, it sounds like you're being honest with us." Virginia rubbed her chin. "So what do you want from us? You considering teaming up or something?"

"Something. I know my detective lost you today. I think, from the way he sounded when he contacted me, and a call from someone I assume was you, I don't think he lost you; you scared him."

"We scared him? We're a couple of academics, not carrier detectives or spies."

"I seriously doubt that, but we'll let it go for now."

"Why'd you need him? You found us without him. How?"

"Yes, but it took some real work and time. As to the how, I have friends all over who see things and report things to me."

"I see." Virginia wet her lips. "Now, what did you have in mind?"

"My government wants that quilt at any cost. We will not let the Golden Crescent have it. Your government obviously knows what it may contain as well, and I'm sure it doesn't want our mutual enemy to have it. All of us are all searching for the same thing. It could get nasty."

Andy chuckled. "Let me see if I got this right. You want us to kill the Golden Crescent people and then compete with you for the grand prize?"

"Not exactly. We both will take them down, then we will work together to obtain the quilt and share in the prize. That way we can do it without looking over our shoulders all the time."

"Interesting offer." Virginia pulled her knees up and wrapped her arms around them. "We are not in the assassination business. We work for the Smithsonian. We are scientists and historians, not killers. If the Golden Crescent gets violent, we will defend ourselves and try to remove them from the playing field. As for teamwork, I'm afraid we must act on our own. I think you, Mr. Abdel Ahsam, are an honorable man, but I'm pretty sure our governments and organizations are not so inclined. So, thank you for the visit and for the offer, but I'm afraid we will have to decline."

Ahsam shrugged and opened his palms in a surrendering manner. "It was a real pleasure to meet you both. I'm sorry we cannot seek our common treasure together, but I fully understand. Now you understand that the gloves are off now."

Virginia unfolded her legs and sat on the edge of the bed, one hand slipping under the pillow. "I understand."

He rose. "Then there will be no hard feelings when I…" he reached under his jacket. As he did, Virginia's hand came out from under the pillow and she pointed her pistol at him. Andy drew his pistol as well.

"I wouldn't do that if I were you. I will kill you if you do anything stupid."

"Yes. I think you would." He slowly withdrew his hand holding a silver card case. He removed a card and set it on the edge of the bed then rebuttoned his jacket. "So much for being just academics. You have my card, should you wish to communicate again. I'll be leaving now. Thank you for the nice conversation. Maybe at some other time when this is over we can talk again."

"I'd like that, assuming we are all still alive."

Ahsam walked to the door. As he opened it, he turned, nodded, then left.

As the door closed, Virginia got up and started to pack. "Andy, get packed, and keep your gun near. The other men you said were in the lobby will probably try and visit, soon. Ahsam didn't mention them so I'm assuming they either weren't with him and he didn't see them, or they're his hit squad." She removed a small white box from her suitcase, hung the box on the door handle, and pushed a little black button.

As Andy threw his things in his suitcase he heard a noise outside the door. It sounded like a scraping near the lock. He motioned to Virginia, switched off the lights, and hid behind the bathroom door. Virginia pulled the drapes closed tighter, blocking out any light from the street, then knelt behind the side of the bed away from the door.

The lock clicked. The knob slowly turned and the door inched open when a loud excruciating, screeching siren sounded from the box hanging on the door. The men outside stumbled back, then charged the door, racing in with their guns in front of them. Andy switched on the lights as Virginia fired two rounds, hitting both men. One dropped his gun and grabbed his arm; the other stumbled backward a few steps and turned toward Virginia when Andy fired. Three bullets hit the man in his side and neck. He stopped, fell on his knees, then face down on the floor. The man with the wounded arm bolted from the room and raced down the hall. Andy and Virginia heard the door to the stairwell slam closed.

Virginia got up and came around the bed and looked at the man on the floor. Blood was pooling under him and seeping out onto the carpet around him. Virginia looked at Andy. "My God. We didn't even get a chance to talk to them and maybe not have a shoot out. How is he?"

Andy stepped to the fallen man and pushed his gun away. He knelt and felt the man's neck for a pulse. "He's alive. Better call 911 and Montgomery for back up. The cops aren't going to like this one bit." He looked at the blood. "Does the Smithsonian cover room cleanup or do we lose our deposit?"

Virginia stared at Andy. "You seem awfully cool for a university professor who just shot someone. Is there another part of your life you need to talk to me about?"

"Last year when we were in Italy and at that maniac's villa, I blew up his equipment and wounded his people and helped you escape, remember?" He got up. "If you can be Miss Adventurous, I can be your wingman."

Virginia smiled and winked. "You can be my wingman any day." She went to the window, pulled the drape aside, and looked at the street. The limo pulled away from the curb. "I'll call Montgomery. Get ready to move out when he gets here. We've got to vanish and think of our next move."

Andy picked up the secure cell phone and dialed Montgomery's number. After a brief conversation, he disconnected and tossed the phone on the bed.

Virginia looked at him. "What did he say?"

"He said not to call 911. He's dispatched help and a clean-up crew. We're to stay until they get here, then go do whatever we were going to do."

"How about the police? I'm sure someone called 911 when the fireworks started."

"He said they have it covered. The metro police won't be responding; his people will arrive shortly. We might as well finish packing."

Within minutes, plain-clothes people, with guns on their hips arrived wearing dark blue jackets with POLICE-FEDERAL OFFICER printed in orange across the back. People looking out from their room doors watched as more men with a stretcher and medical bags arrived.

The lead officer approached Virginia. "Miss Virginia Davies-Clark?"

"Yes, Sir." She showed him her credentials and badge.

"We'll take over now. I think it's best you and your husband leave during the commotion for better cover."

Virginia nodded. "Good idea. Can I ask a question?"

"Sure."

"Your jacket says Police-Federal Officer. Who are you with?"

"The Smithsonian Central Security Service and the medical team is Army."

"Oh. Okay. Thanks for coming so quick. I'll get my husband and we'll slip out."

CHAPTER 7

"Virginia and Andy returned to the Hampton Inn in Warrenton. As soon as they entered the room, Andy hurried to their second floor window, peered outside, then pulled the drapes shut. "That may help keep wandering eyes from seeing in here and cut down on any snoops with parabolic microphones."

"Good idea. Think anyone is out there?"

"I don't think so. I didn't see anything suspicious. There were just some cars in our parking lot, but no people."

Virginia placed their luggage on the folding suitcase stand, then collapsed on the bed. "Okay, assuming we get no more unwelcome visitors, let's do some brainstorming, and figure out our next moves."

"Let's list what we know or suspect so far." Andy sat in a padded chair and put his feet up on a small ottoman.

"Let's start with this mysterious quilt. All I know is that it was made for the Sears contest in 1933 and it won and was at the World's Fair in Chicago. Next, Mrs. Roosevelt had *The Unknown Star*, it was seen by Einstein and disappeared in the early forties. It may or may not contain the wire recorded unified field theory."

Virginia scooted to the headboard and leaned back against it. "That's most of it. The contest, announced by Chicago-based mail order company, Sears, Roebuck and Co., was planned as one of the promotional events for the upcoming fair. At the time it was announced, nobody thought it would become one of the important events in American quilt-making history."

Andy leaned forward. "That much I know."

"But it turned out that, all over the country, almost twenty-five thousand pieces were submitted at the Sears stores and mail-order houses. None of the numerous quilt contests that have been organized in this country attracted so many entries, which makes the 1933 contest unique. Also, Sears Roebuck Co., in 1934, issued a quilt pattern booklet of the prize-winning quilts in the contest. The booklet was *Century of Progress in Quilt Making*. The prize-winning quilt, now *The Star of the Bluegrass* was offered in both kit form and perforated pattern form. It was re-named *Feathered Star* in this publication."

Andy nodded. "So far I'm with you. Is there anything else about it that is unusual?"

"Yes. There is an interesting story behind this winning quilt. Margaret Rogers Caden of Kentucky won. It turned out that she did not actually make *The Unknown Star* or *The Star of the Bluegrass*, but ordered it from three other women in the area, and then just put her name on the entry tag and turned the work in. Margaret Caden ran a very successful business in Lexington, Kentucky, together with five of her sisters. They owned a gift shop downtown, and besides selling needlework and patterns, they also took orders from all over the country to quilt. Caden's story is very unusual. Normally, participants turned in quilts made by them, and most of the time these women were not as well-to-do as the winner from Lexington.

"During the depression, the crafts that women made were sometimes their only source of income. In fact, the gigantic number of entries that the contest of 1933 attracted can be explained by the size of the grand prize offered. At the time, one thousand dollars was a fortune, and winning this prize meant a complete change in someone's life. In 1933, a new Ford cost less than five hundred dollars, a three-bedroom house just three thousand dollars."

"I bet a 1933 Ford would cost a hell of a lot more than that today as a collector's item." Andy rose and walked to the window, pulled the drapes apart a little, glanced outside, then closed them. "No one out there." He turned and leaned against the window ledge facing Virginia. "Is there anything else that may help us?"

"Probably not."

"How do you know so much about all this?"

"I am a quilter. I read up on it before we left and on the way here." Virginia climbed off the bed and went to her red backpack. She opened it and pulled out a book titled *Patchwork Souvenirs of the 1933 World's Fair.* "I was reading this and some notes from the internet."

"Why would Einstein and Mrs. Roosevelt use it to hide something so important or did they? He might have just gone with her to look at it."

"I don't know. But if he didn't stick the little wires into the quilt, why have the Secret Service hide it? We also have no idea where the Secret Service agents took the thing." She returned the book to the backpack.

Andy scowled. "From what Dr. Montgomery said, the government obtained some papers that said he had found the theory and hid it. How accurate that information is, we don't know, but someone high up in the DOD thinks it is true."

"Well, we have the list we started in Washington. Let's see, Fort Knox, Fort Leavenworth, and Federal Reserve banks, maybe a studio or someone in Hollywood. Maybe it never left Washington, which I doubt, or they gave it to someone the agents knew somewhere in the country, or it got returned to Chicago and is in a museum's back room in a box."

Virginia frowned. "Some help you are." She sat on the bed again. "If it is in a box in a museum, it is probably not in good shape or they may have disposed of it by now."

"Well, like you already said, the forts and the federal reserve banks are probably on the bottom of the list." He cleared his throat. "But we did have some federal or military labs around then, like Oak Ridge, Tennessee and a couple in New Mexico and Nevada and, I think, California. Then there are museums. I still like the more personal approach, like they gave it to someone for safe keeping and probably forgot about it when the war started."

"Which would imply the president never knew about the secret that was supposedly hidden in it."

"Right. So it was going to someone Mrs. Roosevelt or the agents knew. I'm betting it was someone Mrs. Roosevelt knew. Also, it was not going someplace that would need the president's authorization." Andy rubbed his chin. "What are we going to do for dinner?"

"You want to eat now?"

"Yeah. I'm hungry, and I don't want to be running around a strange area with who-knows-who out there looking for us at night. I shoot better on a full stomach and when I can see my target."

"Before we go look for a feeding pouch for you, can you tell me again, what this unified field theory is and why it is so important? But do it so I can understand it."

Andy sat on the desk chair, leaned back, put his fingers together in front of himself, and cleared his throat. "Okay. There are basically four forces in nature. Strong nuclear, weak nuclear—they are contained in quantum theory—electromagnetism, and gravity. Each is handled with its own math, and they work quite well in their own worlds. But there is no overall theory to tie them together. Unified field theory attempts to bring these four force fields together into a single framework. Quantum theory seems to limit any interacting deterministic theory's descriptive power. In simple terms, no theory can predict events more accurately than allowed by the Planck Constant."

Virginia shook her head. "Now that's as clear as mud. What's Planck Constant? Wait… don't answer that. Can you translate what you said so I can understand it?"

"There is no mathematical system that ties all the forces together under a unified set of rules."

"Why didn't you say that in the first place? If this were actually done, it would be important, right?"

"Beyond your imagination. Relativity helped develop the atom bomb and nuclear power. This theory could develop either a lot of good or, conversely, a real bad weapon."

"Got it." Virginia slid off the bed. "Let's go to dinner and figure out our next move."

Andy drove out of the parking lot onto US 29. They drove the hilly, tree-lined road past businesses, old buildings to Gainesville and into the Target shopping center. They parked and walked to the Uno Chicago Grill on Atlas Walk Way. They entered and were escorted to a booth.

Virginia looked around at the dark wood trim and sports decorations. "Reminds me of a place you'd see in Chicago or New York. Dark wood, low ceiling, and neat atmosphere." She picked up the menu, noticing Andy busily studying it. "What are you thinking of having?"

"Pepperoni pizza. I think I'll have a Dos Equis dark as well." He looked at Virginia. "You?"

"I was considering a large salad, but if you get a big pizza, I can split it with you. I'll get iced tea, though."

Andy called the waiter and ordered. After the server left, he sat back. "I was trying to watch our tail as we came here tonight. Did you see anyone?"

"No. Maybe we slipped out of Washington fast enough during the commotion and all the traffic to thwart any nonprofessional people trying to follow us." Virginia sat back and glanced around again. "You know, right now I'd like to forget we are looking for the quilt and that there are some dangerous people competing with us and just enjoy dinner."

"Yeah, that would be nice." Andy peered around the room, looking at the various signed photos of celebrities whose pictures adorned the walls. "Look there," he pointed. "In that picture with Cary Grant in it on a far wall. What's that behind Cary Grant?"

Virginia twisted in her seat and stared at the photo. "I can't see it that well. Hang on." She slipped out of the booth and strolled around tables to the wall and examined the picture he mentioned along with a half-dozen others. Grinning, she walked back and slid back into her seat.

"You're good. It's a quilt in the background, all right, but not the one we're after. From the other things in the photo, the picture must have been taken on a movie set."

"Maybe we should check it out. It supports your idea."

"We'll need to determine when it was taken and where. We'll add that to our list and then shake things out. When we leave, take a picture of it with your camera and we can have Washington do some research for us."

The pizza arrived. They ate without much conversation until they were ready to leave. Andy put a tip on the table, scooped up the check, and walked with Virginia to the far wall. "Stand between the one with Cary Grant and the one with Frank Sinatra, and I'll take a picture. This way, if anyone is watching, we may confuse them a little, I hope."

Dangerous Threads

Virginia posed while Andy snapped a couple pictures with his phone camera. Then they walked to the front, paid their bill, and left.

As they exited the building, Andy said, "Did you notice the couple in a booth across the room snapping pictures of you and the photographs you posed with?"

"Yes."

CHAPTER 8

Andy followed Virginia into their hotel room, shut the door behind him, and engaged the deadbolt. Virginia walked to the small refrigerator and removed a plastic bottle of water, then sat on the bed.

Andy grabbed a bottle of water and sat in the upholstered easy chair. "You know, some things have been bugging me since the start."

"What's that?"

"First, if this so-called secret unified field theory was real and so hush-hush, how is it that the Arabs seem to know about it?" He took a drink of water. "Second, how did these Arab factions get the drop on us? Third, just how solid is the information about the unified field theory actually existing and being in that mystery quilt? And fourth, who else knows about it? Fifth, how come our adversaries know about us and we don't know squat about them? And, lastly, why would Einstein put it into the quilt in the first place?"

"I've wondered the same things." Virginia took a swig of water. "I also wondered what they'll do next? For that matter, what are we going to do next?"

"I think we need to get Montgomery to 'fess up on how the Arabs got wind of it and how he knew they did. Is there a leak at the DOD? Where does that put us except in the cross hairs?"

Virginia rose from the bed, walked to Andy, and kissed the top of his balding head. "You use that smart brain of yours and figure out our next move. I'll contact Montgomery."

"Okay." He drank more water as she dug her secure iPhone from her backpack and punch in a phone number. He leaned back and closed his eyes, deep in thought. After a few minutes, Virginia shook him.

"Andy, I talked to Montgomery. It seems there was a leak in the DOD, actually at The Defense Advanced Research Project Agency or—"

"DARPA."

She tilted her head and gave him a quizzical look. "Yeah, how'd you know?"

"I had some grants and contracts from them in my lab at the University of California at Irvine."

"UCI would have been enough, Dear. I went there and we met there, remember?"

Andy gave her a sheepish grin. "Yeah. Montgomery said the leak was at DARPA?"

"Yes. That's what he said. The person who let the information out was a major who was a Muslim convert. He gave the information to someone at the Saudi embassy. He thinks the Golden Crescent has spies inside the Saudi government or the embassy and that's how they found out. The leak's been plugged, but the damage has been done."

"That's why the Russians or Chinese aren't involved." Andy frowned. "You said the spy *was* a major? What's he now, a private and a prisoner breaking big rocks into little ones?"

"According to Montgomery, he was arrested and while being taken to Fort Leavenworth for trial, he tried to escape."

"Let me guess," Andy made the shape of a pistol with his fingers. "He was shot."

"He was shot and killed. The Army saved the taxpayers the cost of a trial and jail and any further exposure of the secret. Nice and neat."

"Did Montgomery know how the Saudi's Al Mukhabarat Al A'amah and the Golden Crescent got wind of us?"

"Not exactly. He figures they were doing some research on their own, and when we went to see that nice old man here in Warrenton, Mr. Carver, both factions happen to be in the area ready to do the same thing. Remember Mr. Carver mentioning that phone call? Montgomery thinks we were unexpected newcomers for both the Saudis General Intelligence Directorate and the Golden Crescent. They kind of ran into us. He thinks, based on the encounters they've had with us, they may take the position of following us and letting us do the hard part then swoop in for the kill when we find the quilt and the wire recordings of the field theory."

"I think he's right." Andy nodded. "But I don't like the part about swooping in for the kill. Definitely not cool."

Virginia hopped onto the bed and sat cross-legged. "Any ideas on what we do next?"

"I think we need to research online. See about that photo we saw in the restaurant and also the background of Cary Grant during that period of time. At least it had a quilt in it, even if it isn't the quilt we want. Maybe there's more where that one came from. We probably should look up what stars or Hollywood celebrities or producers, etc., Mrs. Roosevelt may have known."

"Good idea, but I think we should start that tomorrow. I know how we work, we'll get sucked into it, won't get any sleep, and we've had a busy day." Virginia's cell phone rang. She reached across the bed and picked it up. "Hello?"

"Mrs. Clark?" a soft female voice said.

"Yes."

"This is Vanessa Franklyn. You came to my house in Middleburg."

"Yes, Mrs. Franklyn. How are you?"

"I'm fine, thank you, but I remembered something and thought it might be important. It isn't much, and I may be wasting your time and all."

"That's fine, Mrs. Franklyn. What is it you remember?" Virginia motioned for Andy to come close and listen.

"You got me thinking, and after you left I recalled something that Secret Service agent who returned earlier than the others said to another agent. They were eating some of my peanut butter cookies shortly after he returned."

"What was it?"

"He said the cargo was safe and she was tied up at a secure location. Then he and the other agent walked out. I don't know what that means, or if it is helpful."

"Thank you, Mrs. Franklyn. We'll look into it. Anything you recall may be critical, so please call this number anytime."

"I will. Please give my regards to that nice husband of yours, and good night." She hung up.

Virginia switched off the phone and looked at Andy. "What do you suppose that means?"

He wrote the statement in a small spiral notebook from his shirt pocket. "I haven't got a clue. It is intriguing, though."

Virginia rubbed her eyes. "I asked Montgomery to check with Fort Leavenworth, Fort Knox, and the government labs that existed in those days to see if there is anything in their archives or collective memories about a quilt. That should save us some time."

"Good girl. You're on it. That means we have our internet research to do tomorrow, then we can lay out a strategy."

Haddad Abdel A'hsam, the cultural attaché at the Saudi Embassy and the section head of the Saudi's Al Mukhabarat Al A'amah, sat in his high-backed leather chair behind his ornately carved, polished wooden desk looking at a picture of Albert Einstein. "What did you find, Dr. Einstein? Did you really discover this theory that everyone thinks is so important?" He tossed the photo on the desk blotter and leaned back and stared at the ceiling. The phone rang. He straightened and answered the phone. "Hello?"

"Mr. A'hsam, we found the couple you inquired about," said a man's voice.

Dangerous Threads

A'hsam took a small piece of paper from his center desk drawer and removed a gold-plated pen from his pocket.

"Good, where are they?"

"I don't know. We found them at a pizza restaurant. Then we lost them. But they were in the Gainesville area."

"So, they like pizza. How does that help us?"

"The man, the Mr. Clark... he took some pictures of the woman near some photographs on the wall of the restaurant. We too took photographs of the pictures she stood near. I'm e-mailing them to you shortly."

A'hsam threw the pen on the desk. "You found the couple, then lost them? What am I paying you for? The last idiots I sent to deal with them are in custody someplace in Washington and we can't find them. The Golden Crescent's people have disappeared as well. Now this? You lose them and you want to send me pictures of pictures?"

"Yes... Sir. We... ahh... we thought they might be important."

"What are the photographs on the wall of?"

"Some American cinema or sports celebrities, I think. Most are signed."

"Send them at once and find Dr. Clark and his woman!" A'hsam rubbed his chin. "Do not interfere with them or harm them in any way. Just watch. It is also safer that way. We need to stick with them like dew to a leaf, but be watchful and careful. Do not antagonize them. We have a new strategy now that they are involved and as resourceful as they seem."

"What of the Golden Crescent?"

"I have people looking for those fanatics. If they show up near the Americans, we will handle them. They cannot be allowed to interfere with the Americans."

"I understand. We will continue our search and send you the photographs. Ma'assalama."

"Fi aman Allah," A'hsam replied, then disconnected. He looked at the picture of Einstein on his desk. "Allah alim? Does God really know best in this case? I wonder. Allah be with you, Dr. and Mrs. Clark, Allah be with you. I have a feeling you're going to need it."

CHAPTER 9

Virginia strolled out of the bathroom with a towel wrapped around her, rubbing her wet hair with another. Andy in his pajamas, sat at the desk running his fingers over the laptop's keyboard.

"What are you doing?"

Andy gave her a sideways glance, then returned his attention to the computer. "I've started to research Cary Grant in the late thirties and early forties. Did you know his real name was Archibald Alexander Leach?"

"I think I heard that someplace. Probably on a TV game show or something." She tossed the towel she used to dry her hair on the bed and sat on the end, bending slightly to see the computer screen.

"Well, according to this, he worked for Columbia Pictures and Hitchcock during the time period we're interested in. He was a big baseball fan, originally supporting the New York Giants and then later, the L.A. Dodgers." Andy sat back and stared at the screen. "It says here he was an amateur magician. I didn't know that. He was a fan of Elvis and knew Orson Welles, among others."

Virginia rose and walked to the closet. "Keep searching while I get dressed. So far there isn't much to go on. Did he know the Roosevelts?"

"It doesn't say. But he was a Republican and they were Democrats, so my guess would be no. But I'll check." He tapped some more keys, then settled back in the chair. "No record of him knowing the Roosevelts and in case you're wondering, he was not a member of the OSS during the war. So it looks like he's not on our list to follow up."

Virginia slipped on her jeans and a T-shirt and went back into the bathroom. She stuck her head out. "How about Orson Welles?"

"What about him?"

"Is he a candidate for us?"

"I'll check." Andy banged away on the keyboard. "Well, what do you know? Welles was politically active from the beginning of his career. He defined his political orientation as 'progressive.' He was a strong supporter of Franklin Roosevelt and the New Deal. And guess what? He was a magi-

Dangerous Threads

cian, as well as a radio and movie actor, director, and writer. Wow, he was some guy. He even made movies for the government and Lockheed during the war."

"So he may have known Mrs. Roosevelt?" Virginia asked.

"Could be. We need to follow up on that. What are we going to do about that picture of Cary Grant with the quilt in the background?"

Virginia left the bathroom and walked across the room to the table. "I'll see what I can find, you go get ready. I'm surprised you haven't been complaining about not eating breakfast yet."

"I was just going to mention that." Andy hopped from the chair and hurried to the bathroom. Fifteen minutes later, he walked back into the room dressed in jeans and a red sport shirt. "Any luck finding out about the picture?"

"Sort of." Virginia wrinkled her nose. "I found it online and traced it to the Columbia Pictures studio in California. I was going to call them to see what I could find out, but California is three hours behind us and it's six in the morning there. I'll wait until noon our time. You ready for breakfast?"

"Always ready to eat. Where do you want to go?"

"There's an IHOP down US 29."

"Sounds like a plan." Andy put the .38 Special into its pocket holster and slipped it into his pants pocket. He grabbed his University of Texas baseball hat, wallet, keys, along with a speed loader and headed for the door. Virginia turned off the computer, grabbed her backpack, and followed him out the door.

During breakfast, Virginia's cell phone rang. "Hello, Dr. Montgomery. How are you this fine morning?"

"You seem chipper. Is there a reason for your cheery greeting? You find the quilt?"

"Yeah, there's a reason and no, we didn't find the quilt yet. The reason for my upbeat tone is no one has tried to kill us so far today. Why the call?"

"The Federal Reserve banks do not have the quilt in their vaults and have no records of ever having it. Trust me, they keep records of everything. I also struck out at the federal laboratories."

"How'd you do that overnight?"

"The government never sleeps."

"So you've got nothing."

"I haven't heard back from Fort Knox or Fort Leavenworth as of yet. I'm not expecting much, but I've inquired. Thought you'd want the latest. How are things on your end, besides being alive?"

Virginia told him of the added information from the old White House cook and what they found with their internet search.

"I do have one item for you to follow up on. You're going to like this one," Montgomery said.

"What is it?"

"I located a retired Secret Service agent who worked in the White House in the 1940s."

"He's still alive?"

"Yes, he's still alive. I'm not going to give you directions to Arlington National Cemetery. He's ninety-four and he lives in a not-so-nice neighborhood in North East Washington. Be careful."

"Okay, give me the details and address. We'll go right after we finish breakfast."

Virginia jotted down the information from Montgomery on a napkin and disconnected. "We've got another lead."

"I heard. The old guy may not remember much, but we need to check it all out. You do realize we may never find this mysterious quilt?"

"Yeah, but we'll give it our best shot. I sure as hell don't want the Arabs to find it." Virginia finished her eggs.

Andy glanced around the room again. "Speaking of Arabs, seen anyone suspicious lately?"

"No. Maybe we lost them."

"Or, they are watching and waiting for us to do the leg work like you said last night."

They drove to the address given to them, past a couple cab companies, an auto repair shop, and a number of vacant lots with broken chain-link fences and broken appliances scattered about. Andy slowed the Honda Pilot and cruised down the narrow road flanked on both sides by red brick row homes in various stages of disrepair. Papers blew across the road, catching on the remains of old cars with tires flat, windows broken, parked, and forgotten.

They pulled into a parking space on a side road. Andy turned off the engine. Five black youths approached the vehicle, two on Andy's side and three on Virginia's. Virginia saw Andy slide his revolver out of his pocket and slip it under his right leg. She opened her backpack. One of the young men on Andy's side leaned on the car and rapped on the side window with his knuckles.

Andy slid the window down. "What do you want?"

"Nice car, man. You lost or something?" said the man wearing a red bandana and an old orange flannel shirt hanging loose above some baggy jeans.

"Or something. Like I said, what do you want?" Andy looked him straight in the eyes.

"Tourist stuff is that way," he motioned with his head. "Maybe you should give us some money so you won't have no problems and I'll give you directions."

"We have business here and it isn't with you. We are federal officers."

The black youth looked into the SUV. "She don't look like no fed to me."

One of the men on Virginia's side opened her door and reached for her. He stumbled back screaming and ran down the street with his hands to his face, followed shortly by the second man. The third man started to pull a gun, then stopped and swallowed as he looked down the barrel of Virginia's Walther PPK .380 semiautomatic. She slid out of the car, aiming her gun at his face, then lowered it to his chest. His eyes followed the movement of the barrel. Virginia glared. "Leave the gun alone. Get on the ground, asshole. Put your hands on your head." He did what she said. "Now throw your gun on the sidewalk." He looked up at her with wide eyes and threw the gun away. As she tucked her gun into her waistband and turned her head to look over the car at Andy, the man pulled a knife and lurched up. She grabbed her taser and fired. The man's body jerked and twisted in spasms on the ground. "Why'd you do that? I didn't want to hurt you." She bent down and looked at him. He was unconscious.

Before the man on Andy's side realized what happened, Andy thrust open the door hitting the leader and knocked him backward. As he regained his balance, he reached under his shirt. Andy jumped from the car and leveled his revolver at the man's face. "Don't even think about it."

The man looking down Andy's gun barrel slowly pulled his hand back, empty. "Okay, man, it's cool."

The other black youth pulled a knife. Andy swung his arm around and aimed at him. The man dropped the knife, which skidded away. Andy turned back to the leader.

"On your knees, both of you." Andy shouted.

The men, eyes blazing murderously, slowly knelt. "You." He pointed the gun at the leader. "Now, take your gun out and drop it on the ground."

With a leer, the man did as he was told. "This ain't going to go good for you, man." He gave Andy a scorching wild-eyed look. "This is my hood. You'se a dead man and your woman is going to be mine."

Andy's look could melt iron. "What's your name?"

"What?"

"You heard me. What's your name?"

The man straightened his back slightly. "Dillon."

There was a crackling sound, then a scream of intense pain from a man on the other side of the car. The kneeling Dillon and his friend on the ground next to him glanced at Andy with quizzical looks.

Andy chuckled. "Hmm. Your homey must have tried something."

"Huh?"

"She doesn't like being attacked." Andy smiled. "I think she's about done with him. You're next."

Dillon's lower lip quivered as he slumped slightly. "I... I'm next?" His partner, on his knees, slowly edged away from him.

"Yep." Andy tried to hide his grin as he looked at the second man. "You're probably after him, so stay put."

The second man swallowed. "I've done nothin'. Keep her away from me."

Dillon twisted, looking at the area where the sounds came from. "What'd she do to Hermie?"

"Hermie? You're kidding. That's his name?" Andy choked down a laugh. "This gets better by the minute. If he tried to grab her or pulled a weapon, she responded. You really don't want to upset her. She's probably put fifty thousand volts through your friend."

He bit his lip. "She can't do that."

Andy shrugged. "She did it." *What the hell is she doing over there?*

Sweat beaded on Dillon's forehead. He looked at his friend kneeling on the on the ground near him. "Man, this is bad, Can't we do something?"

"It's too late." Andy leaned against the car. "Dillon, what happened to your macho gang leader act?" He looked around at the deserted street. "I don't see any of your gang coming to help you, either."

Dillon looked around. "Come on... you said you're federal cops. We didn't do nothin'. What are you, DEA, FBI, ICE?"

Andy chuckled. "You wouldn't believe me if I told you."

"Yes... Yes, I would, really... man... who the hell are you people?"

"Smithsonian Central Security Service." Andy displayed his gold badge.

"What? You shittin' me? You're museum cops? There ain't no dinosaurs here. You ain't got jurisdiction here. You're dinosaur cops?"

"Yeah, we're dinosaur cops and yes, we do have jurisdiction here and anywhere in the United States. Just think of us like a Smithsonian FBI. And, right now, we like dinosaurs better than you."

Dillon nodded toward the other side of the car. "Come on, man, you gotta help Hermie."

"Now, this is your turf, right?" Andy waved his gun around. "You're the head man, the big Kahuna, right?"

Dillon's eyes became saucers as they followed Andy's pistol. "Yeah."

"Then, what you're going to do, Dillon, is take your buddy my wife is talking to, and get him to a doctor to make sure he's okay." Andy pushed off the car. "And you'd better find the two girly-men who ran from my wife screaming and get them to a doctor as well, or they may go blind. She used bear strength pepper spray on them. That stuff will stop a grizzly bear. And, my good man, you will leave us and this car alone. Got it? Trust me, you do not want to have us come back and be disappointed."

Dillon saw Virginia walk around the car carrying her backpack. He

Dangerous Threads

watched her, his face etched in desperation. "Wha... What did you do with my friend?" He swallowed. "You not going do that to me, are you?"

"Not if you do what you're told." Virginia smiled. "I tasered your buddy with fifty thousand volts. He tried to stab me. I really didn't want to hurt him. But, he's not very tough any more. Oh, he also needs a change of pants. I gave him quite a jolt into his balls. He seems to have passed out. Next time, maybe he'll think before he pulls a knife." She walked up to Andy. "Now that these young men have seen the light, shall we lock up, and go visit the gentleman we came to see?"

Andy looked at the men on their knees. "The neighborhood seems to have become empty and quiet. You're going to see that it stays that way, aren't you, Dillon? Because if you try anything stupid, you'd better pray someone around here calls the paramedics, because we won't."

Dillon looked at his friend and they nodded. "Yeah. We'll keep things cool."

Virginia picked up Dillon's gun and his friend's knife and stuck them in her backpack. "If you're good boys, I'll give this and the other fella's toys back to you when we leave. Deal?"

Dillon swallowed. "Yes... yes, Ma'am."

Andy locked the car, and they walked a few doors down the street to the house of the elderly retired Secret Service officer. When they were out of earshot, Andy leaned close to her. "Did you really taser him back there? What about the other two?"

"Shot the bear spray into the eyes of the two who grabbed me and then used my new taser—on full power—on the third guy. He pulled a knife and lunged at me. It was a stupid thing to do. What did he think he was doing? I didn't want to shoot him so I used the taser," Virginia said.

"Ouch. What he did was a couple sandwiches short of a picnic. Where'd you learn all this stuff?"

She gave him a mischievous smile. "Home and Garden Television. You were quite impressive back there, Dear. I think you scared the hell out of them." Virginia took his hand and squeezed it. "Not bad for a professor."

Andy smiled. "I watched the Military Channel. What you did is what actually scared them. Especially because they saw the first two run away screaming, then heard the buzzing followed by more screams. Not actually seeing it made it worse in their minds. I just put the frosting on the cake."

"I think you're right." Virginia glanced at the paper in her hand and looked at the addresses on the buildings. "Here it is. I hope he's home and remembers something useful, especially after our encounter with his neighborhood watch."

They walked up the two concrete steps to the red brick building with a dark green door and rang the doorbell.

CHAPTER 10

The green door opened and a short, slightly stooped man with wild, white hair, a handlebar mustache, and arthritic fingers greeted them. He looked behind them at the street. "Hello. Whoever you are, you are more than welcome in my house. Please, come in." He stepped aside and waved them in.

Virginia and Andy looked at each other. Virginia smiled and presented her gold badge and credentials. "Sir, we are with the Smithsonian Central Security Service, and we'd like to talk to you. My name is Virginia Davies-Clark. This is my partner and husband, Doctor Andy Clark." She stepped into the hallway with Andy following.

"I wondered who you were. From what I saw from my window these past few minutes, I figured, in this neighborhood, whoever you were, you are welcome. The old man pointed to the right. "Let's go into the sitting room. Please, have a seat. Can I get you anything? Coffee, tea?"

"No, thank you." Virginia stepped into the parlor and glanced around before sitting on a settee next to Andy. The room looked like it was straight out of a nineteen-forties movie. Floor lamps were arranged near chairs, a wooden and glass coffee table sat in front of a sofa. The chairs were straight from a *Thin Man* movie. The furniture looked new, or at least well kept. The phone on a small desk near a window looked like a black Ma Bell rotary phone only with white buttons arranged in a circle like the original phone dials.

"I'm sorry," the man said as he sat across from them in a worn, polished leather chair. "My name is Richard Van Epps. May I ask a question?"

Virginia nodded.

"What did you do to those young punks out there?"

"We took their weapons. Unfortunately, I had to shoot two of them with a strong dose of pepper spray and tase another."

Andy cleared his throat. "I held the others and when they heard the commotion on the other side of the car, their imagination did the rest."

"I saw it all. Wonderful. You did more in a few minutes than the Metropolitan Police have done in years. Now, how can I help you?"

"Mr. Van Epps. I understand you were a Secret Service agent stationed in the White House in the late thirties and early forties. Is that correct?'

Van Epps nodded. "Yes. I was there then."

"Do you have any recollection of a prize-winning quilt from the 1933 Worlds Fair being given to Mrs. Roosevelt?"

He leaned back in his chair. "Let me think. Yeah, there was a quilt from that fair that she had. I remember because during a couple of his visits, Albert Einstein went to see it. I remember thinking his interest in it seemed strange. Why would a noted scientist and professor be that interested in a quilt? Especially since the president took no interest in it. But it wasn't any business of mine or the service."

"Do you recall it being moved out of the White House?"

Van Epps nodded. "I remember a few agents saying they were moving it, but there was something hokey about that."

Andy's brow wrinkled. "Why do you say that?"

"Because they made too big a deal about it. If my memory serves me, and mind you, it sometimes doesn't, there were three agents who supposedly took it someplace. This was in nineteen-forty-one, just before Pearl Harbor."

"That's what we were led to believe."

"Well, I saw it in January of nineteen-forty-two, being placed in a box for shipment."

Virginia looked at Andy, then back at Mr. Van Epps. "Are you sure? There were duplicates made around the country."

"Oh, it was the same quilt all right. I remember because there was a tag on it and there was an FBI agent guarding it. I remember thinking, for a quilt, a prize-winning quilt at that, it seemed strange that there was an FBI agent guarding it. When I asked about it, I was told the first lady wanted it protected and that was all I could get from them. I had other duties so I didn't pursue it. Seemed strange at the time, especially since it was supposedly already moved to a secure location, but with the war starting and all, it slipped into oblivion."

Virginia leaned forward. "Do you know what happened to it? Where it went?"

"Not really. Like I said, I had other things to do and it didn't concern the Secret Service, or me at the time. I just heard rumors, that's all."

"So it was shipped out of the White House in early nineteen-forty-two?"

"Yes. In February or March. I think the box went to Fort Belvoir, south of Washington, to the President's yacht."

"The President's yacht? Why?"

"That's why I remember the time. The President and Mrs. Roosevelt were going to sail to New York on it with some of the president's staff."

Virginia frowned. "The war had started, why didn't they take the train?

Wouldn't that have been safer?"

"Sure, it would have been safer. I don't know why they took the yacht. I stayed in Washington for that trip. Other agents protected him, along with the Army and the Navy. Did you know the Army owned the yacht?"

"No, I didn't. So, the First Lady went with the president to New York?"

"Yes and I think, from what someone said, she took the quilt with her to see a friend."

"New York? Not Hollywood?" Virginia sighed. "New York?"

"Mrs. Roosevelt had friends there," Van Epps said.

"Did she bring it back?"

"I don't think so, but as I said, I didn't pay much attention to that."

Virginia raised an eyebrow hopefully. "Are any of the agents who went with the president on that trip still alive?

"I don't think so." Van Epps shook his head. "I lost contact with them years ago, but by then most had died."

"Okay, back to the trip. Do you have any idea who Mrs. Roosevelt may have given it to?"

"No. Remember, I wasn't there. But I have some memorabilia from those days, saved in some cardboard boxes. There may be something in some papers I have in them. Most of it is notes and personal stuff. Like I said, memorabilia. They're old and not in the best of shape, mind you, but you are welcome to take a look at them."

"How many boxes do you have?" Andy asked.

"I don't know, a dozen perhaps. There may be something there that can help you. You can take them with you if you like. But please return them when you're done." They trudged down to the basement and found eleven cardboard boxes with papers, journals, and photographs.

Virginia and Andy carted the boxes to the front entrance. Andy went to move the car closer to load the boxes.

When he walked up to his black Honda Pilot, a muscular black youth was leaning on the passenger side door. He looked at Andy. "You the dinosaur cop who owns this?"

Andy grinned. "Rented, and yes I am."

"Okay. Dillon said to keep it nice-like, so I made sure it's okay."

"Thank you, and tell Dillon thanks for me."

The boy looked around. "Where's your old lady? He said there's two of you."

"She's at a house down the street and I need to move the car to load some boxes."

"Okay, dinosaur cop, I'll come with you and help you."

"You needn't do that."

"That's okay. I never met dinosaur cops before and Dillon said you were cool and didn't arrest him or his bros and your lady is a pretty tough cookie. She knocked Hermie out with electricity and sent Roosevelt and Frank to the hospital with something about their eyes. I gotta meet her." He grinned. "Dillon said, for cops, you two are okay. You didn't call the regular cops and have them arrested. You really dinosaur cops?"

"We work for the Smithsonian. We didn't want to arrest him or his buddies as long as they cooperated. We weren't here to harass them." Andy unlocked the car. "Hop in, and we'll go get the boxes."

Fifteen minutes later, they had all the boxes in the double-parked SUV. While Virginia said good-bye to Mr. Van Epps, Andy talked to the young man who helped them. "Thanks for the assistance. My wife has your friends' weapons, and we said we'd return them if everything was cool while we were here. A deal is a deal, so as soon as she comes to the car, we'll give you their weapons, less the bullets."

"Really? I gotta say, you two are real cool."

Andy motioned for him to come closer. "Can you do me a favor?"

The youth stepped closer to Andy. "Sure, Mr. Dinosaur Cop, what do you need?"

"That house where we got the boxes from, there is an elderly gentleman who lives there."

"Yeah?"

"I want to make sure he, his house, and belongings are kept safe. Will you ask Dillon to do that for me?"

The youth smiled. "I don't need to ask him, Mr. Dinosaur Cop. He said to be nice to you and do what you wanted, so consider the old guy and his house protected. We'll protect him and it like we was the Marines."

Andy shook his hand. "Thanks." He nodded toward the house. "Here comes my wife. She'll give you the weapons."

Virginia walked up to them and set her backpack on the ground. She pulled out the knives and three pistols, removed the magazines and took the bullets from the chambers then handed them back to the young man. "Here ya go. A promise is a promise."

He looked at the weapons in his hands. "You're really giving these back?"

"You and your buddies did what we asked, and we gave our word."

He gave them a confused look. "You're really cops?"

"Yep."

"Looks like Dillon was right. You dinosaur cops really are different. We can respect you. Come back any time. And we'll watch out for your friend like you asked." He turned and walked down the street, turned into an alley, and disappeared.

Virginia looked at Andy as she picked up her backpack. "What did he mean by protecting our friend?"

"He and the gang are the new security service for Mr. van Epps. They will be protecting him and from the looks of this neighborhood, that isn't a bad idea."

"Like having the Mafia protect him."

"It worked for you once."

She nodded. "Too true. Shall we take our treasures and see if there is anything in all this stuff that can help us?"

"Get in, and let's go back to the hotel and start looking."

As they drove, a red Mini Cooper pulled out and roared after them. One block down the street, Dillon and seven young men stepped into the street and stopped the vehicle at gunpoint.

An Arab man dressed in a dark suit hurried back to his car, picked up his cell phone and dialed.

A'hsam answered. "What?"

"They just left a house in northeast Washington with a load of boxes. The Golden Crescent tried to follow them and was intercepted by some local gang members. It looks like the locals are assisting the Clarks."

"Where are they going?" A'hsam asked.

"Who?"

"The Clarks!"

"I don't know where they went. I thought it would be best to not try and race after the Clarks right now. The Golden Crescent isn't going to follow them either."

"How did you find the Clarks?"

"I have friends around, and when I was told that two black gang members were in the emergency room and a woman put them there, I figured it might be Mrs. Clark. So I asked where the young men came from and was told around here. I found their vehicle being guarded by a big guy and thought it best to wait and watch."

"Good work, Hassan. Whom were they talking to?"

"I don't know, but it looks like going to see him now might not be a good idea, either."

"Why?"

"A car with three of the local hoods is now parked in front of his house. When I approached, they discouraged me. They're definitely not the congenial types. Looks like the Clarks have them protecting whoever lives there."

"The Clarks have recruited street hoods?"

"It seems so."

A'hsam sighed. "They're resourceful. Give me the address and I'll find

Dangerous Threads

out who the owner is."

Hassan gave A'hsam the address. "Anything else you want me to do here?

"No. You did good, Hassan. We will find them again."

CHAPTER 11

Andy shut the door to their hotel room and sat on the bed. "Good thing they had one of those luggage trolleys; getting those boxes up here would have been laborious." He looked at the cardboard boxes stacked next to the desk. "I'm glad we ate lunch before we began this. Where do you want to start?"

Virginia emerged from the bathroom in a pair of loose fitting pajama bottoms and a large, baggy burnt-orange University of Texas T-shirt. "Why don't we each take a box, start looking through them, and just work our way down the stack?" She stepped to the desk and removed her portable door alarm, turned it on, and hung it on the door handle. Virginia moved to the boxes and with her foot, pushed one on the floor to the side of the bed. She hoisted it and set it on the end of the bed, then hopped on and sat cross-legged as she opened it.

"You're in pajamas in the afternoon?"

"Just wanted to get comfortable. We'll probably be at this for a while."

Andy kicked off his shoes and moved to the desk. "Good idea." He pulled the top box down and set it on the floor next to the desk and started to sort through the papers. "What exactly are we looking for?"

"I don't know. I think we should start with anything related to the quilt, or Mrs. Roosevelt's trip and who she may have seen."

Andy started rummaged through documents and papers, setting aside anything that might have significance for further evaluation.

Andy glanced at the digital clock on the desk. Five p.m. He looked over at the empty box on the floor. Two piles of papers sat on the floor between the desk and the curtains. The short pile contained pictures, notes, and documents somewhat related to their subject. He twisted around and looked at Virginia, asleep on the bed. A notebook on her chest rose and fell with her breathing. On the bed was a small collection of papers. The rest of the documents she had gone through were stuffed back into the boxes.

Andy slowly rose and stretched. As he headed for the bathroom, the hallway door's handle rattled and Virginia's alarm screeched.

He froze for a second then turned toward the desk and his gun. Virginia whipped her pistol out from under her pillow and aimed it at the door. A woman's voice from the outside of the door called, "Housekeeping."

Virginia looked at Andy. "Did you ask for anything?"

"No."

"Get your gun, step to the wall, cover me, and be ready."

Andy grabbed his gun and hurried to the wall, raised his pistol, and nodded.

Virginia moved to the door, shut off the alarm, and looked through the peephole. A small dark complexioned woman stood outside. She fidgeted and kept looking to the side. She held a stack of towels.

"We don't need any more towels, thank you," called Virginia as she continued to watch the woman.

"I... I need to replace the ones you have."

"Leave them, and I'll get them later."

"But—"

Virginia's tone hardened. "Either leave them or just take them away."

The woman looked to the side, then walked away. Virginia watched the hall from the peephole. Not seeing anyone, she slowly opened the door and looked up and down the corridor. Empty. She closed the door and reattached her alarm.

Andy stepped from behind the wall, his gun at his side. "What was that all about?"

"I don't know." Virginia shrugged. "Maybe she was just delivering more towels. Maybe it was a way to see if we were here or to see how well we were prepared."

"I don't think anyone knows where we are, so let's call housekeeping and see what they say."

Virginia walked to him and kissed his cheek. "Always the logical one. I'll call and see if they sent anyone." She moved to the desk and dialed housekeeping and talked to the person who answered then hung up. She looked at Andy. "The manager said they had a request for more towels from this room. He said the call went to the front desk and they relayed the message to housekeeping. I think someone wants to see how well we're prepared."

"That means someone knows we are here. What are we going to do for dinner? Do we trust ordering in or going out? I don't think we should split up, either."

"Just like a man to think of food at a time like this." The phone rang. After answering it and talking for a minute, she hung up. "That was housekeeping again. The maid made a mistake, the call for more towels was from room 311, not our room, 211."

"Do you believe that?"

Virginia wrinkled her nose. "It's possible, but I'm all for going to DEFCON 3."

Andy's eyebrows rose. "You know about the military's alert levels?"

"I've watched TV and movies, and the Military Channel." She put her gun down and moved to the bed and started to package up the papers. "Let's pack this stuff up then take the stuff we need to relook at and get it ready for a quick departure."

"Good idea. Then we should order a pizza."

Virginia chuckled. "Make it pepperoni." She finished stacking her papers and stuffed them into her backpack. She looked at Andy. He stood with a pile of papers in his arms. "Put them in here with mine."

He stuffed his papers in the bulging backpack.

She took the clothes they needed for the next day out of their bags and prepared for an early start in the morning as Andy ordered a pizza. When he was finished ordering, he looked at Virginia sitting cross-legged on the bed. "You want to go through the papers tonight?"

"No. I'm too wound up to think clearly."

After eating their pizza, Virginia made a small opening in the drapes and peered out the window. The parking lot was well lit. Nothing seemed out of the ordinary. She closed the drapes and looked at Andy. "Looks okay. It's eight-thirty, let's get some rest, then attack this problem early in the morning."

"I'll vote for that. Tell you what, I'll stand first watch."

Virginia gave him a quizzical look. "First watch?"

"Yeah. I think we should be alert and ready for anything. Having one of us up and ready will be a good defense plus give the other a chance to wake up and respond or at best—get some rest."

"You've been watching too many westerns. But, it's a good idea." Virginia grinned. "If you're staying up, I have an idea to help pass time."

"Look at the papers?"

"No, dummy. Something a lot more fun." She turned on the TV to a Harry Potter movie on HBO.

At two-thirty in the morning, Virginia slid out from under the covers, glanced at the TV movie Andy was watching, and pulled on her clothes. Andy moved stiffly from the overstuffed chair to the bed and instantly fell asleep. Virginia sat in the chair, picked up the TV remote, and clicked through channels. She settled on an old Bing Crosby and Bob Hope movie, *The Road to Hong Kong*.

Dangerous Threads

At five a.m., Andy stumbled out of bed and wobbled to the bathroom. After shaving and showering, he emerged and changed into his clean clothes. As he stuffed his ditty bag and clothes into his suitcase, he saw Virginia looking out the window. "Things still quiet out there?"

"Yeah, appears so. Finish packing while I freshen up, and then let's get out of here. We can change our hotel this afternoon and in the meantime, let's go over the papers we sorted out."

"Sounds good. Let's get breakfast. Any ideas as to where we should go next? After we eat, that is?"

"I think we can go to Alexandria and check into a hotel there. Once we get things sorted out, maybe New York."

Andy grabbed his computer bag and suitcase. With Virginia carrying her backpack and dragging her wheeled suitcase behind, she followed Andy out of the hotel and to the parking lot. After placing their bags in the back of the SUV, they climbed in, and headed east on US 29 to the IHOP. As they drove Andy's cell phone rang. Virginia answered it.

"Is this Mrs. Dinosaur Cop?" said the voice on the phone.

Virginia chuckled. "Yes. Is this Dillon?"

"Yeah, it's me. We've been watching the man your husband asked us to, and I wanted to tell him a couple things."

"He's driving, can you tell me?"

"Sure. After you two left yesterday, a man approached the house. He looked A-RAB, and we sent him away. Later, five more men came in a big car. You know, one of them Hummers, it was black. They wanted to talk to the old man and wanted to know what you were doing. We discouraged them as well. We sort of... ahh... borrowed some new weapons from them. The old guy came out and talked to us. He's okay. Never met him before in person like, but he was okay. If you dinosaur cops like him, then he's one of us. We'll keep an eye on him and his place."

"Good job. I'll tell my husband."

"One more thing. One of the men had a radio and talked to someone on it, I overheard some of the conversation. They're still looking for you and figured you were in the Manassas area. If you dinosaur cops need anything else, just call."

Virginia clicked off and relayed the conversation to Andy. "It's too early to check into a hotel, but I have an idea where we can safely go to look at what we've got in my backpack—after breakfast, that is."

Splotchy raindrops struck the window. Andy turned on the windshield wipers. "Where?"

"The Smithsonian."

"Great idea." Andy glanced in the rearview mirror and changed lanes. He looked again. "Oh boy! Houston, we have a problem."

CHAPTER 12

Virginia twisted around and peered out the back window. A state police car with flashing lights was behind them. "I wonder what he wants? Are you speeding?"

"No," replied Andy as he pulled the car into a gas station driveway and stopped. He rolled down the window as the officer approached.

The state trooper, in a yellow rain slicker, bent slightly. "Good morning, Sir. May I see your license and proof of insurance?"

Andy handed the officer his driver's license, the rental agreement, and his insurance card. Then he pulled out his Smithsonian Central Security Service ID and badge. "We weren't speeding. May I ask what you stopped us for?"

The trooper examined Andy's license. "Texas, huh? Well, Sir, in Virginia you must turn on your headlights when you turn on the wipers."

"You do?"

"I take it you don't have to do that in Texas."

"No. I didn't know that. Sorry."

"How long are you going to be in Virginia?"

"A few days at most." Andy responded.

"Seeing that the laws are different and you're a visitor, I'll just give you a verbal warning." The officer handed Andy his documentation and credential case. "Please turn on your lights with the wipers and you shouldn't have any problems. I see you're a federal agent."

"Yes. You know of the agency?"

"Yeah. There was some problem in Warrenton the other day and I heard two of your agents were involved. Never heard of you guys before that." The trooper backed away. "You're free to go, Sir. Be careful in this rain, the roads get slippery around here."

"Thank you, Officer. We'll be careful." Andy turned on the wipers and lights after starting the car. He pulled back into traffic and headed for the IHOP.

Sitting in a booth across from Andy, Virginia had her stuffed backpack

Dangerous Threads

on the seat next to her. She ate her eggs and hash browns, while watching Andy devour his pancakes and sausage. She noticed a troubled look on his face. "You seem a million miles away. Anything wrong?"

Andy nodded. "Yeah, something has been bothering me. I know what Dr. Montgomery said about Einstein finding the theory of everything and sticking a recording of it into the Chicago World's Fair quilt Mrs. Roosevelt had. And the people we talked to seem to agree he had an interest in the quilt."

"That's what everyone said. What's the problem?"

"Why would he put it there?" Andy set his fork down and leaned forward. "First, did he really find the theory or did he find something else or nothing? Second, how'd he put equations on an audio tape? Third, even if he did, why put it into the quilt? Why not give it to the army or the government or keep it at Princeton? Fourth, if it isn't the theory of everything in it, why are the Arabs after it? And lastly, why would Mrs. Roosevelt take something that valuable and give it away?"

Virginia stared at him for a second. "Good questions." She finished her hash browns. "What do you think we should do?"

"Finish looking for the quilt. It's a long shot that we will actually find the darn thing, but we're getting paid to look, and we can see what happens. I just wish we knew what was really going on." He finished his sausage, sat back sipping coffee, and looked out onto the rain.

After paying their bill, Andy drove toward Washington.

Andy nosed the SUV into a driveway behind the Smithsonian American History Museum and stopped next to a guard shack.

The surprised guard, in a plastic raincoat, walked toward their vehicle. "This is restricted parking."

Andy handed him their credentials. "We're with the Smithsonian Central Security Service and need to park so the car can't be seen from the street."

The guard bent down, looked into their car, and frowned. "Wait here. I'll call this in." He marched back to the guard shack and made a call, watching Andy and Virginia while he talked on the phone. He hung up, fumbled around on a desk, and strutted back to the car with a document and their credentials in his hands. "Here is your stuff, put this on the dash and park over there." He pointed to a parking spot in an alcove behind the building. "The vehicle can't be seen from the street there."

"Thank you," Andy said. He drove behind the building and eased into the parking spot. He turned to Virginia. "He was a jolly fellow. Mr. Personality."

"Yeah. But cut him some slack. I'm sure his job is pretty boring most of the time, and he's out here all alone. Can't be all that much fun. And, we were obviously a surprise, especially being with the SCSS."

Virginia slung her backpack over one shoulder and popped her umbrella. Andy locked the car, pulled his jacket collar up against the rain. They hurried to the back door of the building. Virginia got there first and stopped. She looked at the keypad and ID card reader as Andy moved next to her.

"What's the problem?"

"I don't have a code."

"We may not need one. Try swiping your credential card. It's an ID card of sorts."

Virginia rummaged in her backpack for her SCSS credential case and removed the ID card. She wiped the coded tape part through the reader. The door clicked and popped open.

Andy grabbed the door, ushering Virginia in ahead of him, and then pulled the door closed behind him. Andy shook water off his jacket as Virginia closed her umbrella. They advanced down a fluorescent-lit, tan painted corridor, past bulletin boards, and closed doors with names on them. A man in a lab coat reading something passed them in the opposite direction. The hallway terminated at a T-junction with another hall. A sign indicated labs were to their left. They turned right, toward some typing sounds and people talking, proceeded to an office complex with a central circular area where three women were typing. Andy approached the counter.

A woman who he figured was in her late fifties looked up at him. "Can I help you?" Her eyes narrowed. "Where's your badge?"

"Here." Andy pulled his ID case out and flashed his gold badge and credential card.

She picked up a pair of glasses and studied it, then smiled. "SCSS agents, huh? We don't see too many of you around here. Welcome to The Museum of American History. What can I do for you?"

Andy leaned on the counter. "We could use a conference room or an empty office for the day if you have one."

She smiled. "Sure thing. There's a small conference room just down that way, number one-oh-nine. I'll put you down for it so you're not disturbed." She typed on a computer keyboard. "Okay, not good. It's already scheduled for the day. I'll try one-twenty-seven." More typing. "Got it. It is halfway down that hall on the left. Room one-twenty-seven. Yours all day. Anything else?"

Virginia stepped from behind Andy. "Is there a cafeteria around here?"

The woman eyed Virginia over her glasses. "Take the elevator down to the first level and you can't miss it."

"Restrooms?"

"Next to the conference room."

Virginia gave her a big smile. "Great. Thank you for all your help."

As they started down the hallway, Virginia heard the woman excitedly tell the other ladies in the cubicle that they were SCSS agents. She smiled. *So much for keeping our visit quiet.*

As they entered the small, carpeted conference room, the light automatically came on. The light green walls had pictures of digs and exhibits. On the far wall was a projection screen. A polished wooden table with leather chairs on castors stretched the length of the room.

Virginia unloaded her backpack onto the table and turned toward Andy. "Shall we get to work?"

He pulled out a soft leather chair and sat. Virginia sat next to him. "Ready to start?"

Four hours later, they had gone through most of the documents. They each took one of the last two folders and sat back. Virginia rubbed her eyes. "Talk about boring. We haven't found anything of value and—"

"We didn't have lunch." Andy pushed his glasses back up his nose. "Should we finish or break for lunch? I vote for lunch."

"Of course you do. You haven't mentioned food for hours, so let's go get a bite to eat and finish this after lunch."

Andy picked up the folder she had and placed it with his. "Let's kill two birds with one stone and finish this while we dine."

"It's a cafeteria. I don't think dining is the right word." She rose, stretched, grabbed her backpack, and headed for the door.

Andy stood. He pointed to the stacks of documents. "What about all this stuff?"

"Leave it. No one will bother it here. We have the conference room for the whole day."

They exited the room and walked to the elevator. After going through the line and getting their food,

Virginia led them to a small table near a back wall. "Here, you take these papers and I'll sort through these. Let's see if what we thought may be helpful really is important."

They ate and sorted through the papers. After finishing his slice of pizza, Andy held up a set of papers that were stapled together. "These might be something. It seems Mrs. Roosevelt took the quilt to New York and gave it to a friend for safe keeping. This corresponds with what Mr. Van-Epps said."

"Why would she do that? Why not just keep it in the White House?"

"I don't know. That's what it says."

Virginia set her ice tea glass down. "Does it say who she gave it to?"

"Yes."

David Ciambrone

"Okay, don't make me guess. Who?"

"Someone at the Metropolitan Museum of Art."

"Who? We need a name."

Andy grinned. "Being the super sleuth I am, I have a name. Doctor Albert Abernathy."

"Well, Super Sleuth. Looks like we're going to New York."

After they had eaten, Virginia and Andy strolled out of the elevator and walked toward the conference room. Virginia stopped outside the room. "Did you leave the door ajar?

Andy shook his head. "No. I closed it."

Virginia pushed the door open and entered. The neatly stacked piles of papers were scattered around the table. She motioned to Andy. "Looks like we had a visitor."

"Well, they didn't get anything. The only stuff that's worth much was with us at lunch. But who would do this here inside the Smithsonian?"

"Either someone at the Smithsonian, or someone else in the government that found out we were here, is working against us. That or maybe someone was just curious about what we were doing."

Andy nodded. "Let's pack up and get out of here before anyone misses us."

"I don't think that will be possible." Virginia started to gather up the papers and put them in her backpack. "Someone who knows what we are up to knew we were here, maybe Dr. Montgomery or others."

"Why would Montgomery be behind this? So far he's been on our side. Maybe it's someone else in the government who doesn't want us to find the quilt or they want to get it first. But how would our nemesis know we're here?"

"You could be right about a new adversary. Think about it; when we entered the back gate, I'm sure the security computer knew we were here and when we got the conference room the secretary used a computer and put our names in it to reserve the conference room. If someone was monitoring the computers for our names, we'd pop up. And the secretary told everyone in earshot that we were SCSS agents and wanted the conference room. Who knows who the guard may have told."

"Great. Big Brother is watching." Andy helped Virginia finish packing the documents. He went to the door, glanced up and down the corridor. Then he led her out of the room. "Let's just sneak out through the main museum entrance like tourists."

"We still need to get our car and when we entered I'm sure the guard logged us into a database. He'll log us out when we leave. There may be security cameras in the lobby as well."

Dangerous Threads

"True, but no one will be expecting us to suddenly drive out without logging out through a security door. By the time they find out we've flown the coop, we'll be lost in Washington traffic."

"Yeah, with a lot of traffic cameras watching for us. You have a point about having a head start." She touched his arm. "Let's go." They hurried up a flight of stairs to the street level. She pushed the crossbar on a set of double doors. They entered the public area of the museum, joined the throng of people milling about. They slowed as Virginia glanced at the quilts displayed on the sidewalls, then headed for the main doors and out onto Constitution Avenue.

CHAPTER 13

Through a cloudburst, Andy led Virginia around the building to the parking lot and their SUV. Getting into the car, Andy shook water off his hat. "Of all the times to pick to run, I pick a downpour."

Virginia tossed her backpack into the rear seat. "It may be a blessing in disguise. Any surveillance cameras will have a harder time distinguishing us from anyone else."

"Good point. Let's get out of here." He backed the car out of the parking space then drove out the gate waving at the guard in the shack as they past. "By the time he does whatever he does when someone leaves, we should be in the mix of traffic. Once we clear the District of Columbia, we should be in pretty good shape. Then we head for New York City."

Virginia pulled a piece of paper from one of the boxes out of her pocket. She leaned forward, and read it. "Andy."

He stopped at a traffic light. "What?"

"I think we have a new destination." He turned toward her. "What?"

"We don't need to go to New York."

"Why?"

"Because according to this paper, the box that went on the president's yacht for that trip to New York didn't really contain the World's Fair quilt. The actual World's Fair quilt was shipped to Los Angeles by an Army courier. The box containing a similar quilt that was on the yacht was a diversion."

The light changed, and Andy slowly pulled ahead through the intersection. "So, someone in the War Department must have known what was contained in the quilt."

Virginia nodded. "Yeah. It looks like we're going back to our old stomping ground."

Andy grinned. "At least there I know my way around. Where in L.A. did it go?"

She looked at the paper. "Warner Brothers Movie studio. Mrs. Roosevelt sent the quilt to then-Lt. Col. Jack Warner."

"Warner Brothers, huh? The question of the day is how do we get there?"

"We fly, of course. It's the quickest way."

"And we have to get permission to bring weapons on a plane; everyone will know where we're going and be there to follow us around." He swerved to avoid an errant cab.

Virginia gave him a questioning look. "Everyone?"

"Yes, including our Arab competition. They seem to know our every move. The rental car company and the airlines use computers, remember?"

"So, what do you have in mind? Drive?"

"No. Take the train." Andy pulled onto the beltway and headed north. "Let's go to a shopping mall and repackage most of the stuff Mr. Epps loaned to us and send it back to him, then turn in the car, and grab a cab to the train station."

"I have a better idea."

"What?"

"Let's go to the Galleria at Tyson's Corner and call Dillon and his gang."

"Huh?" Andy made a turn. "Why?"

"I'll ask them to come and get the stuff and return it to Mr. Van Epps. They seem to like us and are willing to help. And, no one will suspect them of having the materials; they can get it back safely."

Andy exited the freeway and entered the Galleria parking structure. Pulling into a spot on the top level, Andy called Dillon on his cell. "Dillon. This is the dinosaur cop from the other day. I need another favor."

"Sure, Mr. Dinosaur Policeman. What can we do for you?" Dillon said.

"We are on the top of a parking structure, on the south side, at the Tyson's Corner Virginia Galleria. We have the documents we borrowed from Mr. Van Epps—"

"That's the guy we're watching for you, right?"

"Yeah, that's him. I'd like you to send some of your bo... men here to get the papers and safely return them to Mr. Van Epps for me."

"You having trouble with them Arabs again?"

"Yeah, kind of. We may have some others who are interested in us as well, and we could really use your help."

"Okay." Dillon coughed. "I have a request of you, though."

"What is it?"

"One of my homies is in jail and I'd like to get him out."

"What'd he do?"

"Well, Johnson kind of busted the jaw of one of those Arabs last night in Mr. Van Epps' back yard. The neighbors called the cops and even Mr. Van Epps couldn't stop the cops from arresting him. The Arab fellow has diplomatic something or other, and has pull, so Johnson went to jail."

"You send some of your boys here, and I'll make some calls."

"Okay. Where are you exactly?"

Andy gave Dillon directions, then dialed Montgomery and told him of Dillon's problem. After a few minutes, Montgomery called back. "We found the guy you asked about. He busted up an embassy attaché pretty bad. The police are charging him with aggravated assault and assault with a deadly weapon."

"Can you do anything to help him?"

"Per your unusual request, he is, as we speak, on his way home in a military police car. I got the U.S. Attorney to get the charges dropped as well. Some diplomats and the Metro Police aren't happy."

"Thank you very much. That's a big help."

"I hope putting a hood back on the street is a good idea."

"Like I told you, he works for Virginia and me."

"She gets results, so I won't argue. Good luck."

Andy called Dillon. "I just spoke with our contact in the government. Johnson is on his way home, and the charges were dropped."

"Mr. Dinosaur Policeman, you're a good guy. We respect you and your lady. My guys will be there in about a half hour. Call if you need anything else."

"I have a question. Do you know anyone in your... shall we say... line of work... in L.A.?"

"Yeah. In East L.A. My lieutenant has a cousin. Why?"

"Call him, and tell him we may need some assistance shortly."

"You all's going to LA? Nice. *Her* name is Louise Rodriguez and she is the leader of a real badass female gang out there. She put the H in hurt, if you get my drift. I'll have my man call his cuzz and tell her you dinosaur cops are cool and to help you." Andy heard him muffle the phone and talk to someone. "Okay, here's her cell number, 310-555-2384. Good luck, and come back some time."

"Thanks, Dillon." Andy clicked off.

In forty minutes, a bright yellow low-rider Honda Civic pulled next to Andy and Virginia's SUV. The doors opened, and three big, young men stepped out. They pulled up their hoods against the now-light sprinkles. Andy rolled down his window. One of the men leaned on the door. "Dillon sent us. You the dinosaur cops?"

"Yes." Andy opened the door and slid out. Virginia exited the vehicle and walked around the car.

The men's eyes widened when they saw her. "Hellooo, Mrs. Dinosaur Cop. We've heard about you. You're the pretty lady who took out three of our best. You're a legend in our hood. Nice to meet you. I'm Ortiz. You got some stuff for us?"

Virginia smiled. "Yes, I do. We need it safely taken back to Mr. Van

Epps. Dillon said you could help."

"Yes, Ma'am. Mr. Van Epps is pretty cool." Ortiz frowned. "What you got that's so hot you can't take it? It valuable?"

"Monetarily, no. It has nostalgic value to Mr. Van Epps. Our enemy could also use the materials, and they are looking for us as well. So by you taking it, no one knows where we are, and they don't get the documents."

Ortiz grinned. "James Bond stuff, huh?"

"Yeah," She nodded. "James Bond stuff."

"Good. I think we can handle it without any trouble. Once the old man gets his stuff back, Dillon said we're to keep him and his place safe, so no worries, okay."

"Thank you."

Ortiz slipped his hood off. "Dillon said you got Johnson out of jail and didn't arrest or press charges the other day and even gave Dillon's guys back their weapons. So youse are good with us. You showed respect and now we consider you part of us."

The three men loaded the papers into the Civic. Ortiz turned to Virginia. "You're worried about being followed, right?"

"Yes."

"Where you going now?"

"The train station."

"I've got an idea. Why don't you take your car to the airport and give it back, then we'll take you to the train station? After that, we'll take the papers back to their owner."

Virginia looked at Andy. He shrugged. "Okay, let's go." They drove to the Dulles International Airport and turned in their car. They crowded into the Civic and headed back to the district and the train station.

As Ortiz drove away from the train station, Virginia hefted her backpack and smiled. *Even if our competition did get the papers Ortiz has, they won't get far.*

CHAPTER 14

Andy purchased tickets for a sleeper room on the train to Chicago, transferring to Los Angeles for him and Virginia.

Virginia kept watch, from a wooden bench about fifty feet away, for anyone taking undue interest in them. She rose as Andy approached. "You got the tickets?"

"Yep," he nodded. "I booked us a Superliner bedroom suite from here to Chicago and from Chicago to L.A."

"Expensive?"

"Count on it. But I'm not riding coach for over three thousand miles. And the room provides some privacy from the other passengers, except when we eat, of course. They have dining cars. Train leaves at 4:05 p.m. We've got about an hour, so I think we should head for the track."

"Good idea. If we can board early, we are less apt to be seen." She hefted her backpack and dragged her suitcase behind her as she followed Andy. "How long is the trip?"

Andy checked the itinerary. He looked at his watch. "We leave at four-oh-five and arrive in Chicago at eight in the morning. We transfer to the other train at two-forty-five p.m. and arrive three days later at eight in the morning in L.A."

Virginia adjusted her backpack. "Maybe we can get some more information on who we need to contact in L.A. while on the train, and get some rest."

As they walked toward the doors to the tracks, Andy pointed to the architecture. "Did you know that the white granite and classic lines of Union Station set the mode for Washington's classic monumental architecture for the next forty years through the construction of the Lincoln and Jefferson Memorials, the Federal Triangle, the Supreme Court Building, and the National Gallery of Art?"

"Yes, Dear. I was an American history major and I work in a museum, remember?"

Dangerous Threads

Haddad Abdel A'hsam, the cultural attaché at the Saudi Embassy and the section head of the Saudi's Al Mukhabarat Al A'amah, leaned back in his high-backed leather chair and answered the secure line on his telephone. "Hello?"

"Ah... Sir... we found the papers the Clarks took from the old man."

"Good. How did you get them?"

"We didn't, exactly. Our contact in the Smithsonian found that the Clarks were in a conference room at The American History Museum. And while they went to lunch, he searched the conference room they were using. Unfortunately, by the time he found them and started to look at the documents, they returned. He notified me and we were going to get into position to follow them when they fled, with the papers."

A'hsam wet his lips. "Did your man learn anything of value?"

"It looks like they will be going to New York City."

"The documents? Did you get them?"

"Some local hoodlums returned them to Mr. Van Epps."

"What? You didn't stop them?"

"No. They are too dangerous and control the neighborhood. The last person we sent to get the papers from the old man had his jaw and a couple other bones broken by them. And the Clarks had the gang member who broke our agent's jaw let out of jail."

"Who are these people?" A'hsam shook his head. "They can really spoil your day. Have the Clarks followed to New York. Our people in New York must be informed as well."

"We... ah... we kind of lost them again, Sir."

"What!" A'hsam jerked upright in his chair. "What am I paying you for? Two amateurs out-smarted our professionals again? They elude you, recruit criminals to assist them, have people busted out of jail, and are one step ahead all the time. Find the Clarks and stick to them like glue in New York! Inform our people at once. Are they driving or flying?"

"They checked in their car at the Dulles airport, so we're checking the plane schedules and watching the gates, but Dulles is a big airport."

"Hang on." He punched the hold button, then summoned his secretary and told her to find out what flight the Clarks were on to New York. He reconnected to the surveillance man. "I'm having the flight reservations checked. Maybe, if you're not too incompetent, you can make it to the airport and get on the same plane they're on."

His secretary reentered. "Mr. A'hsam. The Clarks are not on any flights to New York. But I ran a quick check of the long-distance buses and trains and found them on a train to Chicago with a transfer to Los Angeles."

A'hsam nodded and smiled. "Nice to see someone around here is competent. When does it leave?"

"It left fifteen minutes ago. And there are others on that train as well."

"Who?"

"I'm not sure, sir, but the reservations were made within minutes of the Clarks."

A'hsam wiped the back of his neck with his hand, took a deep breath and spoke into the phone. "Did you hear that? They're on a damn train. One *you* missed. It seems our competition found them even if you couldn't. Now, fly to Chicago and get on the train they're taking to L.A. And, it's a train; they can't get off if it's moving so try not to lose them on it. Find out where in L.A. they are going and who they are seeing. Then find out who else is on that train with them and eliminate them. If you don't, I swear by Allah, I'll see to it that you're stationed in an outpost in Hell… if you live long enough to get there." He slammed down the receiver.

Virginia put her backpack on the table and slid her suitcase near the sofa in their suite, then exited with Andy to explore the train. After they had located the dining bar and lounge cars, they returned to their room and changed for dinner. When they left their room, Virginia pulled out a hair and wet the ends then placed it on the side of the door. She glanced at Andy. "This way we can see if anyone has entered our room while we are gone."

"You watch too many spy movies."

"Maybe so, but we have to be careful."

They walked to the dining car, keeping an eye peeled for anyone taking an undue interest in them. They were seated in the middle of the car at a white cloth-covered table and ordered drinks and their food selection. Virginia watched the people entering from the front of the train while Andy, sitting opposite her, watched people entering from the rear. She and Andy continued observing people as they ate dinner.

As they finished their desserts, Virginia touched Andy's hand. "The couple with the olive complexions, three tables across and behind you, is keeping an eye on us and trying to look like they're enjoying their food."

Andy glanced at the window, noting their reflection in the glass. "I see them. What do you want to do?"

"There may be more of them, so we should head back to our room and see if we had any unwelcome visitors there… but be careful in case they try something funny."

"They may be just passengers."

"They could be the Easter Bunny, too."

They signed the bill, rose, and strolled out of the dining car toward the rear of the train. Two cars back, they slowed as they heard the doors between cars open and close and someone talking softly. Virginia slipped her hand into her pants pocket. Andy removed his baseball hat and hid his taser under it in his hand.

Dangerous Threads

Halfway down the empty corridor, a room door opened and a dark-skinned man stepped into the hall facing them. He stepped toward them and started to raise a pistol when Virginia pulled her hand out of her pocket and fired her taser into the man's chest and pulled the trigger. He fell, twitching violently.

Andy turned and fired his taser into the black-haired woman holding a pistol in the lead of the couple behind them and pulled the trigger. The woman convulsed, dropped her gun and tumbled to the floor.

Andy, now holding the fired taser, looked at the man behind her.

The man lowered his weapon. "Dr. Clark?"

"Yes."

"I am Joseph Goldman. I'm with Israeli Foreign Intelligence. The man your wife just put down is a member of the Golden Crescent. It is an organization involved with radical and violent Jihad." He slipped his semiautomatic back into a holster under his jacket.

"You're Mossad?" Andy looked at the unconscious woman on the floor. "Her, too?"

"I'm afraid so, Sir." Joseph knelt and pulled the taser darts from his partner and looked up at Andy. "I'm sorry we didn't identify ourselves before. We were going to talk to you in private, but it seems things got out of hand."

"Ya think?"

"Help me move her to the room just down the corridor." Joseph looked at Virginia and the man on the floor she was disarming. "Mrs. Clark, we can move him in the room as well." He looked around. "We'd better do it before someone comes."

Virginia stood holding the pistol she took from the presumed Golden Crescent man on the floor. She looked at Joseph with a frown. "How do we know you're who you say you are?"

The man stood and pulled a leather case from his pocket. He opened it, displaying his credentials in English and Hebrew. "Can we get them out of the passageway now, please?"

Andy, Joseph Goldman, and Virginia hauled the woman and the Golden Crescent man into the designated room then closed the door. Virginia examined them. "They'll be asleep for a while but otherwise sore and probably okay." She sat and faced Goldman. "Why are you here?"

He leaned forward. "We had intelligence that the Golden Crescent and Saudis are after something of incredible importance, and it could be used as a new and powerful weapon. We also learned that you were the focus of their activities. So we tried to find out what it is they're after and where you were. We found you, and it looks like the Golden Crescent did, too."

Virginia smiled. "So, you're the good guys?"

"We want to make sure neither the Saudis nor the Golden Crescent get their hands on whatever it is you and they are after. Even better, we'd like to get it first."

CHAPTER 15

Virginia sat back on the seat in the railroad car compartment and looked at Goldman. "So, Mossad actually found us when the Saudis couldn't? How did you and this supposed Golden Crescent guy manage to find us? I'm not sure our government even knows where we are."

Goldman settled into a chair across from her and Andy. "We were told by our sources that you had recruited some street thugs to be your deputies in a certain neighborhood. We tried to interview one of them and came out the worse for wear. But our man overheard one of them on a cell phone mention that you were at the train station. He notified us. We were close to the area, found you, and purchased tickets on this train. We were planning to make contact, but not the way things happened. I must ask, what is a dinosaur cop?"

"I'll get to the dinosaur cop thing in a minute. The Golden Crescent guy?" She glanced at the man on the floor. "How'd he get here? Has he got friends on board?"

"My partner, Sarah, spotted him watching the ticket booths. He must have recognized you and followed before we could intervene. As to any back-up he may have, we do not have any knowledge."

Andy adjusted his UT baseball cap. "You have any idea what you're looking for?"

"Only that it could be very dangerous. I want to know exactly what you are looking for."

Virginia chuckled. "A quilt."

Goldman's eyes narrowed. "A quilt? Like what my grandmother would have made?"

Andy looked at Goldman. "They make quilts in the desert?"

"Yes. We make a lot of things."

Virginia grinned. "I make quilts and belong to a quilt guild. So watch the grandmother references, bub."

"Bub?" Goldman frowned. "I don't know this term."

"It's American slang," Andy said. "And she's right. We're looking for a quilt."

"You are? Why?"

Virginia leaned forward. "It's from the 1933 Chicago World's Fair and was lost. The Smithsonian wants it and they sent us to find it. Like I said, we work for the Smithsonian Central Security Service. As you now know, we're, as our young street gang friends like to say, dinosaur cops. We're not CIA or NSA, BATF, FBI, Secret Service, Homeland Security, DEA, or DIA or any other alphabet soup agency, or spooks. We work for the Smithsonian. In case you didn't notice," she held her arms wide apart, "it's a set of really big museums in Washington, D.C. You should go there sometime."

Goldman gave her a blank stare. "So that is why the street gang called you dinosaur cops. You work for a museum."

"Right. A really, really, big one." Virginia pointed to the man moaning on the floor. "Now, how are you, or he, going to use a quilt to build some sort of new weapon? Smother the enemy to death with it?"

Goldman studied Virginia and Andy. "If what you say is true, what's really on, or in the quilt that my government or these extremists would want?"

Virginia rose, nodded to Andy, and started for the door. "You tell me; you're the spy. In the meantime, we're going to our compartment to spend a quiet night. You can do what you like with your new friend here cluttering up the floor next to your partner." She and Andy opened the door and left the compartment.

They hurried through two more railcars to their compartment and once inside, locked the door.

Virginia collapsed onto the sofa. "Wow. Do you believe what just happened?"

"No." Andy tossed his hat onto the table and plopped next to her. "Was that guy really Mossad?"

"I don't know, but it wouldn't surprise me, especially with all the Arabs trying to interfere with us. I'll check with Dr. Montgomery in the morning."

Andy nodded. "Plus, how'd he and the Golden Crescent really know we were on this train? If the Saudis found out, they'd be here, too. That, or join our entourage and us in Chicago for the trip to L.A. You have any ideas as to what to do next? What is Goldman going to do about the Golden Crescent guy?"

"I'm not sure what they will do with him. I'm not even sure he's what Goldman said he was. Maybe he was one of them, but I know what I'm going to do now."

"What?"

"Call my friend Donna in Newport Beach and ask her for some help."

Andy shrugged his shoulders. "Okay, I guess. What can she do? Why not call Montgomery first?"

"Montgomery can figure out about Mr. Goldman and company tomorrow. It's not like they can run away. Donna can do some preliminary legwork in California for us before we get there. And she's three hours behind us." Virginia slipped her secure satellite phone from her backpack and dialed Donna's number.

"Bolette Travel," a soft female voice answered. "How may I direct your call?"

Virginia sat back. "Ms. Donna Bolette, please. Virginia Davies-Clark calling." She waited for a few seconds counting the clicks on the line.

"Virginia! How are you? How's Andy?" screamed Donna's voice in the receiver. "Better yet, where are you? Or, don't I want to know?"

"Hi Donna. Yes, Andy's with me and we're on a job for the—"

"Smithsonian Central Security Service, if I guess right."

"Right." Virginia smiled. "We're on a train to Chicago and then on to L.A. In the meantime, we need some help."

Donna's voice rose in excitement. "Do I get to shoot anyone?"

"No, at least not yet. You are good at other things, though."

"Oh. Well, I guess I can live with that, for now. What can I do for you?"

"I need to find someone who was close to Jack Warner during the early 1940s at Warner Brothers. Someone still alive."

"What's this about?"

"A 1933 Chicago World's Fair Quilt that won the national Sears quilting contest."

"That's it? Nothing dangerous?"

Virginia heard Donna taking notes. "Oh, it's plenty dangerous."

"Oh, goody. How soon do you need the contact?"

"If I wanted it today, I'd ask tomorrow."

"That quick, huh? Okay, I'll see what I can do. How do I reach you? Use your normal cell number?"

"No." Virginia sighed. "I'll have to contact you."

"Got it. I'll get people right on this. Any chance I can help when you get here? Where are you staying?"

"We haven't any reservations yet; care to make some for us?"

"Using your money or our uncle's?"

"Uncle's."

"Excellent. Call my office before you arrive. We'll have you some discreet reservations, a car waiting, and your information. Remember, if you need back-up, I'm always available. I still have my Beretta and other toys left over from Italy. And, say hello to Andy for me."

"Oh, can you do the reservations without using our names?"

"Of course. I do it all the time for some of my rich clients. Call when you get here."

"Thanks, I'll be in touch." Virginia hung up.

Andy watched her put the phone away. "She's going to help?"

"Yep. She'll also make our hotel and travel arrangements. She said hello to you, too."

"Good." Andy climbed up. "Okay, better call the steward and get this room made up for the night."

"Just a second." She rummaged through her backpack and pulled out her Glock. "Better get yours too, just in case."

Fifteen minutes later, the room was in its sleeping configuration. Virginia slipped into a pair of pajamas. Andy put his bright burnt orange UT T-shirt on with a pair of fire engine red pajama bottoms.

She shook her head as she looked at him. "Your fashion sense is overwhelming. I need sunglasses."

"Wait 'til the lights are off."

Virginia grinned. "What happens then? Something exciting, I hope."

"Watch." Andy switched off the lights. The UT symbol on the shirt glowed an off-green color while his pajama bottoms gave off a red swirl pattern on both legs. "How about that?" He turned the lights back on.

"You're... you're... the words escape me. This is really—"

"Cool, don't you think?"

"Cool isn't exactly the word I was looking for. Where did you get them? Whoever sold them to you should be in a mental ward, along with you."

"The campus store. They were on sale."

Virginia smiled as she shook her head. "I just bet they were. It's always amazed me how at one moment you can be a really focused, serious, engineering professor and researcher, and the next a complete nut."

He smiled. "It's a gift. Anyway, it's just a way to let out some of the tension of looking for grant money, teaching, and research. People expect professors to be absent-minded and somewhat nuts. It's our image."

Virginia chuckled. "If you say so, Professor. Shall we try and go to sleep? Maybe I need to cover my eyes." She slipped under the covers and placed her pistol under her pillow.

Andy checked the door, switched off the lights, and climbed into bed. "Don't forget to call Montgomery in the morning."

Goldman sat in his compartment. His partner, still sore and somewhat groggy, sat next to him. Across the small space on the floor rested the highly bruised and bloody Golden Crescent agent, his hands secured behind his back with white plastic ties. His feet were likewise bound. A gag and blindfold partially covered his face. With muffled sounds, he twisted around on the carpet.

Goldman nudged the man on the floor with his foot. He turned toward his partner. "Sarah, what should we do with him?"

Sarah shifted in her seat and grimaced in pain, then glanced at the trussed-up man. "Since he either won't cooperate with your interrogation, or you did a poor job of it, Joseph, I suggest we dispose of him. Dead, he can't interfere." She watched Goldman's reaction.

"Maybe we should try again, first."

"You said he resisted your... your enhanced methods of interrogation already, right?"

Goldman's eyes shifted down to the left. "Yes."

Sarah steeled him with her dark brown eyes. "Then we kill him and dump the body."

Goldman shifted in his seat. "We're on a train. Not the easiest thing to do."

"According to the schedule, we're due for a stop shortly. We dump him then."

Goldman shrugged then leaned forward. "You hear what she said? You're going to die unless you tell us what we want to know. Nod your head if you understand."

The man nodded.

"You willing to talk?"

Again he nodded.

"Good." Goldman turned to his partner. "Sarah, sit him up and remove his gag."

Sarah knelt next to the man and pulled out his gag. "Help me, Joseph, he's heavy and I'm very sore from the taser that Clark woman hit me with. I'm still twitching."

Goldman rose, stepped to the man, and bent to help set him upright when he gasped and jerked. His eyes widened as he looked down to see a knife up to its hilt under his ribcage. Sarah twisted it. He started to speak but fell onto the floor.

Sarah untied the Golden Crescent man. He rolled out from under the Mossad agent.

The man sat on the sofa rubbing his wrists. "You didn't stop him from using so much force during his interrogation. I will inform the Golden Crescent that you were aiding him."

"Get real, Mallah. In case you didn't notice, I was groggy and extremely sore. I didn't count on the Clarks using tasers on us. Anyway, he was doing his job. I killed him, didn't I?"

Mallah looked at Goldman and the knife in his side. "Okay. I am wrong. I do not like taking a beating from a Jew."

Sarah sat opposite him. "What are your plans now?" She pulled her purse close, removed a compact, and a handkerchief.

"We sit him up and leave this compartment. We can go to yours. Do you know which room the infidel Clarks are in?"

"Yes."

"Let us get some of our tools from your room and go eliminate the Clarks as well. We do it tonight."

"That's your plan? I don't think that is a good idea, Mallah. They are leading us to what we want. Killing them will impede our quest. There is also the small problem of all the dead bodies on this train that will be discovered."

"Allah will provide. I say we eliminate the infidels now!"

Sarah shook her head. "Your problem, Mallah, is—you don't think."

"Quiet, woman! Allah will provide and guide us in our holy jihad."

"You're right, Mallah, Allah will and did provide."

She smiled as she tossed fluid in his face from a small vial. The edges of her lips turned up. "Pig's blood." He wiped his hand across his forehead and looked at the blood when Sarah fired the small .25 caliber semiautomatic.

Mallah's head popped back against the sofa as a hole appeared in the center of his forehead.

"Too bad you can't enjoy paradise." Sarah pulled out a satellite phone and dialed. A few moments later, a computerized voice told her to leave a message. "I made it onto the train with the Clarks. The Mossad agent and the Golden Crescent jihadist are both dead. I'll continue to follow the Clarks and await further orders." She hung up.

She put the pistol, and her other items back in her purse. Sarah wiped off the hilt of the knife and other surfaces she touched, then rose, stepped to the door and switched off the lights. Opening the door, she peered out. The corridor was empty. She closed the door behind her and strolled toward the bar car.

CHAPTER 16

Morning light spilled into Virginia and Andy's room as they watched the Chicago train station slowly slide into view. A voice came over the loudspeaker. "We are arriving at Chicago station. Due to special circumstances, please remain in your seats or compartments until further notice, as police will be boarding the train to investigate a situation and conducting some interviews. This should cause only a minor delay in disembarking. We will keep you informed of developments." The train jerked to a halt. Virginia looked out the window at a rush of uniformed and obviously plainclothes police moving toward the train from the platform. Two teams of what looked like ambulance attendants pushed stretchers to the rail cars.

She turned to Andy, who just closed his suitcase. "Looks like there was some serious trouble aboard last night. Lots of cops and two ambulances."

Andy stepped around the suitcases and backpacks and looked outside. "The men you thought were ambulance attendants are from the Cook County Medical Examiner's office. Coroner's deputies." He pointed out the window. "That fellow's jacket has it on the back. I wonder who died?"

"I bet we find out soon enough." Virginia sat on the chair as Andy continued to watch. She pulled her satellite phone out and called Dr. Montgomery. He answered on the third ring.

"Hello, Virginia. How are you doing?" Montgomery replied in a tired voice.

"We're doing pretty well but need some information, and I have some news for you, too. We may also need some help. You sound tired. Pull an all-nighter?"

"Close. I got here at four this morning. What have you got for me?"

"We're on a train from Washington to Chicago. We just pulled into the station," Virginia said. "Last night we met some people. A man supposedly from the Golden Crescent, along with a man and a woman who said they were Mossad. I didn't know our Jewish friends were on to this caper as well as half the Arabs in the world. You got anything on that?"

Montgomery's voice escalated. "Did you say Mossad?"

"Yep. The guy's name was Joseph Goldman and the woman's name was Sarah something or other."

"I didn't think the Jewish security forces were onto this."

Virginia tightened her grip on the phone. "Why not? Who the hell isn't? The Boy Scouts?"

"I don't know. I'll have the CIA do some checking on that. Now, what happened?"

"The Arab pulled a gun on me and the Mossad woman drew on Andy. We tazed both of them. We left them last night unconscious with the Goldman fellow."

Andy motioned for her attention. "Just a second." She looked at Andy. "What's up?"

"They just removed two bodies. One of the men out there from the Coroner's office, I think he's a doctor, opened the body bags and looked inside. I got a glimpse. I think it's Goldman. I'd hazard a guess the other is the Golden Crescent fellow from last night. This will screw up their train schedule as well as ours."

"Any sign of the other Mossad agent? The Sarah woman?"

Andy shook his head. "No. I'll keep watching."

Virginia spoke into the phone. "Looks like we have a situation."

"Yeah, I heard your husband. I'll start to make inquiries and will call you back. Be careful." He disconnected.

She put the phone away and stood next to Andy, watching the commotion outside the train. There was a knock on their door.

Virginia opened the door to three men in suits. "Mrs. Clark? I'm Detective Warner, Chicago PD," said the man in a wrinkled off the shelf brown suit. "This is Special Agent Reynolds of the Amtrak police."

The third man in a dark blue suit with white shirt and red and gray regimental tie—government-issue federal agent uniform—moved closer and flashed a gold badge. "Special Agent Metzger, FBI. May we come in?"

Virginia looked at the three men. "Why?"

Detective Warner spoke first. "We'd like to ask you some questions."

"About what?"

"Can we do this in your room? It would be easier that way."

"For whom? If you can't tell me why you want to talk to me, then I see no reason to invite you in, or, for that matter, to talk to you. Now, do you want to tell me what this is about, and why do you want to talk to us?"

Special Agent Metzger said, "There was a murder on this train last night. You were seen leaving the dining car just ahead of one of the victims."

She titled her head. "Oh. You mean the guys being taken off the train in body bags?"

They nodded.

"We've been looking out the window." Virginia looked inside the room, then back at the three men. "With the three of you, me, and my husband in here, it would be most uncomfortable."

Detective Warner cleared his throat. "Look lady, we can talk here or downtown. Make up your mind now."

She glared at him. "You arresting us?"

"If necessary."

"If you're going to be an asshole, then I'll call our lawyer now and we'll just shut up. No information, nada, nothing. You really don't understand the art of conversation, do you?"

The officers looked at each other. Special Agent Reynolds spoke. "No need for all that, Ma'am. We could move to the dining car. It is fairly close and more comfortable, or a lounge car, if you like. We just have some basic questions at this time."

Detective Warner grunted.

Andy stepped behind Virginia. "The club car would be fine."

Virginia stepped back and straightened her blouse tight across her ample chest. "You guys don't have any problem with that, do you?" The officers stood staring at her chest with their mouths open, then into the cabin.

Andy and Virginia wore their backpacks and pulled their suitcases ahead of the officers toward the club car.

After getting comfortable in the club car, Special Agent Reynolds asked Virginia and Andy if they knew the people in two photographs he slid across the table.

They examined the pictures. Virginia looked up at Agent Reynolds. "This guy said his name was Joseph Goldman. I recognize the other man from last night on the train, but we don't know his name. There was a dark-haired woman with them. Did you find her?"

Agent Reynolds shook his head. "No. There was no one in the compartment when the porter opened the door. He mentioned seeing a woman similar to the one you described earlier. Do you know her name?"

Andy spoke up. "Sarah, I think. Can't be sure, but that's what I heard Goldman say."

Detective Warner rubbed his chin. "How did you come to know these people?"

Virginia chuckled. "We tazed them."

"You what?"

Andy sat back in his chair. "Like she said, we tazed them."

The three men exchanged puzzled glances, then Agent Metzger asked, "Why? What did they do? Did you report it?"

Virginia shrugged. "They pulled guns on us. Not a very nice thing to do. And, no we didn't report it. Who, on a moving train, do you report these things to?"

"The conductor, that's who." Warner scribbled more notes as Agent Metzger spoke. "Why would they pull guns on you? Were they trying to rob you?"

"No." Virginia eyed each man, then smiled. "You don't know who we are, do you?"

Detective Warner looked at his notes. "You are Virginia Davies-Clark, a curator at the San Gabriel Museum in Georgetown, Texas and," he pointed to Andy, "you are Doctor Andy Clark, a mechanical engineering professor at the University of Texas at Austin."

Virginia and Andy pulled out their credentials, showed their IDs, and gold badges to the three officers. "We're with the Smithsonian Central Security Service," Virginia said.

"I'll check this out." FBI Special Agent Metzger rose from the table, walked a few feet away, pulled his cell phone out, and made a call. After a couple minutes, he returned to the table where everyone waited. "Your credentials check out." He turned to the other officers. "They are federal agents. I was just told that they are not to be questioned any further or interfered with." He looked at Andy and Virginia. "Whatever it is you're working on seems to have attention and authorization all the way to the White House. My supervisor said things have heated up and to extend you any help you need and to keep the murders under wraps. That part may be a little hard right now with everyone on the train and station watching the goings-on, but why didn't you tell us this when we were at your room?"

Andy shrugged his shoulders. "We weren't sure we'd need to. We're not advertising who we are. We try to stay under everyone's radar."

The Amtrak Special Agent Reynolds sat wide-eyed. "You're working on a case? Can you tell us what it has to do with the two murdered men? Any idea who may have killed them?"

Virginia spread her hands on the table. "We're on a case, but we can't tell you much about it. Goldman said he, as well as the woman, were with Mossad. The other guy is an Arab. He was with a group called the Golden Crescent, it's a radical Islamic organization involved with Jihad. But we had just Goldman's word on that."

Andy sat back in his chair. "You might start with the woman if she wasn't in the compartment. She's about five feet five inches tall, slender, weighs about one ten or so, short black hair and brown eyes, olive complexion."

Virginia wet her lips. "She has a small birthmark just below her left clavicle, she's right-handed, and wears contacts, and has a black, nine millimeter semiautomatic."

The three officers stared at Virginia and Andy, then rapidly scribbled more notes. "Good. Anything else?"

Andy wrinkled his brow. "I think the Goldman guy was for real. He wasn't from this country and had a slight accent. He didn't understand some of our slang words. I'm not sure about the woman or the other man. They didn't get a chance to speak while we were around."

FBI Agent Metzger's phone rang. He answered it at the table. "Metzger here." He listened and nodded, then said, "Yes, Sir. I'll take care of it." He closed his phone and looked at the group. "That was my supervisor. The FBI is taking the bodies and all evidence. I'm to ask Special Agent Reynolds to escort you to your next train as additional security for you two until you depart on the rest of your trip."

"What do you mean you're taking the bodies and evidence?" Detective Warner slammed his hand on the table. "Like hell! And, these two aren't going anywhere until I say so. This is Chicago, not Washington D.C."

His phone rang. Warner flipped it open with more force than necessary. "Warner. What?" He listened then said, "Yes, Sir, but... yes... but there's been a murder in our... but... yes, Sir, I understand, sir. Yes, Sir." He closed his phone and looked at Virginia and Andy. "The mayor got calls from the Pentagon and the White House. He called the commissioner and he, in turn, called my captain. You are free to go and..." he looked at Metzger, "...you get the evidence and bodies. I have another homicide on the west side to look into."

He looked at Virginia and Andy, then shook his head. "Whatever it is you two are investigating, it sure must be important to garner all that heat from so high up. I guess I'm lucky not to have to get involved in this mess after all. I've got to head out to my new murder. Good luck to you."

He got up, said good-bye to the other officers, pulled a walkie-talkie from under his jacket, and spoke as he left.

"Looks like I need to get my people searching the train for this Sarah woman." Agent Metzger rose, thanked Andy and Virginia and, also talking on a radio, followed the detective out of the rail car.

Amtrak Special Agent Reynolds sat facing them. "Looks like I'm your bodyguard while you're here. When is your next train?"

"This afternoon, the two-forty-five to Los Angeles." Andy said.

Reynolds smiled. "Any place you'd like to go in the meantime?"

CHAPTER 17

Virginia fished her ringing cell phone out of her backpack. She answered it as she looked out the front window of the Amtrak agent's car from the rear seat. Andy rode in the shotgun seat next to Agent Reynolds. She could see the reflection of the red and blue flashers in the window. "Hello?"

"Virginia! Montgomery here. I had an Air Force executive jet redirected to O'Hare. You're to meet the plane at the FedEx terminal. So you're good to go. Do you want my office to get you a hotel there or a car?"

"No. Thanks for all your help." She waited for the yelp of the siren when Agent Reynolds ran a light, then continued. "I have a friend in California who is taking care of those details."

"Okay. Good luck."

Virginia scrunched her nose. "Any word on how Mossad and the Golden Crescent found us?"

"Yeah. You won't believe it, though," Montgomery said.

"Try me."

"Mossad was following the Golden Crescent operative and they both ran into you accidentally." Montgomery cleared his throat. "It seems the Golden Crescent was there for another reason. The Arabs got word of you coming to the train station and so they followed you."

Virginia knitted her brows. "Do you really believe that?"

"Not a word. We really don't know what happened. But, as they say, that's the word on the street."

"Thanks. I'll tell Andy." She punched end and stuffed the phone back into her backpack.

Andy twisted around. "Montgomery? We good at the airport?"

"Yeah. We're to go to the FedEx terminal." Virginia said. "He's got us an Air Force executive jet and cleared us to get on the plane armed. He said the word he's getting is Mossad and the Golden Crescent agent found us by accident. He doesn't believe that."

Andy shook his head. "I don't buy it, either. You know Golden Crescent and the Saudis will figure out pretty quickly that we are not on that

Dangerous Threads

train to L. A."

Agent Reynolds chuckled. "Yeah, they'll be pulling their hair out. You've effectively dropped off the map." He glanced over his shoulder. "FedEx terminal, right?"

"Yes. We'll meet the plane there."

Andy smiled. "I love it when a plan comes together."

Virginia sat back. "You're right, Agent Reynolds, we are dropping off the map. My friend, Donna, is making our hotel reservations and getting us a car, but not using our names. She's arranging for us to disappear once we get there. She and I have been through a lot of adventures together and believe me, she's good at it."

"She's right. I've seen the two of them in action." Andy fidgeted in his seat.

Agent Reynolds glanced over his shoulder again. "You've done this a lot?'

Virginia nodded. "More than you could ever guess."

"This friend of yours in California, she cute and single?"

Andy raised an eyebrow and grinned. "Oh yeah, she's really a quite a doll, but she's married."

"Too bad. I may have asked to go along with you." The unmarked police car, emergency light flashing, jerked to a halt in front of the FedEx terminal at O'Hare International Airport. With workers staring at them, Virginia and Andy scrambled out as Agent Reynolds pulled their bags from the trunk.

A tall man in gray slacks and an open collared blue shirt rushed up to the car. "What's going on? What's wrong?"

Agent Reynolds displayed his badge, "Amtrak Police-Federal Officers." Virginia and Andy did the same.

The man looked at their badges and identification cards. "I'm Jason Ambrose, the station manager. Can I be of assistance?"

Virginia stepped close to him. "Agent Reynolds needs to get back to the railroad; maybe you could have someone help us with our bags." She gave him a smile. "We are waiting for an Air Force plane that supposed to come here.

"Oh. So you're the package they're picking up." Ambrose nodded. "Yes Ma'am. The plane is on approach. It'll be here in about ten minutes. Let's get you inside and ready."

Agent Reynolds shook Andy's hand and Virginia gave him a hug. "Any time you guys have another adventure in Chicago, please let me know. You two are really something." Reynolds returned to the car and drove off.

Virginia and Andy turned and followed Ambrose and two men pulling their bags into the building.

They settled into a couple padded chairs and, sipping some coffee Ambrose provided, watched the tarmac out the large window. In ten minutes, a white and blue Air Force Gulf Stream executive jet rolled to a stop outside the terminal. The door opened and the stairs lowered.

An officer disembarked and walked into the building and toward Virginia and Andy. "Are you the Clarks?"

Andy stood. "Yes, Major." He produced his badge and ID card. "I take it you're our ride."

"Yes, Sir. I'm Major Tom Simmons, the pilot." He glanced at the bags. "I'll get a couple crew members to handle your suitcases."

Virginia stood. "We can pull them, Sir."

"That's okay, Ma'am. I'll have the crew take them and put them in the hold. If you will follow me, we'll get you situated and be on our way. I was told to make the turnaround as quick as possible."

Virginia nodded. "Okay. I'm sorry if we interrupted your plans."

Major Simmons looked at Virginia with a smile. "No problem. We were in Michigan about to take a self-centered, egotistical, obnoxious congressman to Minnesota for some sort of hearing. Being redirected to take you to southern California is not going to upset me, or my crew one bit. As far as we're concerned, that bag-of-wind congressman can walk to Minnesota. He doesn't like the military, but he enjoys our free rides. Will you follow me, please?" He raised the walkie-talkie in his hand and mumbled something.

They strolled behind Major Simmons as two enlisted men rushed into the terminal and pulled their suitcases toward the plane.

Virginia sat in a soft leather chair next to a polished wooden table. She slipped off her shoes and wiggled her toes in the plush carpet. Andy sat across the aisle in a similar chair. On the bulkhead in front of them were two televisions. Virginia put on a set of earphones and fiddled with the controls set into the table. *This is neat. I could get used to this.*

They strapped in as a Senior Master Sergeant checked their seatbelts. "Can I get you anything before we take off?"

Virginia shook her head. Andy asked for water. The sergeant returned with a glass of water and a small bottle. "Okay then. I'll check on you after we take off. Restrooms are to the rear." He disappeared into a rear compartment.

Five minutes later, the major's voice came over the speakers in their cabin. "We are ready for takeoff. Sit back and enjoy the ride. We will be landing at the Orange County airport in a little under four hours." The Air Force executive jet rolled out onto the taxiway, then sped to the end of the runway, turned, roared down the runway, and shot into the air, turning southwest.

Virginia turned to Andy. "That was fast, I didn't see another plane in front of us."

Dangerous Threads

Andy released the lock on the swivel and rotated his chair toward Virginia. "That's because this is a military plane. It has priority over all other aircraft except a hospital plane."

Virginia released the swivel lock on her chair and rotated around. "This kind of treatment could spoil a girl."

Haddad Abdel A'hsam, the cultural attaché at the Saudi Embassy and the section head of the Saudi's Al Mukhabarat Al A'amah, answered the secure line on his telephone. "Hello?"

A voice in a broken accent responded. "Sir, we have a couple of small problems."

"What type of problems? How small?"

"Have you seen the TV? There were a couple of murders on the Clark's train from Washington to Chicago. A Mossad agent and an operative of the Golden Crescent were killed."

A'hsam nodded. "Yes, I heard about it. The Clarks didn't kill them, did they?"

"From what I've learned, no Sir, they didn't. No one seems to know what happened."

"Where are the Clarks?"

"That's the second problem, Sir. I don't know. They were last seen leaving the train station in an unmarked police car."

A'hsam jerked upright in his chair. "Are they still ticketed on the train to L.A.?"

"Yes, Sir. I checked and they are still ticketed for a room on the train."

"Okay." A'hsam relaxed. "Maybe they are going to a police station to give their statements."

"Possibly. I'm trying to find out as we speak, Sir. I'll let you know when I have more details. In the meantime, we have people ready to get on their train and be in position to watch them when they arrive."

"Any chance they've switched method of transportation?"

The man on the phone coughed. "I don't think so. I've also checked the airlines and rental car agencies and the Clarks do not have any reservations on any flights nor have they rented a vehicle."

"Good work. Then they'll probably be on the train when the police are done with them. Keep me posted." A'hsam hung up and stared at a picture of Virginia on his desk. *What are you up to?*

Andy sat at his table playing cards with the sergeant and Captain Johnson, the co-pilot, while Virginia, sat in the co-pilot's chair, with Major Simmons next to her. After a few minutes, Andy watched as Virginia climbed out of the seat and returned to the main cabin. She asked the sergeant for a phone and called Donna to let her know when they would arrive. After Andy folded, the sergeant and co-pilot finished the poker hand and paid their bets in toothpicks, Captain Johnson returned to the cockpit.

Andy leaned toward Virginia. "Did you get hold of Donna? Is everything arranged?"

"Yeah, she'll meet us at the airport. She has the information about Jack Warner I asked for as well."

In an hour, the red seatbelt sign illuminated and Virginia returned to her seat across from Andy. Major Simmons' voice came over the speaker. "LA Approach has handed us off to Orange County Air Traffic Control and we are on our descent into Orange County. Commercial aircraft have been diverted and are in holding patterns while we have a direct approach. The tower will pick us up shortly and we will be on the ground in fifteen minutes. Sit back and relax."

They looked out their windows as the plane flew over Saddleback Mountain, then circled around and lined up with the runway, descending over Irvine and the I405 freeway. It touched down and taxied to gate at the main terminal. When the engines wound down, the sergeant opened the door and lowered the stairs. A crewman exited ahead of Virginia and Andy and secured their suitcases from the hold. Major Simmons and the co-pilot, Captain Johnson, saluted them from the cabin door and said good-bye. Andy and Virginia walked up a set of stairs, into the building to be confronted by two TSA officers and an Orange County Sheriff's deputy.

CHAPTER 18

Virginia and Andy froze. The TSA officers stood in the middle of the tiled walkway with the Sheriff's deputy behind them. People at the last gate watched the unfolding confrontation. Andy stepped forward. "Is there a problem?"

One of the officers straightened. "Yes Sir, there is. This is a secured area and we don't know where you came from. You'll have to go with us for a search."

Andy shook his head. "I don't think so. We just got off an Air Force jet. We're federal agents and we're on official business. We're also armed."

The deputy stepped forward puffing up his chest. "You will surrender your weapons."

"No, we won't." Andy produced his badge and ID. "Federal officers."

Virginia displayed hers. "As he said, we're on official business. We're with the Smithsonian Central Security Service." She started to walk forward.

"I've never heard of it." The deputy said. He stepped in front of Virginia and put his hand on her arm. "You're coming with me."

Andy raised an eyebrow. "There are a lot of things you never heard of, deputy, that doesn't mean they don't exist. And," he shook his head, "grabbing her was a big mistake."

Virginia shot her hand forward, grabbed the deputy's left elbow, and squeezed a nerve. The deputy stiffened and released his grip on her. She pressed harder as he rose on his toes. She glared at him. "You just assaulted a federal agent. We were not a threat to you or anyone else, but you had to go and try to show off your so-called authority. Not too smart. I can charge you with federal crimes. Now, if I let you go, will you behave?"

Through his clinched jaw he mumbled, "I'm a sheriff's deputy, you are under arrest." She squeezed harder. His voice squeaked. "Let me go!" His right hand reached for his pistol.

"You touch that gun and I'll break your elbow along with a few other things. If I do it right, you won't be able to shoot, walk, or probably talk for some time. Got it?" She rolled the nerve. His back bowed; his right arm went straight.

"Sto... stop." His eyes bulged.

Andy looked at the people watching, then noticed the two TSA officers talking on their radios. One of them smirked. "We have radioed for assistance. You'd better surrender now before things get worse."

Andy heard a noise and glanced over his shoulder. Major Simmons, Captain Johnson, the sergeant and one of the airmen had entered the terminal. The major and captain had side arms and the sergeant and airman had M16 assault rifles. They walked up to Andy and Virginia, nodded, then turned to the TSA officers and the deputy who was obviously still experiencing the pain Virginia was inflicting.

Major Simmons cleared his voice. "Gentlemen. These two federal agents are cleared by the U.S. Air Force to go through this airport unmolested. Any attempt to hinder them will result in your arrest; we are here to enforce that order."

"Hi, Major." Virginia released the deputy who sank back onto the soles of his feet and staggered backward a few steps, rubbing his arm.

The deputy wet his lips. "These officers have requested back up. We'll see who hinders who."

Major Simmons stepped in front of the deputy. "Get this straight, mister, leave them alone. Neither you, nor TSA, have any authority to hold or hinder them. If you do not back down, now, I'll place you under arrest."

The deputy stiffened. "You can't do that. This is not a military base."

Everyone turned as they heard people running down the carpeted walkway. The deputy sheriff smiled. "Here comes my back-up. Now we'll see what's what."

The two muscular men, sporting brush cuts, wearing tight, dark-blue T-shirts and jeans with round, silver badges suspended on chains around their necks and black semiautomatics on their web-belts stopped before the group. One turned toward the TSA officers, the other toward the deputy sheriff. Across the back of their shirts were the white letters USMS with POLICE underneath. The one facing the sheriff's deputy said, "United States Marshals. These two federal officers are to come with us."

"I've placed her under arrest for assaulting a sheriff's deputy, resisting arrest, violating the secure area of an airport, and being armed in the security area. Now stand aside."

The marshal stood inches from the sheriff's deputy. "They are federal officers and we are here to escort them. Do not interfere. You can be arrested for assault on federal officers, interfering with a federal investigation, interfering with federal marshals, and violation of national security, and these armed, Air Force gentlemen will back us up. *They* can shut down this airport until the Department of Defense investigates. Now, either you stand

Dangerous Threads

down or the Air Force will close this place and inconvenience a whole lot of people. You will be lost in the federal judicial system for years, sheriff's deputy or not. I hear Gitmo is nice, but humid this time of year."

He turned to Major Simmons. "Sir. We thank you for calling us. We appreciate the support until we arrived."

Simmons nodded. "No problem, Marshal. Do you need us to assist you while we are here? My orders are to protect Doctor and Mrs. Clark as long as necessary."

The marshal looked at the crowd that was watching and the deputy sheriff. "Thank you, Major. Looks like we generated a small crowd. I'm not sure about the local cops being cooperative. So, if you and your men could help us escort the special agents to where they need to go to get their belongings and transportation, we would appreciate it." The marshal stepped to Virginia and Andy. "Mrs. Clark, Doctor Clark. We are United States Marshals and we have orders to assist you. If you will proceed to the baggage claim—"

Virginia pointed to their suitcases and backpacks. "We have everything, Marshal."

"Yes, Ma'am," the marshal said. "There is another Smithsonian Central Security Service officer impatiently waiting for you in baggage claim. We will take you to her."

Andy smiled. "Donna's here."

The marshal nodded. "Yes, sir. We asked her to wait at baggage claim. She wanted to come, but we assured her we would take good care of you. If we don't, I bet that lady could do a lot of serious damage."

Virginia shouldered her backpack. "You wouldn't lose that bet, Marshal."

The deputy sheriff and TSA officers walked in front, of Virginia and Andy Who were sandwiched between the U.S. Marshals and the armed Air Force men. They proceeded down the long carpeted walkway toward the exit. The people seated at gates watched them march down the wide aisle while people walking parted to let them through. At the escalator the deputy sheriff broke off and hurriedly talked to two other sheriff's deputies, both sergeants. They stood aside, solemn-faced. The TSA officers likewise went to a supervisor and then walked to the security checkpoint. The marshals and Air Force men continued to baggage claim where Donna was pacing. She saw them coming and raced to Virginia and Andy.

Donna looked at the marshal. "Thank you, Marshal. Are we good to go or should we expect more trouble?" She spotted the airmen and gave them a five-hundred watt smile. "Hi, boys. Thanks for watching out for my friends." The airmen stood staring wide-eyed at Donna, dressed in a form-fitting, bright-red blouse, which contrasted with her olive complexion, tight jeans and red track shoes. Her outfit emphasized her figure. Her black hair bounced around her shoulders.

Major Simmons smiled and nodded, "Our pleasure, Ma'am." He saluted and they started back for their plane. After a couple steps, he stopped and turned. "Ms. Virginia, if you ever need another ride, we'd be happy to oblige."

"Thanks, Major."

"The marshal smiled at Donna, "Ms. Bolette, I don't think there will be any more trouble, so I'm turning them over to your care. From what I saw Mrs. Clark do to that deputy sheriff, I have the feeling if there were to be more problems, you, and they, will be more than sufficient to handle it. But, we will escort you all to your vehicles anyway. I'm not sure I trust that deputy to give up easily." Donna led them across the airport driveway to the parking structure and to the roof where their silver Honda Pilot waited. The marshals looked around, said good-bye, and left.

Andy lowered the third row seats to give more cargo space, put their bags in the rear of the SUV, and closed the tailgate. He walked around to the driver's side where Donna and Virginia were talking. They looked at him as he approached.

"Thanks for the help, Donna. I think we all made an impression inside. We're probably already on YouTube and being carried by a number of news agencies." He glanced around. "So much for sneaking into town. Maybe we should get out of here before the press or more sheriffs' officers arrive. What hotel have you arranged for us?"

"It's the Grand Californian at Disneyland."

"Not near the beach?" Andy sighed. "I guess that'll do."

Donna put her hands on her hips. "When you lived here that was all you could talk about… how much fun it would be to stay there. You love the lobby. Anyway, it's been foggy and chilly at the beach lately."

He beamed. "You're right. I've always wanted to stay there. Thanks."

Donna turned to Virginia, "You have to put up with this all the time?"

"Yeah, what's a girl to do?" They laughed.

"Okay, then," Donna leaned on the car. "I thought we'd go directly to the hotel. I'll get you registered under your alias and safely in your room. Then, I'll brief you on the people you'll be seeing who worked with Jack Warner during the war. Oh yeah, the car is a rental and I set up a special way to pay for it so the transaction can't be traced."

Virginia wet her lips. "Good job. Who are we at the hotel?"

"Mr. and Mrs. Strangefellow."

"Oh, great," Virginia rolled her eyes. "No one will figure that it's a fake name."

"I don't think anyone will be looking for you at Disneyland, either. Oh yeah, your room keys are your passes to Disneyland and California Adventure. It's part of the package."

Andy hugged her. "Donna, I love you."

Virginia hit him on his arm. "Watch it, buster. You're married and so is she."

Donna chuckled, then tossed Andy the car keys. "I'll meet you at the hotel. After we go over everything, let's have dinner at the beach."

Andy continued to smile. "See you at the hotel."

A half hour later, they stood in a short line at the registration desk in the lobby of the Grand Californian. Virginia noted the hotel looked and felt like a National Parks Service Lodge, with rock foundations, and shingle siding.

As Andy, with Donna's assistance, registered. Virginia walked around the spacious, woodsy lobby that looked and felt like the towering Ahwahnee Hotel in Yosemite National Park. She gazed at the roaring fire in an oversized stone fireplace that warmed and accented the lobby. She noticed the massive rock foundations, Craftsman-style décor with polished floors, rustic carpets, darkened wood paneling, and soaring beams and crossbeams. Chandeliers inspired by California woodlands glowed above the vibrant yet rustic hues of the lavish lobby.

Virginia sat in one of the large, overstuffed chairs and took in the feel of a mountain lodge. After they were done registering, Andy and Donna joined her.

Andy helped Virginia up. "Let's get settled in and Donna can brief us on who we'll see."

They took their bags up to their room. Entering, Virginia noticed the room was outfitted with Craftsman-style furnishings and early twentieth–century Californian decor. The room included wood furnishings, carved headboards, and leaded-glass lights. There was a flat-screen TV, a mini-bar in a wooden armoire, and a multi-line phone with voice mail. The rooms even offered complimentary wired and wireless internet access. The bathroom had illuminated makeup mirrors. Virginia moved the drape and looked at their private balcony. She turned and looked at Donna and Andy. "This is great. I may not want to leave."

Donna plopped into a chair and pulled an iPad from her bag. "Shall we get to work? I have the names and addresses of the people you wanted to see."

Virginia pulled a small notebook out of her backpack and sat on the sofa.

Andy plopped on the bed and leaned against the headboard. "Okay, who are we seeing?"

Donna consulted her notes. "There are three people still alive who may be able to help. One is a gentleman. Name's Jason Van Heart, ninety years old. He lives in a small bungalow near the La Brea Tar Pits in L.A." She gave Virginia the address. "Next is Mary Lindstead, age eighty-nine and she lives in Newport Beach. And the last person is Heriberto Vasquez and he lives in east L.A. Tough neighborhood." Donna gave the address to Virginia.

Virginia scribbled the information into her notebook. "You've been busy. Thanks for the help."

Donna shut off her iPad and slipped it into her bag. "If you need anything else, call me right away. I'll help all I can. Be careful in east L.A. It'd be nice if you had someone from there to give you some support."

Andy slid off the bed. "We do have a contact there. Louise Rodriguez. She's a cousin to one of Dillon's lieutenants. She's expecting a call from us."

Donna looked at Andy with a raised eyebrow. "Who is this Dillon fellow?"

"He's a gang leader in Washington. He and his gang are assisting us and keeping an eye on a friend of ours."

"You have a street gang helping you? How'd you do that?"

"We were nice."

Donna looked at Virginia. "Who'd you shoot?"

"No one. I managed to put down one of their big guys and ran two other large gentlemen off, all three needed a hospital and we didn't have them arrested. Matter of fact, we got one of their boys out of jail. They call us the dinosaur cops because we work for the Smithsonian. Nice guys when you get to know them."

Donna stared at Virginia for a minute. "You're kidding, right?"

"Nope. They've been helping us since then."

"Well, that's one for the books." Donna rose from the chair. "So, where are you taking me for dinner?"

Virginia's cell phone rang. She rummaged for it in the bottom of her backpack. "Hello?"

Dillon's voice sounded strained. "Ms. Virginia. Thought you should know. Some men from an A-RAB embassy tried to get to Mr. Van Epps. We stopped them like you asked."

"What did they want and how'd you stop them?"

"They tried to break into the old gentleman's house around dinner time. Rosa, she's my lady, was cooking him some dinner, and she threw hot grease on one of them. The second guy, I hit a few times with a baseball bat."

"A few times?"

"Okay, a dozen, and it was an aluminum bat. I cleaned up afterwards."

"Where are they now?"

"We figured out who they were and that they wouldn't be arrested because of some sort of immunity shit. So, we sort of reemphasized with the bat and some steel-toed boots that they should stay away from the gentleman and then dumped their sorry and broken asses outside a hospital emer-

Dangerous Threads

gency room. Trust me, they needed to be there."

"Are you and your lady friend okay?"

"Yeah, we're cool, but laying low. I've got Mr. Van Epps covered, though. He's pretty cool. We enjoy talking to him. He's taught us a lot about history and stuff. It's really interesting. He has great stories and it's more interesting because he was actually there, not a boring teacher who just got it from books. So, he's become our adopted member, like a borrowed grandfather type, ya know? And we take him shopping, to his doctor, and places, and my lady likes to cook for him. So, I get to eat there and talk to the old guy. He even told us how to handle the A-RABs so we wouldn't get arrested. Oh, one other thing. While we were having a kind of a… conversation… with the A-RABs, with the help of the bat, they said their people were looking for you and they know you are on your way to L.A. But, they don't know how since you missed your train or who you are going to see."

"Okay. Good work. I'll tell my husband. Thanks for all you've done."

"No problem. Don't forget to contact Louise Rodriguez when you get to L.A. She can arrange for some muscle for you. She's expecting your call."

"Thanks, Dillon, we're going to contact her soon."

"One more thing, Ms. Virginia, I think you should turn off your cell phone. They can find you with the GPS chip in it."

CHAPTER 19

Early the next morning, Virginia stepped out of the shower, her blonde hair clinging to her head, grabbed a towel and dried herself as she watched Andy trying to shave while wiping the condensation from the bathroom mirror. "I told you to do that after I showered."

Andy turned, grinning, his face half-shaved and half-soapy. "I know but I'm anxious to get started interviewing the people Donna set us up with."

"Yeah, me too. I thought we'd start with Mary Lindstead. She lives in Newport Beach and is closest."

"I agree." He finished shaving and rinsed off his face. "Let's get dressed and head downstairs for breakfast, then we can call her and make an appointment."

After breakfast, Andy strolled around the mountain lodge, Craftsman-style décor lobby waiting for Virginia, who was sitting in an overstuffed chair, finishing a call on her cell phone.

After a couple minutes she rose and joined Andy. "If I can break you away from all this, we have an appointment at ten with Mrs. Lindstead."

"Did you get directions?"

"No. That's what the navigation system in the car is for. We have her address. She said she remembers Jack Warner well."

Andy led the way to their car. "Did you mention the quilt or that we are with the Smithsonian?"

"No, I didn't tell her about the quilt, but I did tell her we are with the Smithsonian. I told her we had something important to discuss with her."

Andy opened the car door for her. "Hop in. You can put the address in the nav system."

They headed down Harbor Drive to I405, then south to State Highway 55 into Newport Beach. When the freeway ended, they followed the road downhill to the Pacific Coast Highway and turned north. A short drive and they turned inland and, after several more turns, found the small, yellow bungalow with white shutters. The street was still full of parked cars, so they parked a block away and walked to the house. It had a little front yard

Dangerous Threads

and manicured shrubs around the house. A concrete walkway led to a diminutive porch and a stained wooden door. Virginia rang the bell.

In a few moments Mrs. Lindstead opened the door. "Hello. You must be Dr. and Mrs. Clark. Please come in." She stepped aside and let them enter. The entrance opened into a small, neat living room. It was decorated in early American style, except for the large flat screen TV mounted on a wall between two windows.

Mrs. Lindstead pointed to the sofa. "Please have a seat. Can I get you anything?"

They sat, then Virginia responded, "No, thank you, we had breakfast a little while ago."

"Oh. I do have fresh butter croissants."

Andy perked up. "That sounds good." Virginia poked him.

"Good. I'll be right back." Mrs. Lindstead hurried to

the kitchen and returned with a platter piled high with croissants and set it on the coffee table. She scurried back to the kitchen and returned with a pitcher of iced tea and three glasses setting them next to the platter. She sat on a chair across from them and poured the tea. "Help yourselves to the croissants."

Andy took one and bit into it. "Ohh... this is really good."

Virginia sipped some tea, then spoke. "Mrs. Lindstead, we are here to ask you some questions about what may have happened at Warner Brothers in the early nineteen-forties. Especially about something Jack Warner may have had."

Mrs. Lindstead nibbled on a croissant. "He was a nice man. Did you know the President commissioned him an officer in the Army to make films to support the war effort?"

Virginia nodded. "Yes. Mrs. Lindstead, what did you do at Warner Brothers during the war?"

"I was young then. I had a lot of jobs at the studio. But at the time, I was a property manager."

"What did you do as a property manager?"

"I was one of the people that inventoried props, assigned them an ID number, and determined where to store them, then put the information into our property management files. When producers or directors needed some props, I made sure the right ones were on the set and in the proper location when they needed them."

Andy reached for another croissant. "That was a pretty important job. There must have been hundreds of props."

Mrs. Lindstead smiled. "Tens of thousands, actually. I never lost one."

Virginia leaned forward. "Did you ever see or hear about a special quilt given to Mr. Warner?"

Mrs. Lindstead sat back and stared at the fireplace for a minute. "Well, kind of. I remember hearing that he got a special quilt and some other things from Washington, but I never saw them or knew what happened to them. For that matter, I never knew if they were real. There was a lot of talk about 'secret' things in those days."

"Do you have any idea where he might have put them?"

"If we didn't get them in property management, then I have no idea what he might have done with them." Mrs. Lindstead sipped some tea. "You mean the quilt was real? Why the interest in it today?"

"The Smithsonian is interested in it because of its historical significance. It won the Sears quilt contest and was at the 1933 Chicago World's Fair. We'd like to have it at the Smithsonian."

"I see. I don't know anything that will help you, I'm sorry. I still know some people at Warner Brothers today. Would you like me to call and ask them about it?"

"No. Not yet. We have a few more people to contact. If that doesn't prove fruitful, I may take you up on that offer."

Mrs. Lindstead nodded. "I'll be happy to help any way I can. I visited the Smithsonian and enjoyed all the museums, so I'd like to help if possible."

Virginia and Andy rose. "Thank you for the refreshments and your help."

As they walked to the door, Mrs. Lindstead stopped, tilted her head and asked, "Why are Smithsonian people carrying guns?"

Virginia turned and looked at Mrs. Lindstead for a long moment. "We are with the Smithsonian Central Security Service. We are federal agents and the quilt has national security significance. So, I must ask you not to mention the quilt or our visit with anyone. Can you do that?"

Mrs. Lindstead grinned. "Honey, during the big war, some of us were involved with the Army and we kept secrets, so if you like, and as they say on TV, you were never here, unless of course you need anything else."

Andy put his hand on Mrs. Lindstead's arm. "Thank you very much for your help and understanding. And thank you for the croissants, they were really good."

"You're welcome, Son. Stop by anytime."

Virginia and Andy left and strolled back to their car. After getting in and starting it, Andy looked at Virginia. She dug a paper out of her backpack. "Okay, next we go see Jason Van Heart. He's ninety years old and, according to Donna, he lives in a small bungalow near the La Brea Tar Pits in L.A." She punched the address into the car's navigation system. A female computer voice said, "Turn right and go one mile then turn right."

Andy pulled into the street. "Okay, one down, two to go."

Dangerous Threads

An hour later they pulled in front of Jason Van Heart's bungalow. Virginia stood facing the front of the faded pink stucco house. It looked like a home in an old nineteen-thirties or forties Hollywood movie. The dark wooden front door opened as they approached. A small elderly woman smiled at them as they walked up. "You must be the federal agents I talked to."

Andy produced his badge. "Yes, Ma'am. We have a few questions for Mr. Van Heart. Is he available to speak to us?"

"Yes, he's expecting you. But, please, Jason's not well, don't excite him unduly."

Virginia stepped up to the door. "I'm Virginia Davies-Clark. We won't keep him long. Are you Mrs. Van Heart?"

The woman chuckled. "No. I'm Mary Scott; I'm a friend. Mrs. Van Heart died three years ago." Mrs. Scott stepped aside. "Please, come in. Jason is in the dining room sorting his mail."

They entered the small house. The living room had an old but well maintained, red couch, two padded chairs, a coffee table, and a small brick fireplace. A flat-screen television sat on a cherry wood cabinet. A rug was centered on a polished, wooden floor. They took the short step up into the dining room. The bald, stoop-shouldered Jason Van Heart sat at a round table with a crocheted, white, tablecloth and mail sorted in front of him. A walker stood next to the chair.

Mary called to Van Heart. "Jason. You have company. They are the people from Washington."

Van Heart looked up. "Yes, yes, please, come in. Would you mind joining me here at the table?"

Virginia, Andy, and Mary Scott sat down at the table with Jason Van Heart.

Virginia looked at the tablecloth. "This is beautiful. The workmanship is outstanding."

Van Heart nodded. "My wife made that over seventy years ago. I've always liked it. Now, what can I do for you? You've come a long way to see an old man."

Virginia cleared her throat. "Sir, I understand you worked for Jack Warner during World War II. Is that correct?"

"Yes. He was Lt. Col. Jack Warner then. I was head of the film processing area. We developed all the film. In those days the editors worked in that organization, too."

"Did you have any direct dealings with Colonel Warner?"

"Yes. We were making our movies, but his attention was on the movies for the War Department. He had me make sure they had priority."

Virginia leaned on the table with her arms folded in front of her. "Do you have any recollection of a special quilt being given or loaned to Colonel Warner in the early forties?"

Van Heart jerked up straight. His breathing quickened. "Yes. I remember an Army officer giving him a package from the White House. It came while we were having a meeting. It was a big box. I figured it was materials for the movies he was making, but when he opened it there was a quilt inside. He got nervous and called his secretary, and then had us all leave his office."

Andy rubbed his chin. "Then what happened?"

"We left the office. There was some talk about state secrets being hidden in the quilt and for a while, word spread throughout the studio. But with everything going on there, talk about it slowly died down. We were busy and heard nothing more about the quilt or other things that seemed to arrive at odd hours. I never saw it again. Just about everyone I knew then is dead or I've lost contact, so I'm afraid I'm not much help."

Andy nodded. "Do you know if security was called to help protect it?"

"I don't know for sure." He fidgeted in his chair, "But I don't think so."

Virginia smiled at him. "Mr. Van Heart, Do you have any other information about the quilt or where it may have gone? Do you know something and haven't answered because we didn't ask the right questions?'

Van Heart hesitated. "Well, I remember one night I went to Colonel Warner's office late and he was handing the box, now resealed, to a woman I didn't recognize. She was very pretty. Latin type. I thought she was maybe an actress or something, but I never saw her before or after. He told her to guard it until someone from the government comes for it. I assumed it was the mysterious quilt, but I couldn't swear to it. When he saw me, he asked that I never breathe a word about it to anyone. That was over seventy years ago. I don't know if anyone in the government came for it or not."

Virginia shook her head. "No, Sir. Not until now."

Van Heart wrinkled his brow. "Why was the quilt so important, and why are you looking for it over seventy years later?"

"It is important to national security," Andy answered.

"Oh." He raised an eyebrow. "I see. I wish I could be of more help."

Virginia reached across the table and patted his arm. "You've been more help than you know. Thank you so much for your time."

Virginia punched the last address into the navigation system as Andy called Louise Rodriguez.

"Hello?" a soft voice with a slight Spanish accent answered.

Andy cleared his throat. "Ms. Rodriguez? My name is Dr. Andy Clark. I was told you're expecting our call."

"You're the dinosaur cops my cousin called me about, right?"

"Yes. We are heading your way and could use some support."

"Where are you going? I'll meet you there with some friends. My

Dangerous Threads

cousin said you are cool and to protect you."

Andy gave her the address. "We'll be there in about two hours. Need to make a stop on the way."

"I'll meet you there, Dr. Dinosaur Cop. Is your lady with you?"

"Yes."

"Good, my cousin said I had to meet her."

"Thanks. We're driving a silver Honda Pilot."

"I'll tell our people. See you at the address in two hours. How can I reach you?"

Andy gave her his cell number and hung up. He looked at Virginia. "Got Heriberto Vasquez's address in the system?"

"Yep. Where are we stopping on the way, may I ask?"

"Lunch."

An hour and a half later, Andy parked the SUV a block down the street from Heriberto Vasquez's home. The small, wood-sided, one-story houses on the street had bars on their windows, short chain link fences, and dogs in the yards. One had a vegetable garden in the front yard. Some had low-riders parked in the driveways just wide enough for one car. An empty lot had refuse amongst the weeds. A few young men in white or dingy tank tops over low, baggy jeans hung around, leaning on cars in the street or against fences. Loud, deep, pulsating bass sounds assaulted their ears from a number of the cars around the block,

Virginia peered out the window, then slid her 9mm out of her backpack, jacked the slide, and set the safety. "Looks like a friendly neighborhood."

A Hispanic woman, who appeared to be in her mid-twenties with short black hair, pushed off from a low rider and strolled to the SUV. Andy lowered the window as she approached.

She leaned on the vehicle and looked inside. "You the Dr. Dinosaur Cop I talked to?"

Andy nodded. "Yes. I'm Dr. Andy Clark and this is my wife, Virginia. We are with the Smithsonian Central Security Service. We're Dillon's friends. You're Louise Rodriguez?"

"Yes. My cousin said you're okay and to help you, so," she pointed to Vasquez's house. "The man you're looking for lives there. My friends will watch your car and keep an eye out for other gangs and any trouble. While you're here, you're safe."

"Thank you for your help."

"Just go see the old guy and then get out of the neighborhood," Rodriguez said. "Cops and outsiders are… well… they're not greeted with open arms, if you follow me."

"Trust me, we won't stay longer than necessary. We don't want any trouble and tell your… err… friends, we are not interested in anything they may have done or if the local law is interested in them. It's none of our business."

"That's what my cousin said you'd say. And, he said you were straight with them, so you're good here, but just the same, you know." Louise stepped back from the car to let Andy out. "I have a question, Doc. Did you really get one of my cousin's homies out of a Washington jail?"

Andy nodded. "Yes."

"You really are strange for cops, but I like you."

Andy and Virginia got out of the car, locked it, and walked to Heriberto Vasquez's house. They opened the short gate and walked up the uneven concrete walkway. Andy knocked on the door.

Heriberto Vasquez answered and after seeing their ID, ushered them inside. "I see you've met the local welcoming committee. I'm surprised they let you just walk up here."

Virginia smiled. "Right now, they kind of work for us."

Vasquez frowned. "They do? How did you arrange that? They are some real bad people, and they don't like or trust outsiders, especially cops."

"It's a long story. Mr. Vasquez, we have some questions we'd like to ask you about when you worked for Warner Brothers in the early forties."

"Yes, you mentioned that on the phone. Please, come in." They walked into a small living room decorated in a retro, nineteen-fifties style. They took seats on a worn couch across from him.

Vasquez sat back. "What exactly do you want to know?"

"We are looking for a quilt that was given to Lt. Col. Jack Warner in the early forties. We were hoping you could shed some light on how we can find it."

Andy pushed his glasses up on his nose. "We were told it was given to a pretty Hispanic woman by Colonel Wagner."

Vasquez sat looking at them, then smiled. "It was over seventy years ago. My wife and I worked for Colonel Wagner. Hispanics were either film stars or relegated to lesser roles then. I was his driver and go-to man. When he needed something done quietly, I did it for him. My wife worked in costuming, and she was also an extra in some movies and sometimes entertained dignitaries. She was very pretty."

Virginia nodded. "I see. Can you tell us anything about a special quilt that was secretly given to Colonel Warner during that time?"

"You are really federal agents? You work for the museum, in Washington?"

"Yes, Sir. The Smithsonian."

Vasquez sighed. "Finally."

Virginia leaned forward. "Finally? I don't understand?"

He looked at her with a haunted expression. "My wife was given the quilt by Colonel Warner for safekeeping. He said some federal agents would come for it. She hid the box and never mentioned it to anyone. She died five years ago and no one ever came for the box. I thought everyone forgot about it."

Andy took a breath. "Do you still have it?"

"Yes. It's right there." He pointed to an old travel trunk dating from the thirties. "It's inside the trunk."

Virginia's eyes widened. "May we take it, Sir?"

"Please do. I'd like to get rid of the burden of keeping the secret all these years."

Virginia stood, stepped to the trunk, and opened it. Inside was a wooden box. She lifted it, carried it back to the couch, and sat as she held it. "I'll examine it later, then contact Washington and ask them to send you some compensation and recognition for keeping this safe for so many years."

Vasquez nodded. "Thank you. It isn't necessary. Colonel Warner was very generous to us. He made sure we would be taken care of after we retired. After all this time, the studio still takes care of me."

Virginia nodded. "I understand, Sir, but I think the government owes you something, and we will see what we can do to get you some recognition."

"Thank you. I know my wife would be happy."

Virginia and Andy stood. "Thanks for your help. We'll—"

They heard three shots. Andy's cell phone rang. He pulled it out of its holder and punched the talk button. "Hello?"

"Doc. Get out now! There is trouble." Louise Rodriguez said in a strained voice.

"Another gang?"

"No. They look like they are from... well, they look dark like Arabs. My cousin said they were after you. If you come out now, we can get you out of here."

"We're leaving right now."

"Use the back door. I'll meet you."

"Mr. Vasquez, I'd recommend you stay low for a while. Virginia, hang on to your box, we're going out the back." Andy drew his gun as she hurried behind him. Andy carefully opened the door. Louise Rodriguez, crouched low, motioned for them to follow her. They sprinted across the yard and over a fence, ran across another cluttered yard and through a gate to an alley. As they entered the alley, two more young men with pistols ran out from behind some parked cars and joined them. The men led the way to the street. Their SUV was parked five cars down.

Louise Rodriguez motioned for them to stop and pulled out her cell phone. She made a call and said something in rapid Spanish. A few seconds later there was more gunfire, then more rapid Spanish over her phone.

Louise Rodriguez turned to Andy and Virginia and pointed. "Go to your car and turn around and go back that way. I'm having some of my boys follow you. In a block, you will see a dark blue Honda Civic low-rider with four men in it. Follow them. They'll take you to the freeway. The others will make sure no one follows you. My cousin said we're to take care of the old man you talked to. So don't worry about him. He'll be well protected. Now go, before the LAPD finally arrives and really screws things up."

CHAPTER 20

Andy steered toward the low-rider ahead. As he approached, an arm holding a black semiautomatic waved them to follow. Another vehicle with four male occupants tucked in behind them. They picked up speed as they wound through neighborhoods, each looking a lot like the last one. A few turns later, Andy heard police sirens. He saw the freeway, but not an entrance until they rounded another corner. The lead car pulled to the side and the driver motioned for Andy to take the on-ramp.

Andy slowed as he pulled alongside and yelled, "Thanks for the help."

The driver smiled. "No problem, Dinosaur Cop. You're always welcome. Now, get out of here before there's more trouble."

Andy sped up the on-ramp to the I5 South and headed for Orange County. As he slid into the number two lane of the seven southbound lanes of the freeway, he glanced at Virginia. She had her cell phone in her hand. "Virginia! Turn that damn thing off, pull out the battery, and toss the pieces in the back seat. Now!"

Virginia looked at him. "Andy, I…"

"Get that battery out now or I'll toss the damn thing out the window!"

"But—"

"How do you think our detractors found us in South Central LA? Google? The Auto Club? No! They used the GPS chip in *your* phone. The one Dillon told you to keep off."

Virginia turned pale. She switched off the phone and undid the back cover, removed the battery, and tossed everything on the rear floor. Virginia slumped in her seat. "I could have gotten us and everyone else seriously hurt or killed."

Andy glanced back at her, and then patted her leg. "What's gotten into you? You know better than to use that phone. Use the secured cell phone Doctor Montgomery gave you."

"I think it's the quilt and all we've been through. I just wasn't thinking. Sorry. I need to plan more."

"Virginia, do you know what generals use detailed combat plans for after the actual battle starts?"

She gave him a quizzical look. "No. What?"

"Toilet paper."

"Well, a good documented plan can help us avoid disaster and getting shot."

Andy switched lanes and passed a truck, then swung back into the second lane. "First, when did you ever make a detailed plan for any of your capers? You fly by the seat of your pants. You're good at it. Very good, or the government wouldn't have us doing this. And, General MacArthur once said, 'Whoever said the pen is mightier than the sword, obviously never encountered automatic weapons.'"

"I get it. You're right." Virginia twisted around and looked out the rear window. After a minute, she settled back, "I didn't see anyone following."

"How could you tell in all this traffic?"

"Wishful thinking."

After an hour and a half in slow-moving traffic, Andy pulled the Pilot into the Grand Californian Hotel and gave the key to the valet. They lugged their backpacks and wooden box to their suite. Virginia locked the door as Andy dropped his pack next to the bathroom door, took a few more steps, and fell across the king size bed. Virginia slid her backpack into the closet and set the box on the coffee table. She plopped onto the sofa, rested her chin in her hands with her elbows on her legs, and stared at the container.

Andy raised his head and looked at her. "You going to stare the thing to death or open it?"

She straightened and sighed. "I guess this is the big moment, isn't it?"

"Yeah. It's either a moth-eaten rag, just a faded old quilt, the real deal, or it's a prop and the real quilt is in someone's attic or Goodwill. So, let's find out."

"Nothing like positive reinforcement." Virginia retrieved her backpack, pulled out her Swiss Army knife, and used various tools to undo metal straps, screws and glue before prying open the lid. She tossed it on the floor.

As she reached inside, Andy rose and put his hand on her shoulder. "Wait." He stepped to the window, closed the thick drapes, and switched on the desk lamp. Virginia quickly turned on all the room lights.

She sat next to the box. "Did you see something?"

"No. But at this moment we don't know if our enemy knows about the hotel. You used your phone here, remember?"

"Right. Okay, let's see what we have here." She unfolded the thick, white cloth that wrapped whatever was inside. Andy leaned over the box with her. Inside rested a folded quilt. She pulled a small box from her suitcase and removed a pair of white cotton gloves and slipped them on. She carefully lifted the quilt from its resting place and set it on the bed. Next she gently unfolded it.

Andy stepped close with a book, *Patchwork Souvenirs of the 1933 World's Fair,* in his hand, opened to a marked page. He compared the quilt on the bed to the one in the picture. He looked at Virginia. "I think this is it. The Sears contest winning quilt, *The Unknown Star.* I guess lab tests will verify that."

Virginia wet her lips. "I never thought we'd really find it. It's been missing for over 70 years." She put her hand to her chest. "My heart is really racing. We did it, Andy."

"Looks like it. Now we need to protect it and get it to Washington."

Virginia leaned closer to the quilt. "Do you see any of the record wires?"

"No. But they'd be extremely thin and I don't expect to see any without magnification."

Virginia sat next to it and looked at Andy. "Okay, we've got what we think is the real quilt. Now what? Do I just 'Special Delivery' mail it as certified mail with a return receipt and insure it for ten billion dollars, just UPS, or FedEx it?

"Or, we could hand-deliver it to the Pentagon, or the Smithsonian, or to a National Laboratory, or a military base." Andy touched the quilt's binding.

Virginia looked at the quilt again. "I'd better use my sat-phone to call Montgomery."

Andy sat next to her. "As much as I like that idea, of maybe having him send a detachment of Marines from Camp Pendleton to guard us and all, I think, if we do that, you should not call from this hotel or from anywhere near here."

She frowned. "Why not?"

"Think about it. Every time we've let the DOD know about what we were doing, even using their sat-phone, our adversaries seem to end up close or even trying to kill us."

"You don't think Dr. Montgomery is a spy, do you?"

"Maybe not him, but I wouldn't be surprised if there isn't a mole in their organization. The government is using us and not DOD or DOE people."

"Because of our unique qualifications and cover?"

"Maybe."

She sighed. "If I believe that, you've got a bridge you'd like to sell me, cheap?"

"Something like that." Andy turned Virginia's head toward him and brushed a short strand of blonde hair out of her face. "Now, My Dear, is the time for some of your devious, dangerous, and crazy planning."

"You said they use battle plans for toilet paper."

"Last year, you and Donna outsmarted some real dangerous guys in Italy who tried to feed us to fish. You've outdone intelligent villains in Scotland and the Mafia in part of Texas and out-witted crooks in California. You've got a lot of experience at this. This should be fun for you."

She looked at him with a blank expression, and then she began to smile. "Okay, let's assume Doctor Montgomery's organization is compromised, like you said. My Dear, we've got work to do."

CHAPTER 21

Virginia moved to the desk and used the hotel phone to dial Donna's number. Donna answered on the fourth ring.

"Bolette Travel. Donna Bolette speaking. How may I help you?"

"Hi. Andy and I need some more help. You game?"

Donna's voice picked up a notch. "Virginia, Dear, I'm always up for another of your misadventures. Do I get to shoot someone this time?"

"Could be."

"Goody, what do you need?"

"You said you still have some of the toys Luigi gave us in Rome last year when we were after the Crystal Skull, true?"

"Virginia! A private citizen in possession of some of those military and automatic weapons and surveillance items would be subject to all sorts of legal problems from the ATF, FBI, Customs, State Department, DOD, and who knows who else. Would a nice girl like me smuggle those weapons, or what was left, into this country and keep them?"

Virginia chuckled. "Yep."

"You know me so well. What's up?"

"We found the item we've been searching for."

"You did? Great."

"Yeah, but we've been compromised. Our adversaries keep showing up where we do. It's been really helpful to have our own private army of street gangs to help us, but we're kind of on our own now."

"Street gangs?"

"It's a long story." Virginia switched the phone to her other ear. "I'll tell you later."

"This ought to be good. On your own? What happened to your private army? Why do you need me?"

"You ask lots of questions at once like I do. It frustrates Andy. But to answer one of your questions, you're a one-girl army and the three of us—"

"Will get into all sorts of trouble. What's wrong with your Washington contact?"

"Andy and I think our Washington contact's organization has a mole."

"So, what are you going to do, mail it? And where do I, and my toy collection, come in?"

"We need to get the package to Washington. We can't count on government or military help. I'm afraid to mail it, or let it out of my possession."

"Not even those cute air-boys in blue I saw at the airport with you?"

"I can't contact them and change their orders to pick us up. That has to come from their headquarters."

"Too bad. That pilot was cute."

"And you're married."

"A girl can have a fantasy life, can't she? I'm picturing him and me at twenty thousand feet getting it on. Maybe I'd become a member of the four-mile-high club."

"Get your mind back down to earth, Girl. Can you meet us here at Disneyland, in downtown Disney, for dinner to go over some ideas?"

"Sure." Donna's voice perked up. "How about at *Naples Restorante e Pizzeria*? I know the head chef and I can get us a reservation upstairs so we won't be interrupted. How does seven sound?"

Virginia turned and looked at Andy. "How about six? Andy is ready to eat the curtains. The poor boy didn't have much of a lunch. He's not happy."

"The poor guy. Okay, I'll shoot for six. If there are any problems I'll call you. Should I use your cell, the sat phone or the hotel number?"

"Use the hotel land line. I'm not sure how secure the sat phone really is, and my cell is what I think helped the bad guys."

"Okay. See you at six."

Virginia hung up and turned in her chair toward Andy. "We're meeting Donna at *Naples Restorante e Pizzeria* at six."

Andy nodded. "I heard. Good; I'm starved and I love Italian. I take it the toys you mentioned are some of the weapons you two used in Italy. How'd she get them into the country?"

"I haven't a clue as to everything she did and I doubt she'll tell you. Probably involves charming some poor government official. I figured she still had some of the items."

"Care to share what is going on in that pretty, but devious, head of yours?"

"Later. I'm still thinking. But, now we should get dressed for dinner and go see the sights in Downtown Disney until it's time to meet Donna."

A little before six, Virginia and Andy walked under a wooden trellis into the green building with NAPLES above the door.

Andy took a deep breath. "I love the smell of an Italian restaurant. Can't you smell all the mouth-watering sauces, the spices, and… the pizza?"

"I knew you'd get pizza in there somehow."

They approached a pretty young woman standing at a tall wooden desk. She had dark hair past her shoulders, olive complexion, and a black, low-cut dress that displayed her attributes at their best. Virginia told her they had reservations upstairs at six.

The girl looked at a book. "The name?"

Virginia wrinkled her forehead. "Bolette, I think."

"Ah, yes, here it is. Private party, upstairs." She made a call on an intercom, then gave them a warm smile, and winked at Andy. "Will you please just walk up the stairs and someone up there will assist you."

"Thank you." Virginia started for the stairway, then turned, and spotted Andy, with a big grin, chatting with the young lady. Virginia grabbed his shirtsleeve and tugged in the direction of the stairway. "This way, Romeo."

At the top of the stairs, they were greeted by another attractive young woman who escorted them to a small room Virginia had never noticed when she'd eaten there before.

They were seated and ordering drinks when Donna sauntered in. She stopped the waiter and ordered a margarita with lots of salt. Then she took the chair Andy had pulled out for her.

Donna looked up at Andy. "Thank you, Sir. Chivalry is not dead as reported by MSNBC." She looked at Virginia. "Well, you're still alive, that's always a good sign."

Virginia gave her a demure smile. "Yeah, well, we had our challenges, but we got it."

"The quilt? You actually found it when no one else could? Wonderful!" Donna frowned. "Oh, by the way, there was a short piece on the news this afternoon about some trouble up in East L.A. Some Arab types and a Hispanic gang had a brief tumble and when the police got there the Arabs were found, with serious injuries, and some illegal automatic weapons and a huge pile of illicit drugs. Did that have anything to do with you two?"

Virginia leaned closer. "Did the Arabs claim diplomatic immunity?"

"Nah. They're in the county jail pending more state and federal charges, at least according to the news."

Virginia and Andy exchanged glances. "The Golden Crescent," they said at once.

Their drinks arrived. After a couple of sips, Donna asked, "Who's the Golden Crescent and who else is involved with you and your quilt?"

Andy took another drink, then straightened up in his chair. "The Golden Crescent is, we are led to believe, an Arab terrorist group and our other playmates are the intelligence service of the Saudi government. The Mossad may be somehow involved, too, but we're not really sure. That's all we know about at this point."

"How'd the Golden Crescent or the Saudis find you?"

"Good question." Andy gave her a furtive look. "We believe the Saudis have a mole in our DOD contact's organization. The Golden Crescent may have followed the GPS chip in Virginia's cell phone."

Donna took a long sip of her margarita. She looked at Virginia. "The phone is off now, isn't it? You didn't bring it here, I hope."

"No. It's in pieces on the floor of the car. I took the battery out and removed some other things so it won't work anymore."

Donna took another long sip of her margarita. "Oh that's good. The drink, I mean. I'm sure dismantling your phone was good, too, but this is *really* good. I needed this."

"You needed it? Think about where we were today and guess who really needs another drink?" She looked at Andy. "Get the waiter's attention. We need another round." Donna set her drink on the white, crisp cotton tablecloth. "Were you there when the Arab group met the gang? Was that your handiwork?"

Andy ordered more drinks. "Well, sort of. We enlisted the gang to help us. They saw the trouble shaping up and helped us get out, then took care of the problem."

Donna's mouth hung open. "You really recruited a gang in East L.A. to be your foot soldiers? How the hell did you do that? Even the cops are nervous about going in that area."

"We have another gang in Washington assisting us. One of the leaders of the gang in L.A. is a cousin of one of the big shots in the Washington gang."

"The gangs don't know you work for the Smithsonian Central Security Service do they?"

"Yeah. They know. They refer to us as dinosaur cops."

"Dinosaur cops? Now I've heard everything. I know there's a story in there somewhere. Later, you have to tell me how you pulled this off." Donna polished off her second margarita and waved the waiter over to order another. "If you've got support like that, what do you need from me?"

Virginia wet her lips. "I'll explain over dinner. But, let's say we can't count on the DOD for support because they've been compromised. I don't want to just mail the quilt, send it by UPS, or a commercial shipper. Not after what the quilt, and we, have been through. I don't want to let it out of my possession. So we're going to hand-deliver it. That's what I need to talk to you about."

Haddad Abdel A'hsam, the cultural attaché at the Saudi Embassy and the section head of the Saudi's Al Mukhabarat Al A'amah, answered the secure line on his telephone. "Hello?"

A voice in a broken Middle Eastern accent responded. "Sir. The Clarks are in Los Angeles. We know they got here when we heard about the scuffle at the Orange County Airport. It seems they flew in on an Air Force plane. TSA and the local Sheriff weren't too happy about their unexpected arrival and them being armed. During a standoff between them and the officials, the airmen came in to support them and they entered the terminal armed as well. When U.S. Marshals arrived, the Clarks left the building with them."

A'hsam cleared his throat. "Where did they go? Did you track which car rental agency they used? What type car do they have? Where are they staying?"

"That's the problem. They have disappeared."

"Disappeared? How?" A'hsam tightened his grip on the phone. "They must have left a trail. Credit cards, phone records, something."

"They have vanished. But we believe they did turn up briefly in East L.A."

"Why?"

"We think the Clarks were doing something in that area. The Golden Crescent is also here in L.A., and they seem to have located the Clarks in East L.A., but they ran into problems with a Hispanic gang. The Crescent people lost the fight and are in the county jail and the jail section of the county hospital."

"They being held for a gang fight?"

"No, Sir. They're charged with possession of automatic weapons, a federal offense, and for possession for sale of a huge stash of illegal drugs."

A'hsam sighed. "Have the Clarks recruited another gang to assist them? How in the name of Allah do they do that?"

"Yes, Sir, I think they did, and I don't know how they did it, Sir."

"Do you know what they were doing in that part of L.A.?"

"We assume they were talking to someone, but we have no idea who. We don't know why they're in L.A. at all."

A'hsam leaned back in his chair. "I'll see what our people at the Pentagon can tell me, and I'll call you back."

"Thank you, Sir." The man hung up.

A'hsam sat staring at the poster of Albert Einstein on the far wall. "For a couple of amateurs, they are sure devious, lucky, or the best operatives I've ever seen. I wonder who else they'll get to help them?"

As he reached for the telephone and dialed, his mind raced. *How did you fall off the grid? Where are you? Ms. Virginia, you are a crafty woman, and you are embarrassing me with my superiors, but I'll find you and when I do, you will be a guest of mine in my country under very unpleasant circumstances. That I promise.*

CHAPTER 22

Drying herself off from her morning shower, Virginia heard a commotion in the bedroom. She wrapped a towel around her waist and pulled her .380 semiautomatic from inside a sealed baggie and cautiously opened the door. She heard a man's voice and movement around the corner. She stepped into the room with her pistol raised. Andy and a bellman stood staring at her through an empty baggage cart. The bellman dropped a box he was holding and raised his hands. His eyes widened as he stared at her.

She slowly lowered her weapon and stepped around the cart, looking at the boxes. She turned slightly to Andy. "What are you doing?" She looked at the bellman. "You can lower your hands."

Andy cleared his throat. "These are the boxes Donna sent. She's on her way up with the other items you asked for."

"Good." Virginia glanced at the still-staring and grinning bellman. "I think you're done. Let me get a tip for you."

"That's quite all right. Not necessary. If there is anything else I can do for you, please call down and ask for Benny."

"Okay." Virginia led him to the door and opened it. As he pushed the empty baggage cart out, a couple walked by. The man's face lit up when he noticed Virginia standing in the doorway topless with a towel around her waist; his wife frowned. Virginia closed the door and walked back to Andy.

Andy sat on the bed next to the boxes. "You can put the gun down now, Dear."

Virginia wrinkled her nose. "The bellman didn't want a tip?"

"He got one."

"Huh?"

"Virginia, you were standing here with nothing on but a towel around your waist and holding a gun. I'm sure he got over the gun part pretty quick and, by the look on his face; I'd say he enjoyed looking at you. You even walked him to the door. By now, you're the talk of all the bellmen and male employees of this hotel."

Virginia turned and headed back to the bathroom. "I might as well finish getting ready. I bet we don't have any problem getting help around here now."

"No bet. You'd better hurry; Donna should be here soon with the rest of the stuff you requested."

Andy heard the knock, hurried to the door and peered through the peephole. Seeing Donna, Benny, and another bellman with two carts loaded with boxes, duffle bags, and a suitcase, he opened the door and ushered them inside.

Donna, dressed in a pair of tight denim shorts and an even tighter red tank top, led the procession into the room. She pointed to a corner of the room as she tossed her tote bag on the bed next to the boxes. "Just put the things there, please." She looked around then at Andy. "Where's Virginia?"

"Right here." Virginia walked in from the bathroom, her damp hair pulled into a small ponytail. Her khaki shorts and safari blouse disappointed the two bellmen. "Hi, Benny. Back already?"

"Yes, Ma'am. This lady needed help with her stuff. When you need help, remember to ask for me."

Andy led the two men out, giving them a tip as they left. He returned to where the girls were standing. "Okay, I know what the boxes are for and I assume those other containers have the fake quilts. What's in the duffle bags and suitcase?"

Donna unzipped one of the duffle bags so Andy could look inside. He bent over, reached in and moved a couple items, then stood up. "You've got an arsenal in there. What's in the other two?"

She quickly undid the remaining duffle bags and Andy peered inside. "I recognize some of the things in there, but not all of them, and why are tubes of lipstick and watches, perfume, and hairspray in there?"

Donna smiled. "The items inside these bags all go boom or do other nasty things to people or electronics. This collection is most of what I was able to smuggle back home from Italy after our quest for the crystal skull. If you remember, we used some of these to destroy a good part of our enemy's computers and other expensive electronic toys." She pulled a couple small grenades out. "These babies, or ones like them, we used to get rid of some really bad guys trying to kill us."

Andy hefted a grenade. "How'd you get them into the country? Aren't they illegal for civilians to have?"

"Oh yeah. They're really illegal. The ATF, DOD, FBI, CIA, and local cops would have kittens if they knew I had them."

"But how—"

"Remember when we got back to Italy after the Navy came to rescue us, even though the SEALs thought they weren't needed after seeing Virginia take out some of the bad guys?"

"Yeah."

"Well, I kind of went to see Luigi, the CIA guy who gave them to us, and asked for his help. I told him I'd send people to his restaurant—as I am a travel agent—if he'd assist me."

"He agreed to that?"

Donna gave him a coy smile. "I used my wiles and I prevailed."

Andy sat slack-jawed. "You're married."

"Yes, but I really wanted these play things and figured Virginia and I could use them for something someday. Anyway, I didn't do anything all that bad. As long as Luigi was happy, I got my way."

"What does 'not all that bad' mean?"

"You really don't want to know."

He looked at Virginia, who was trying to look inconspicuous. "What part did you play in all this?"

"I knew she was going to try to get them so I helped some, but didn't really know if she succeeded. Looks like she did."

Andy shook his head. "You two are dangerous, daring, immodest, and uninhibited as any women I've ever met."

Virginia lifted one shoulder in a semblance of a shrug. "You knew that when you met me. Remember, I was a naked Miss August center-page foldout one year, and Miss July center-page foldout the next for the engineering school's monthly magazine you were the faculty advisor for at UCI. I was in it a few more times as well. And, you've known Donna for a number of years now and how immodest she is about baring her boobs and everything else. This shouldn't come as a surprise."

A sly grin spread across his face. "I know. Those issues sold more copies than any we ever had. You were quite popular with all the male students and the male professors."

Virginia rubbed her hands together and winked at Donna. "So, now we get down to business."

Andy sat on the edge of the bed. "I do love the way you two operate together. I don't think our adversaries have any clue just how diabolical you two are. Now, what's next?"

Donna pulled the first quilt—one she got at a department store—out of a bag. "Hand me that flat box next to you, Andy." She stuffed the quilt into the box and with some strapping tape from a duffle bag, she sealed it. She glanced at Virginia. "Where do you want this one to go?"

"Mail it to my office at the museum in Georgetown."

"Got it." Donna wrote the address on the box with a black marker.

Andy hauled another quilt from a bag and found a box to fit it.

"Wait!" Virginia scribbled a note and placed it on top of the quilt. "Okay, go ahead and seal it."

He folded the quilt and placed it inside the box, along with the note, and sealed it closed with the strapping tape. "Where does this one go?"

"To Doctor Montgomery at the DOD in Washington." Virginia rummaged through her backpack and came up with a business card. "Here's his address." She handed it to Andy.

Donna held the last of the quilts she purchased. "How about this one?"

"Just put it into a box and fold the flaps closed." Virginia stepped to the desk and pulled the 1933 Sears contest-winning quilt from a shopping bag. "This is the real thing, I think. This one goes in my other suitcase."

Donna rose and stretched. "Okay. Now how are we going to handle the trip east?"

"Andy and I are going to drive using the credit cards you arranged for us that get back charged to the one issued to us by Doctor Montgomery. That way there is no way to trace our progress. I want to take some of your toys as well."

"Don't I get to go, too?" Donna gave her a forlorn look. "I kind of miss our adventures."

"Oh yeah, you get to come. You are following us and watching our six o'clock and come running when there's trouble."

"Good. Wait a minute. When there is trouble? You're expecting trouble even though we've taken precautions?"

"Expect the worst and hope for the best. Yep, I'm expecting our Arab friends to locate us, but we're going to do it on our terms."

"Okay, when do we leave?"

"Tomorrow morning. But first we need to send the two fake quilts." She looked at Donna and Andy. "Did you put your travel agency return address on them like I asked you to use?"

Donna and Andy nodded.

"Good. Then someplace along the line, either here in California or at the Pentagon or at my office, some spy will note it and start to ask questions and then try to follow us. Your staff knows what to do?"

"Yep. All briefed. I was hoping that I'd get to come along, so I made sure things were as you asked and told them how to respond to inquiries while I was gone. Also the credit card transfers are rigged by me personally and the bank,. No one has access to that."

Andy moved to the bag of weapons. "Besides the ones issued to us by the Smithsonian and DOD, what treasures have we in here?"

Virginia and Donna stepped beside him. "We'll show you. But first we need to mail the boxes."

Donna picked up one and started for the door.

"Wait. Donna, did you bring your bathing suit like I asked?"

"Yeah. We're going to the pool?"

"Yes. Let's change and Andy, call for Benny to come up. He can take the boxes to be mailed by the hotel."

Donna wrinkled her brow. "Why the bathing suits?"

Andy smirked. "Because when he gets here, you two will be topless. He already saw Virginia that way and I'm sure he's hoping for a second chance. You two will be the talk of the male staff when he leaves and when you get to the pool you will be the talk of the male employees who will flock to see you there. This is also bound to get out and attract any people snooping around the area. Too bad you can't be topless at the pool. That really would get their attention."

When Benny arrived, Donna answered the door in only her bright red bikini bottoms. She invited the wide-eyed bellman in and led him to the bed where the two boxes were stacked. He wet his lips when he saw Virginia standing next to them in only her blue bikini bottoms.

She smiled at him. "Will you take these to the front desk and have them shipped for me, Benny? We're going to the pool."

Andy strolled into the room from the bathroom carrying their tops. "Here you go, ladies. You'll need these for the pool. Hi, Benny."

Benny turned slightly, then went back to look at the women. "Hi. Yes, I'd be happy to ship the boxes. Is there anything else I can do for you?"

"No. That'll do it. Oh, yeah, there is one more thing. Please tell the front desk we will be checking out tomorrow."

"Tomorrow?" Benny voice sounded dejected. "Are you sure you wouldn't like to stay longer?"

"No, Benny. Tomorrow."

"Yes, Ma'am. I'll tell the front desk and get these boxes taken care of for you. I can have a cabana ready for you at the pool if you like?"

"That would be fine, Benny, Thanks."

Virginia walked him to the door and opened it so he could get through carrying the boxes. She tried to hand him a tip, but he declined. She watched him hurry down the hall, then stepped back into the room and closed the door. She looked at Donna and Andy. "That went well. It won't take long for the news of us leaving tomorrow and that we'll be by the pool to get around. Shall we finish getting ready for the pool?"

After donning their tops, Virginia, Andy, and Donna went to the pool. Andy carried the duffle bags with the weapons, Donna had a large cloth beach bag, and Virginia had another bag like Donna's and a shopping bag. Each was armed.

They found the cabana Benny had hastily reserved for them and were immediately descended upon by male staff wanting to get them drinks, more towels, or anything else they could think of to get a glance at the two women with the tiny, neon-bright bikinis.

After they settled onto three lounge chairs, with Andy between Donna and Virginia, Andy said, "Do you seriously think anyone will really search the room?"

Virginia shrugged her shoulders. "Not right away. But I'm willing to bet the box with the other fake quilt will be gone by the time we get back. I'm pretty sure that there are phone calls being made to friends about us. At a Disney hotel, Donna and me are not what the staff is used to. Here, they're used to families."

Andy nodded. "Yeah, you may be right. Having topless women around their staff is something out of the ordinary here."

"Might as well get attention." Donna jumped up. "Last one in the pool is a rotten egg." She dashed for the pool and dove in. Every man in the pool area watched.

Andy leaped up and followed Donna. Virginia slowly rose and strolled around to the pool steps and walked into the water. She looked around. There were half a dozen families, three middle-aged men, six male, and two female staff around the pool. She swam to Donna and Andy at the far edge of the pool. "Looks like most people are at Disneyland or California Adventure. That's good."

Andy looked around. "With the tops of your bikinis acting like wet T-shirts, you two are the star attraction for the men around here and you're getting the evil-eye from the women."

Donna leaned forward and kissed him on the cheek. "You're right, and I bet they envy you."

After two hours, they returned to the room. The box with the fake quilt and a marked-up map of the U.S. were gone.

Virginia smiled. "Okay. Phase one is complete. When they discover it's a fake, we'll be on the road and ready for phase two."

CHAPTER 23

Andy closed the tailgate of the idling SUV and walked to the driver's side, slid behind the wheel, and pulled out of the hotel parking lot. He headed for Interstate 5. Virginia, belted into the right passenger seat, fiddled with the vehicle's navigation system.

In the rear seat, Donna arranged their weapons in the duffle bags and sorted out the maps. "I'm glad you changed your mind, and I get to be with you instead of following in another car."

Virginia twisted around. "You're the official navigator, travel agent, and weapons officer. We had to have you here with us."

"You have a nav system, why do we need a navigator?"

"Because, when the shit hits the fan, and it will, we will quickly need alternative routes and trying to get a car nav system to cooperate is almost impossible. You're also our travel coordinator and a crack shot."

Andy turned onto the ramp for the freeway and accelerated up to the speed of the heavy traffic. He glanced at Virginia. "When do you think we need to be on our toes and watch for our Arab friends?"

"I'm guessing when we get close to, or in, Arizona."

Haddad Abdel A'hsam grabbed the private phone on his massive embassy desk and answered it. "Hello?"

His field agent responded. "Sir, we found the Clarks, but too late."

"Explain."

"I learned the Clarks lived in Orange County here in California before moving to Texas. That's why they flew there. So, I figured they would use this as their base of operations. It seems, Mrs. Clark and a friend created quite a stir at a hotel at Disneyland. One of my operatives heard from a friend about a couple of topless girls at the hotel, he went and checked it out. He showed her picture to some of the bellmen and they confirmed the Clarks were there, especially Mrs. Clark."

"Good work. You didn't intercept them, did you?"

Dangerous Threads

"No. You had said to leave them alone for now, but just follow them. But we did get into their room and took a box with a quilt in it and some maps."

"Send me the quilt as soon as possible."

"I don't think that will be necessary, Sir. I went to a library and looked up the 1933 Sears contest quilt and compared it to the one we took from Mrs. Clark's room. It isn't the one we are after. It's like she knew we'd break in and take it to set us up. She mailed two others. One to her museum and one to the DOD."

"You have done well. The other two may be decoys as well. I'll have them checked out. If she has the actual quilt, it's probably with her. Where is she now?"

"The Clarks checked out of the hotel. From the look of the maps we took, she's heading for the I-10 toward Texas."

A'hsan sighed. "Send agents along Interstate 40 and Interstate 8 as well as Interstate 10. I think the maps you found are a ruse, but we can't be sure. She is crafty."

"One more thing, Sir. She has a friend with her."

"She does? Who?"

"A travel agent."

"A travel agent? She has her own travel agent? Why?"

"She is a friend of Mrs. Clark and the other woman who caused the commotion with the male staff at the hotel."

"Right. You mentioned something about that. What did they do exactly?"

"They were topless in front of the hotel men. They also wore extremely revealing swimsuits. Their bathing suits were very bright and very small and when their tops got wet, you could almost see through them. They should be whipped for exposing themselves. It is against Allah's will."

"They're not believers in Islam, my friend. In the case of Mrs. Clark and her friend, I think Allah will understand. Anyway, I'd love to have seen them myself."

"Sir?"

"Never mind. Good job. Get agents on the road and find them; but do not intercept them. Watch for the Golden Crescent and eliminate them as a threat to the Clarks."

"Understood, Sir. I'll keep you informed." He disconnected.

A'hsan dialed another number. A woman answered. "Yes?"

"Sarah, we may have found the Clarks. The Golden Crescent has probably located them, too. Be ready to move out."

"Same arrangements as before?"

"Yes." A'hsan cleared his throat. "The Golden Crescent needs to be eliminated along with anyone else interested in or who interferes with the

Clarks. I want the Clarks and a friend who's with them in good condition until I know they have the right quilt. Then we move in."

"I'll be ready when you send word." She hung up.

Donna clicked off her cell phone. "Looks like you were right. Out little topless act got a lot of attention from your Arab friends. They're seriously looking for us. It looks like there are at least three or maybe four different organizations interested in our whereabouts. We'd better be on our toes."

Virginia looked over her shoulder at Donna's set-up in the rear of the vehicle. An iPad was plugged into a power jack, along with her laptop. Two cell phones rested on the seat next to her. Her duffle bags, with the weapons, sat behind her seat in the cargo section, within easy reach. Maps were organized and stacked in an open briefcase. "How'd you get all that?"

"My agency has been monitoring reservation searches for anyone looking for us. The Saudis and another organization have conducted internet searches for us. I also got a text message from Benny, the bellman at the Disney hotel. He said there were Americans looking for you, as well as some desperate Middle Eastern types. He said the Americans had dark suits and guns, and suspects the others did, too."

Virginia frowned. "Americans?"

"That's what his message said. Americans and another Middle Eastern group, probably Israeli."

"That's four groups. We've become popular," Andy said as he moved the car to the right lane to transition to I-5 freeway north.

Donna looked at her computer and a map. "They hopefully will think we're taking Interstate 10 and not Interstate 40."

Andy shook his head. "Why? If I were them, I'd cover both freeways and I8. And, who is the new group, and why are our own people looking for us?"

Virginia looked at the traffic in front of the car. "We've been off the grid for a while. No one can track us, and I think that's made Washington nervous."

"You mean Dr. Montgomery, and why hasn't he just called on the satellite phone?" Andy said as he transitioned from I5 to California 91 east.

"I've had the satellite phone off so no one can track us, including Montgomery's office." Virginia wet her lips. "I didn't want the mole there at the DOD to be able to find us. And we haven't been using their credit card directly so they have effectively lost us. I think that's made them nervous."

Donna opened a bottle of water and took a drink, then resumed looking at her computer. "It looks like someone is trying to crack my credit card scheme and find out how it is being charged without you moving."

Virginia looked back at Donna. "Can they do it?"

"Given enough time and money, yeah. But it won't happen soon, unless the NSA gets involved. Then we're toast in about three or four days. Anyone else will be at it for some time. Long enough for me to retire."

Andy accelerated onto the new freeway. "What if the Saudis are the ones looking?"

"I doubt it. They wouldn't... oh boy."

Virginia twisted around. "I don't liker the sound of that 'Oh boy'. What's up? They crack your scheme?"

"Not exactly. The Saudis are looking for the Golden Crescent and they've found some of their people waiting for us in Flagstaff. The Saudis have dispatched a hit team to take them out before we get there. They don't know which route we're taking, but with the Golden Crescent in Flagstaff, they're not taking any chances."

"The Saudis are eliminating their competition, at least those they know about. But how did you find out?"

"I asked my dear husband Dean to help me hack into their secure system and I'm on line in the background at the embassy."

"That's illegal as hell. Especially with a foreign country's embassy and their secret intelligence service."

"Yep." Donna grinned. "And it may save our bacon. I'll check for alternative routes. Oh, and Andy, please don't get a ticket or all of them will find us."

Andy glanced at the rearview mirror again, then accelerated as he wove through the heavy traffic. "I think we may have company."

CHAPTER 24

Virginia and Donna turned and looked out the rear window of the SUV. Virginia looked at Andy. "Which car is following us?"

"The black Camaro. It's been back there for some time. Every time I speed up, it does too. When I slow down, he still hangs back. I don't think he'll do anything on the 91, but when we get to Interstate 15 and head out of the populated area he may do something. Be ready."

Donna rubbed her nose. "If he's going to try anything it will be when we get just past the Grapevine and into the desert. We can have a warm welcome prepared."

Virginia sat back. "Maybe he's just following and reporting to someone. We'd better be prepared for an ambush when we reach the mountains or desert. Whoever it is found us pretty quick. Oh yeah. No alternate route. I want to go directly to Flagstaff."

Donna looked up from her computer, "Okay. I'll get us a hotel reservation in Flagstaff. But first I'll get some of our weapons ready just in case."

Virginia lowered the visor and opened the makeup mirror and watched the Camaro behind them maneuver through traffic to keep pace with them. "He's not gaining on us yet."

Andy angled right onto the northbound I15 freeway and accelerated. The traffic was lighter than he expected, so he pushed the speed limit slightly.

He looked at Donna in the mirror. She had unfastened her seatbelt and was rummaging around in the cases behind her seat in the cargo area. She lifted three boxes and set them on the rear seat, then turned and refastened her seatbelt as a California Highway Patrol cruiser eased by. She waved at the two officers who grinned back. After they had pulled ahead, she sighed. "I'm glad they didn't stop us because I wasn't strapped in."

Andy nodded. "I'm not sure they were looking at your seatbelt. What have you got back there?"

"I have no idea what we can expect, so I pulled out a box of flash bang and real grenades, a couple mini-flair guns on steroids. They're small, but

Dangerous Threads

very effective."

Andy jerked the wheel, then recovered. "You have mini-flair guns on steroids? What are they, really?"

"Yeah. They're kind of like small RPGs."

Virginia looked at Donna in her mirror. "When did you try that one? We didn't use rocket propelled grenades in Italy."

"In the desert a few months ago. The ones with the red launchers will take out an armored car with no difficulty. Imagine what I could do to a passenger car."

Andy took a long breath. "You're having way too much fun with those things. How about that one there on your lap with the yellow launcher?"

"Explodes with... ah... thermite, or whatever that is. The directions that came with it say it can burn through just about anything. Also it is bright, so don't look at it.

Andy swallowed. "That'll burn through iron. They're dangerous."

Donna looked at the weapon. "Yeah, but I know how they work."

"What else have you pulled out?"

"MP5K compact submachine guns." Donna ran her hand over the weapons. "And extra magazines."

Andy stiffened. "A machine gun?"

"Two, actually."

"How the hell did you get those?"

"From Luigi in Italy. He only gave me these two, though."

"Now I am curious as to what you two did to get all these things."

"Can we take the fifth? I've got lots of other gadgets, too. Luigi was very cooperative."

Virginia scratched her head. "Any EMP devices?"

"Yep. I've still got four from our last adventure, but we can't use them and drive at the same time."

Andy glanced at Virginia. "Didn't you two use those in Italy last year when you were searching for the crystal skull? They knocked out everything electronic for six blocks."

"Yes." Virginia nodded. "They're small and really effective." She heard Donna punching keys on her computer. "Getting us our reservations?"

"Yeah," Donna nodded, "I asked my people at the agency to book us and let me know where. Oh yeah, according to my tap in the Saudi embassy, they have activated a team from their L.A. Council General's office to fly to Flagstaff to take out the Golden Crescent operatives and look for us, but with orders not to interfere with us. Want to change plans?"

Virginia shook her head. "Nope. Let them remove one set of bad guys and we can then deal with just them. How many are joining the party?"

"Doesn't say. Uh oh. Looks like someone else is hacking into the embassy's spy computer's back door. It's getting crowded. I hope this doesn't trigger some alarm or computer analysis."

Andy checked the rear view mirror again. "Our tail is still back there. Any suggestions?"

Virginia perked up. "Yes. When we get to Barstow and before we turn onto I-40, let's stop for a snack at Peggy Sue's. If our friend back there stops too, we take him or them out before they cause us any real grief."

Donna smiled. "I like the way you think."

Andy flexed his fingers on the wheel. "How do you plan on doing that? Shoot them?"

Donna chimed in. "No silly boy. I've got two dart guns with knockout drugs in them. Of course they're for really big zoo animals, but what the hell, they may not be fatal. They can't be traced at any rate."

"What's the drug called?"

"Acepromazine or something like that. I was told the drug could deck a full-grown male grizzly in seconds. I didn't load these darts with that much, I don't think, so I hope the amount I used isn't lethal, if we have to use them. I added just a little more than was probably necessary, if a little is good and a lot has to be better, right?"

Virginia smiled. "Sounds good to me. Which one of us acts as the distraction? You, I hope."

Donna nodded. "Okay, it's usually you, but it's only fair I do it, especially with Andy along."

"What are you two talking about?" Andy's voice went up. "What have you done for distractions? What did you two do to Luigi?"

Virginia patted his arm. "Nothing you haven't seen us do before, Dear, so relax."

"That's what I'm afraid of."

Andy pulled into Peggy Sue's parking lot. The vintage nineteen-fifties restaurant stuck out like a sore thumb in the desert, but it was a favorite hangout for the Marines at the nearby base as well as frequent travelers on I 15. They parked near the corner of the building away from most of the windows and exited the SUV.

Andy and Virginia slipped out of the car and moved behind some parked cars. Donna had changed into her skimpy red bikini top and khaki shorts. She stood by the SUV's rear fender, her hands behind her back. The Camaro pulled into a spot at the side of the restaurant next to a dumpster and two men with dark complexions got out. They immediately noticed Donna smiling at them. They stopped, ogled her, looked around, and then grinning, marched toward her. One had an open, dark blue shirt over a white tank top. He reached under his shirt and started to pull out a black

Dangerous Threads

semiautomatic when his body jerked, then fell to the pavement. The second man stopped and looked at his partner spread out on the ground.

Donna brought her arms out holding a small .380 semiautomatic. He froze. Donna stepped closer. "Have a good look, then 'nighty night'."

He snapped his hand to his neck, his eyes bulged, and then he went down.

Andy moved from behind a car and helped Virginia and Donna pull the men the few feet needed to stuff them into their vehicle and lock the doors. He looked at Donna. "I'd suggest you change before we go inside. It's a family establishment."

"Yeah, but with a lot of Marines." Donna pointed across the parking lot. "See all the Hummers parked over there."

"I still think you should change." He pointed to the unconscious men. "How long will they be out?"

"I have no idea. Maybe a couple hours, maybe a day or they may never wake up. It's a veterinary sedative the CIA uses, remember? I'm not a vet or doctor or in the CIA, so I just hope I didn't use too much." She looked around and at the windows. "I hope no one noticed."

"Great. I suppose you think going in like that, in a skimpy bikini top that doesn't cover a whole lot and very short shorts is a patriotic thing to do for the Marines."

"Yeah. The poor lads do need our support, you know."

"Donna!" Andy took a breath and slowly let it out. "Think of what your husband would say. Anyway, if we killed the two men over there, we don't want to attract undue attention to ourselves."

"Okay, party pooper." Donna stuck her tongue out. "I'll change. You go in and get us a table while I change and Virginia puts away her dart gun and gets the quilt." She tucked her gun in her belt.

"Fine." Andy marched into the restaurant as the women returned to their car.

While they ate, Virginia kept a close eye on the large cloth bag she placed on the chair next to her. She noticed the three tables of Marines looking at her and Donna, still in her shorts but with a tight light blue T-shirt. Virginia leaned toward the table, "It's nice to have all those Marines watching us. I bet we could get their support if anything happens."

"I think you're right." Donna pointed to the front window. "Looks like someone noticed the two guys we drugged and stuffed in their car. Nice idea Andy, putting their guns in plain sight. But the tourists who saw them are really upset and on their cell phones. We'll have cops crawling all over the place shortly. Maybe we should ask for the check."

Andy secured the check and paid for their food while Virginia and Donna watched the front parking lot.

Donna pointed to the window. "Sheriff just arrived along with the

Highway Patrol. We'd better act cool and see if we can duck out before they get too interested in us."

"Yeah, we need to stay off the grid if at all possible," Virginia agreed.

They casually walked outside toward their car. Andy noticed a black and white CHP cruiser blocked it. He motioned to the officer. "Officer. Can you move your car, we'd like to leave?"

The officer pointed to their SUV. "This yours?"

"Yes."

He pointed to the Camaro. "Did you see this vehicle arrive?"

"No. We were inside eating. No one was parked there when we got here. What's wrong?"

"The two men inside are in serious condition and they are armed. We're trying to figure out who they are and what happened to them. You didn't see anything?"

"No. We were inside for a while. You can ask the Marines in there. They saw us."

Virginia and Donna joined them. Virginia smiled at the CHP officer. "Can we go?"

"No, Ma'am. Not just yet. Let's go back inside. The Sheriff's deputies are going to want to talk to everyone here."

"Hold this, please." Virginia handed the cop the bag with the quilt and rummaged through her backpack. She withdrew her SSCS ID and presented her credentials to the officer. "We are federal agents and we need to leave—now." She took her bag back.

The officer looked at her badge and ID. "All of you feds?" He looked at Donna and Virginia. "Really?"

"Yep. And we need to roll."

Andy and Donna displayed their credentials and badges.

The officer looked at Donna, then her credentials she was holding up to him. "You too, huh?"

"I'm kind of a reserve agent. I became part of the SCSS last year on a major case I worked with Virginia."

"Oh. Just a minute." He walked to his patrol car to call in their ID. In a couple of minutes he returned and handed Virginia her badge case. "Okay. I never heard of your agency before, but it seems you're for real and have some serious pull, especially with the DOD. So, you can go. I'll move my cruiser." He looked at Virginia and Donna again and sighed. "I think I need to change the agency I work for. We don't have too many officers like you."

Virginia smiled at him. "Oh, by the way, those two men in the car over there you're concerned about, are with the Golden Crescent, an Arab terrorist organization. You can tell the Sheriff, but you didn't get it from us. May save you some time figuring who they are. I'm sure the FBI or CIA can help you."

The officer looked stunned. "Huh? Terrorists? Here in Barstow?"

"There's a huge Marine base right behind us, isn't there?"

The cop nodded. "Terrorists, Marine base... holy shit, I'd better let the Sheriff and my headquarters know about this."

"Fine, but please move your cruiser first, we've got to go."

They climbed into their SUV while the CHP officer backed his car up. Virginia chuckled. "So much for stealth. Now Washington knows where we are and so do the Saudis."

Andy started the car and pulled out onto the road. "Looks like the Golden Crescent already did."

CHAPTER 25

Donna finished talking on her phone, then pushed the off button. She leaned forward. "Okay. I've got us reservations at the Pony Soldier Inn in Flagstaff. I used the cover credit card, so your official one won't lead to us. But, I think everyone looking for us already knows we'll be either staying in Flagstaff or passing through. That California Highway Patrolman in Barstow assured that."

Andy glanced at her in the rearview mirror. "What if we switched direction up ahead and went to Las Vegas?"

"Why would we do that?"

"To throw them off."

Virginia wrinkled her nose. "I think it's about time we turned the tables on these people. The Golden Crescent has been right behind us all along. The Saudis are formidable and we have our own people looking for us. This doesn't include the leak at the DOD. So we go to Flagstaff, and we get ready to face our nemeses, at least those who show up."

Andy looked at her. "How do you propose to do that?"

"They'll come sneaking around searching for the quilt. We set some traps."

"How are you going to protect the quilt?"

"What was it you told me about magic when you took it up as a hobby? To hide something—"

"Hide it in plain sight." Andy turned onto I-40, heading deeper into the desert.

Donna looked at the map, then at the gun on the seat next to her. "Think we'll need more of our toys between here and Flagstaff?"

"Count on it." Virginia stared out the front window, then turned to Donna. "I think one of the groups may try something when we get into some real desolate areas. So we'd better figure out who gets what weapons and be ready for anything."

Donna looked around. "When we get to some desolate areas? Looks pretty desolate to me now."

"You're right. Figure out what we need while we drive and then what we may need in Flagstaff."

Donna nodded. "Got it." She rummaged through the duffle bags and withdrew an array of weapons. "Okay, when we stop for gas, let's go over these, so we know what to do when necessary."

Andy pulled into a gas station in Needles, California, and stopped next to a pump. He got out and, using one of Donna's untraceable credit cards that the charges bounce back to the original government card Virginia had, he started to fill the tank.

Virginia stepped out and stood by the open back door to the SUV looking at the weapons Donna had pulled from the duffle bags. "I like the smoke and flash bang grenades and the MP5 machine guns, even if there are only two. The super flare guns or mini-RPGs are good, and I see you have the MP devices. Got anything we can use to really slow a car down that's a little less lethal?"

"Yeah. These babies. I have these goodies that look like softballs. When you throw them and they hit the ground, they open and very sharp metal pieces fly out. Our Italian friend said they would reduce rubber tires to elastic bands in seconds. If we used the smoke and flash bang grenades, then tossed a few of these I'm sure anyone behind us would be seriously inconvenienced for a while."

"Okay. When Andy's done, show him how to use the steroid flair guns, and we can handle the rest."

Donna tilted her head, then looked at Andy. 'You sure you won't mind being given just the little RPGs when we have the guns and grenades, would you?"

"No." He shook his head. "The RPGs are fine. You two can have the machine guns. I'll finish topping off our tank while you two get things organized."

Virginia put the MP5 down. "Anyway, he's driving. He can't use the guns and other things, but we can. If we get into a pickle and have to stop, his RPG may be our ticket out of trouble."

"Good point. Okay." She looked at the back of the car as Andy rounded the rear fender. "Here he comes. I'll show him the ropes on the launcher, but we'd better be quick. More cars are coming in." She gave Andy a short course in rocket launching and then slid back inside, closing the door as another vehicle pulled up to the next set of gas pumps. She waved at the middle-aged man who slowly climbed out and stretched. He smiled at her and went around his car toward the pumps.

Andy kept looking at the rear view mirror at the road and the high desert brush after he drove out of the gas station and continued up the highway to the entrance of I40. A half-hour later, they were well away from any cities or houses. Outside was nothing but desert sage, sand, bare stone mountains, and heat. Andy reached over and turned down the radio. "Looks like we have company."

Virginia looked back. "The white trucks back there?"

"And the one in front of us. May be nothing, but then it could be they're going to try the squeeze play."

Virginia looked at him. "Huh?"

Andy glanced at the mirror again, then at Virginia. "With the squeeze play, one truck gets behind us, one directly in front, and one to the side. Then they force us off the road and try to rush the car before we have much chance to respond."

Virginia smiled. "Where did you learn all this?"

"Computer games. There is a hell of a spy one that is—"

Donna called out. "Guys, looks like Andy was right. How fast are you going, Andy?"

"Eighty."

"Well the trucks behind us are catching up fast and one just moved into the left lane." She wheeled around and looked out the windshield. "Look, the truck in front has slowed."

Virginia watched the trucks rapidly gain on them. Heat waves rose from the roadway making the trucks shimmer until they were close. "You're right." Virginia unbuckled her seatbelt and turned to Donna. "Give me some of the grenades and be ready to hand me the ball gizmos with the tire shredders in them. Open the sunroof, please, Andy."

The sunroof buzzed open. The hot air rushed inside. "Wow, it's hot out there. What is it, a hundred degrees?" Virginia asked as she hefted two grenades.

"According to the car, it's one hundred and twelve," Andy replied. "They're about thirty yards back, better do something soon."

Virginia popped up through the roof and lobbed two smoke grenades then pulled the pins on two flash bang grenades and tossed them at the trucks. Next, she threw four of the special balls behind the car as Andy accelerated. The smoke and flash grenades stunned the truck drivers long enough for them to hit the tire shredders at well over eighty-five miles an hour. They swerved out of control and in a screech of metal, crashed into each other.

One truck came to a jarring halt sideways in the road, wavered side to side, then settled, its tires gone; the second rolled to its side, and with the sound of grinding metal, slid into the sand and gravel on the side of the highway.

Virginia turned and looked at the truck in front of them. The back door was going up. Two men knelt inside. One held a pistol, the other a rifle. "Andy! Hit the brakes and close your eyes." As the car leaned forward, trying to stop, Virginia closed her eyes and threw a flash grenade at the truck in front. The grenade went off a few yards from the vehicle. When she opened her eyes the truck was further down the road, but one of the men from the back was bloody and rolling on the pavement. "He must have fallen out. Get going, Andy, I don't want to be here in case he recovers."

Andy pushed the accelerator and the SUV lurched forward around the stricken man on the ground. "That truck raced off and left him. Which group was responsible for that, do you think?"

Virginia slipped back into her seat and pulled her seatbelt back on. "I don't know, but they weren't as dark as the other guys who've given us trouble."

Donna sat back, holding a silver tube with a handle and cord coiled to a small black box. "You know something? We could have used this laser thingy and put out their radiators back there and then blinded the two guys in front and it wouldn't have caused as much damage for the police to clean up."

Virginia sighed. "Now you think of that."

Andy started to close the sunroof when he stopped and listened. "Houston, we may have another problem." Virginia looked around. "Now what?"

"First, no cars coming in either direction. This is an Interstate highway, that's strange. But I think I hear what could be rotors, like a chopper."

Donna looked at her map, and then leaned forward. "About two hundred yards ahead is a dirt road off to the right. It goes into those mountains over there. Turn on it, and hightail it to that confluence between those two hills."

"Huh? Oh. Okay." Andy slowed, then turned onto the dirt road. A large cloud of dust trailed their car as he bounced over ruts racing toward the small valley Donna had pointed to.

"What do we do when we get there?"

Donna set the map down and switched off her computer. "Stop, and prepare to take down a chopper if necessary."

"With what?"

"Your RPGs. We can back you up with the MP5s, but they are not made for long shots or downing aircraft. I don't think they are, anyway."

Andy gave her a quick look over his shoulder. "You're kidding, right?"

"No."

"I've never fired one of those things before. For that matter, I don't usually go around shooting people either."

"Relax, we'll be here with you, and we've got a little experience at it."

"Great. Ma Barker and Janet the Ripper." He pulled to the side of the dirt road and parked the car between two looming masses of dark volcanic rock.

They jumped out of the car. Donna picked up her MP5 and gave Virginia a machine gun, then handed Andy the RPG with the yellow launcher. "If a chopper comes after us, we can shoot it down, but first I'd like to try the MP device. Our car is off so we won't hurt it, and I've shut down my computer and cell phone. I'd turn off anything electronic you've got, like right now."

Andy, Virginia, and Donna moved to the entrance of the valley and peered out at the highway.

Virginia watched a dark, olive-colored chopper with no markings fly low just above the highway through her binoculars. It passed the dirt road, then stopped and hovered, turned and followed the settling dust cloud. She lowered her glasses. "Looks like the type you see in bad spy adventure movies. They're looking for us, and the side door just slid open. "

It continued toward them, then stopped about fifty feet above the ground. Ropes flew out the side and men in dark suits started to repel down.

"Here we go." Donna flipped the little red switch and pushed the green button on the device in her hand. Nothing happened for a second, then the chopper started to whine. The engine stopped. The helicopter started to swing around, wobbled, then rolled on its side with the rotors almost perpendicular to the ground, throwing the men on the ropes to the terrain below. The chopper hurtled to the earth a second later.

Andy grabbed Virginia and Donna pulling them down as the rotors struck the dirt and shattered, hurling sharp metal across the desert. The chopper landed on two of the men in black with a loud crash accompanied by the screams of the men inside. The pilot appeared either dead or unconscious while the observer struggled with his seat restraints. Gas poured out of the fuel tank onto the side of the fuselage and spilled onto the ground.

As the men inside struggled to get out, the fuel hit the engine manifold and burst into flames, catching two of the four men on the ground still alive on fire. They ran screaming into black smoke as it billowed into the sky. In a few seconds the chopper exploded, sending hot metal and burning plastic across the desert, setting small fires.

Donna put the little box on the ground, picked up her gun, and stood. "That was easier than trying to shoot it down."

Virginia got up and trotted forward, holding her machine gun on the remaining two men, clad in black cargo pants, black T-shirts, and jump boots, struggling to get up. Donna quickly followed. Andy held his RPG in his left hand and his .38 special in his right as he followed Virginia and Donna.

Virginia stopped, aimed her gun, and smiled. "Okay, boys, drop your weapons and get on your knees. Hands behind your heads."

They looked at her and Donna and chuckled. "Like hell, girlie," the biggest one with a blond buzz cut said as he raised his pistol.

His body jerked and twisted. Blood, tissue, and bone sprayed out behind him as the MP5 Virginia held stitched holes from his right hip up through his chest and left shoulder. He fell back onto the bloody sand.

His partner's eyes bulged, his grin gone. He dropped his pistol and fell to his knees. "Okay lady, anything you say."

Donna and Andy caught up with Virginia and looked at the man sprawled out on the ground. Andy lowered his weapon. "I don't think we need to check for a pulse. I take it he didn't play nice."

"You could say that." Virginia stepped a few feet closer to the man on his knees. "Hello."

"Huh?"

"I said hello. You hard of hearing?"

"Ahh, no, hel... hello. Did you bring down our chopper?"

"Yes." She pointed to Donna, who waved. "Really, she did."

"How? You didn't shoot anything."

Virginia smiled. "She did it compliments of Uncle Sam. Now who the hell are you?"

He just looked at her.

"I don't like the quiet type. Either tell me what I want to know or we'll make the rest of your life very, very painful. I'll end your love life while I'm at it, too." She aimed her machine gun at him.

He just looked at her.

Virginia looked at Donna. "You want to blow off his elbows or should I do it?"

"You've had some fun already. I'll do it."

Andy stepped around them. "Donna, you brought down the chopper. Virginia got to shoot the other guy. He's mine."

They looked at him with wrinkled brows. Virginia shrugged her shoulders, then stepped back.

"He's all yours, Dear. When you get done with his elbows, if he doesn't talk, we can blow off some kneecaps. That hurts like hell. He'll never walk right after that, and the surgery to repair them is very painful. Then we'll remove his ability to father children."

The man on his knees had perspiration beading on his forehead. He swallowed.

Andy raised his revolver and pressed it to the man's right elbow. "Last chance. In case you missed it, we're serious. Look at your buddy over there."

"Okay! Okay! I'm a contractor. We do special jobs for some people in Washington and corporations overseas. We are mostly ex-military or ex-CIA. We were hired to stop you, obtain some sort of quilt, and then kill you. Why someone would pay to find a quilt and kill for it, I don't know. We were paid a lot to find you and do it. No witnesses."

Virginia nodded. "Who hired you?"

"A suit in Washington. He had to be military or ex-military, though. You can tell; a real command type. I only saw him from a distance. Our leader did the negotiations and talked to him."

"How much?"

"Three million dollars in gold."

"Three million in gold, wow." Virginia smiled and looked at Andy and Donna. "We're worth three mil to someone if we're dead. Not bad. Too bad we'll have to disappoint." She turned back to the man. "Who's your leader?"

"He was in the cockpit of the chopper you brought down."

"Nuts. I see you have three pairs of handcuffs. Slowly drop them to the ground and the keys with them, then lay flat on your stomach."

He quickly did as he was told.

Virginia placed the three cuffs on his wrists behind his back and Donna tied his legs with plastic cable ties from her duffle bag, then she pulled his legs up and they secured them, via more plastic straps, to his wrists.

Virginia stood. "Now, I'm sure within some reasonable time your colleagues, wherever they are, will have released normal traffic on I-40 and will come looking for you and your friends with the trucks we left back on the freeway. They'll find you when they spot all the smoke from your chopper. Firefighters should be arriving as well as the police. You can explain your predicament and this mess to them. We'll be leaving you, so have a nice afternoon."

He pulled his head up. "How about some water? It's hot and these black suits are even hotter."

"You wore them, not me. Ask the firemen for water. They probably have a truck full."

"I'll kill you when I catch up with you, bitch."

Andy shook his head. "Big mistake, fella. Big mistake."

Virginia stood next to him. "That wasn't nice or very professional." She spoke through clenched teeth. "No one calls me a bitch, asshole."

She aimed her machine gun at his right knee and fired. His pant leg and knee shredded. Blood and bone spewed over the sand. As he jerked around and screamed, she turned to the others. "We'd better get out of here fast. There'll be more cops and government types here sooner than we need." She looked at the man and bent down. "You'd better pray the cops and paramedics arrive pretty soon. Otherwise you'll bleed to death or a hungry coyote will assist you down that road."

"Call for help! Oh God. Please!"

"After you tried to kill us? Guess again, buddy boy."

They walked back to their car. Donna turned and glanced at the man on the ground. "Do you think it's our people that sent him?"

Andy looked at the man on the ground as he got into the SUV. "He

Dangerous Threads

wasn't Arabic and he said they are ex-military or ex-CIA and he said a suit in Washington paid them, so it looks like we've got some homegrown problems, too. You should never totally trust the government." He looked at Virginia. "Call 911?"

She nodded.

CHAPTER 26

Virginia fished her satellite cell phone from her backpack and dialed Dr. Montgomery's number as their SUV sped through the one hundred and twelve degree desert. They had crossed the Colorado River earlier and were now in Arizona, heading rapidly toward the mountains and Flagstaff. The phone connected. "Dr. Montgomery, This is Virginia Davies-Clark. It's been a while since I touched base."

"Virginia? How... how are you?" Virginia heard a click on the line. "I've gotten word that you've had some more nasty encounters on your mission."

Virginia held the phone away from her ear and pointed at it. Donna nodded, then went back to her computer, plugging the cable from Virginia's phone into her laptop. Virginia continued, "You could say that. The guys trying to spoil our work came out on the losing end each time. You'd think they'd learn after a while."

"Yes, well ahh... I received the box with the quilt you sent. It isn't the one we're after."

"Yeah, I know. I sent a few of them out to help throw our adversaries off for a while."

"Good idea. Did you find the quilt we are looking for yet?"

"Yes. I know right where it is." Virginia smiled at Andy.

"You do? Where is it? Do you want me to send back-up for you? For that matter, where are you?"

She read the scribbled note Donna held up. *There is a hot trace on your phone.* Virginia nodded. "Yes. I know where it is. It's safe for now. We're heading for Flagstaff and will spend the night there and rest up from our day's incidents. We don't need back-up, at least not yet. I can't say as much for the other guys, though."

Montgomery's voice sounded strained. "Do you have the quilt in your possession?"

"Let me just say it's safe. I know where it is."

"Are you sure you couldn't use some assistance? Maybe an escort once

Dangerous Threads

you get the quilt?"

"No. We're doing okay. Thanks anyway."

"Okay. Keep me posted. I can get people to you quickly, if necessary."

"Oh, I know you can, and tell the guy on the line listening in to have a nice day." She hung up.

Andy glanced at her. "You going to shut that off?"

"No. They're trying to trace it. Based on our last encounter, I'd say doing that is overkill."

Andy looked at the mirror again, then pushed his glasses back up his nose. "I think they're trying to ascertain if we're really going to Flagstaff or Las Vegas."

Donna giggled. "They've got you. They are using the GPS in the phone to track us. Let's hope we get to the hotel before they can mount another roadside welcome like we just had. Maybe I can slow them down a bit." She went back to work on her computer.

Andy sped around a slow-moving truck. "They don't know exactly where we're going in Flagstaff and I think we destroyed a lot of their assets back there. It'll be a while before they could mount much of an offensive. It's the Golden Crescent and the Saudis that worry me now."

Virginia handed her sat phone to Donna then looked at Andy. "You still think it was Montgomery's people who attacked us back there?"

"Him, or another faction in the DOD, or DOE, or CIA, or whatever other alphabet soup organization is working for or against Montgomery. In any case, they have a lot of power and firepower as we saw."

Donna punched a few keys on her computer, and then took a breath. "Yes, but we have a couple advantages. They don't know what weapons we have, and they don't have our conniving and cunning personalities. They are trained to think certain ways; we're not. We're wild cards to them. We're probably considered armed and dangerous, especially now. And, I just reprogrammed your GPS chip to say we're not here. We're back down the road a bit, quite a bit actually." She turned off the phone.

Andy pulled off I-40 and onto US 66 into Flagstaff. "Route 66, the Mother Road. It goes from—"

Virginia looked at him, "—from Chicago to LA, I know. You've also said a million times it becomes Foothill Boulevard in L.A. You've been telling us that every time you see the darn Route 66 highway signs since we got on I-40-US 'Route' 66 back in California. You mention it again and I'll shoot you."

He gave her his little-boy expression and watched the road. A few miles down the highway through pine trees and the business section, he swung the SUV into the Best Western Pony Soldier Inn and pointed to the Route

66 sign across the street.

As they drove under the covered entrance, Donna twisted in her seat. "I like the statue of the pony out there. This could be fun." She slipped out of the car and took a deep breath. "Ahh, the smell of a pine forest is always nice."

Virginia and Donna registered and dragged their bags down the hall to their suites as Andy parked their SUV toward the rear of the parking lot.

When Andy entered their suite he heard the air conditioning hum. Virginia was turning on the television. She pointed down their little hallway. "We've got a bedroom, living room with microwave, fridge, and two bathrooms. Nice."

Andy looked around then plopped on the sofa next to her. "Where'd you hide the quilt?"

"I remade the bed. It's under the covers like a blanket."

He nodded. "Good idea. You hid the box with the spare fake one someplace?"

She pointed to a door. "It's on the shelf in that closet over there behind some pillows."

"Nice." He quickly turned toward the TV. "Hey, look at that."

The news reporter, from a station in Needles, California, was reporting on location. He was talking about a mysterious truck smash-up and a helicopter crash near each other along I-40 in a deserted area of the desert. The cameraman was using his telescopic lens to bring the pictures of the wrecks and the downed chopper site to the viewers. The reporter kept pointing down the road past police and what appeared to be Army personnel keeping people away.

According to the report, six men were killed in the helicopter crash and one was hospitalized. In the truck incident, four men were slightly injured and another was found on the road in critical condition. A security cordon and blackout had been placed around the actual sites of the accidents and the men are under guard in the hospital. He said the military had taken over the investigation, but no one there would tell him why. The local police were cooperating with the federal authorities. The reporter continued to give the usual statement: "More on the six o'clock news or as it breaks."

"Well, we made quite the stir today." Virginia sat back with her hands behind her head. "Terrorists in Barstow, and we helped screw up I-40 for the rest of the day, downed a secret helicopter, and killed at least six men and injured a lot more. I'm not sure we signed up for all this. Why are our own people after us? I bet those men died not knowing why. I'm not happy about this."

They jumped at the knock on their door. Virginia grabbed her nine-millimeter semiautomatic as Andy pulled his revolver from his belt. They went to the door. Andy peered through the peephole. Donna fidgeted in the

Dangerous Threads

hallway. He opened the door and let her in. They went into the living room.

Donna sat on a chair as Virginia and Andy resumed their spots on the sofa. "Did you guys catch the news?"

"Yes. We just saw it. We seemed to have left a path of destruction behind us the authorities are trying to make go away," Andy said.

"Yeah, I saw that, too. But I meant the Golden Crescent guys in Barstow. The news story says it seems they had cyanide with them and used it. The cops and Homeland Security are royally pissed and they're looking for the federal agents who were there before the Sheriff and CHP. It seems the DOD, and the Smithsonian have stymied them. Turf battles rage. This is getting out of hand. Did we sign up for all this?"

Andy smiled. "That's what Virginia said a minute ago. You two are scary."

Virginia rose and went to the window, pulled the drape aside, and looked out. "I don't see anyone from here and it's a nice afternoon, not too hot at this altitude. Want to explore Flagstaff?"

Andy pulled the SUV out of the Lowell Observatory parking lot and followed the navigation system toward the Outback Steakhouse.

"How'd you like the tour, ladies?"

"I enjoyed the shops in Flagstaff and going to the observatory."

Virginia put the folded brochure onto the seat. "I really liked it. Kind of makes me want to get a telescope."

"Yeah, and I found Pluto in those images they used originally when they found it. I still think Pluto's a planet. I don't care what the astronomers say." Donna looked around at the road and terrain. "I didn't see any bad guys either."

Virginia looked at a log cabin-style building as they passed. "I haven't seen anyone suspicious either. I wonder how long until someone catches up with us." She pulled the visor down and looked into the mirror. "Maybe we should go to the hotel first and freshen up, then go to dinner."

"Sounds good to me," Donna said from the back seat. "I know you just want to check on the quilt, but I'll take the time to maybe change and wash up before dinner."

"Okay, hotel it is." Andy made a U-turn and drove back to the hotel. As they approached the hotel, he slowed and moved over for a passing police car with its emergency lights on and the siren sounding. "I wonder where he's going?"

Virginia watched the police car race ahead. "With our luck, our hotel."

After a couple miles, they saw more police cars, an ambulance, a crime scene unit truck, and a fire engine at their hotel. They slowed, then turned into the parking lot on the opposite side of the building from their room and the other parking lot. They walked around the front of the hotel to see what the commotion was about.

Andy approached a fireman standing by the yellow tape across the entrance and parking lot. "What happened?"

"I can't address that with the public, Sir."

Andy pulled out his Liberty Hill, Texas Volunteer Fire department credentials. "Just curious."

The fireman looked at the badge and credential, smiled, then pointed toward a low, black Chrysler being examined by some people in jumpsuits. "Looks like someone didn't want the people who were in that car to leave. They're dead."

"Shot?"

"Executed would be more like it." The fireman removed his helmet. "According to the paramedics who examined them first, they were shot with a small caliber weapon in the back of their heads."

"How would someone do that in a car?" Andy squinted as he looked at the vehicle. "I don't see any bullet holes in it."

"You'd have to get the detectives to answer that, but I don't think they know at this point."

"Were they Arabic? Did they have a quilt with them?"

The fireman jerked his head toward Andy. "How'd you know?"

"Just a guess."

"You'd better wait here. I think you need to see the detective in charge." He stepped to a uniformed officer and talked. The cop used his radio in a hushed voice, and then he and the fireman approached Andy.

Virginia and Donna walked up to Andy and looked at the scene, then at the cop in front of Andy.

The officer straightened to his full height and tried to look intimidating. "Okay, what's your name and why do you think the victims were Arabic? And, why do you think they had a quilt with them?"

Andy stared at him. "You're the head honcho around here?"

"Huh?"

"You're not the detective in charge, are you?"

The officer's eyes narrowed. "I asked you a question, mister. You show me some ID and answer the question."

Virginia fished her SCSS badge and ID out of her backpack and displayed it to the officer. "We're federal officers. This may have a bearing on what we are doing, so we can't answer your questions. But you will answer ours."

He looked her over, then looked at Donna. He returned to Andy. "If you're federal cops, I'll eat my badge. Now either answer my questions, or I'll arrest you."

Donna pulled her ID out of her purse along with a packet of ketchup

Dangerous Threads

from Jack in the Box. She showed her badge to the cop and handed him the packet. "Your badge will taste better with a condiment."

Andy opened his display case, showing his badge and ID. "We are with the Smithsonian Central Security Service and we're going over there to that gentleman who seems to be in charge. You get in the way and these two ladies will make you wish you never got up today." They put their badges on their belts, then Andy pulled the yellow police tape up so Virginia and Donna could slip under. Then he followed.

The officer started toward them. "Now just wait one minute here. You can't just walk onto a crime scene. And, I don't know if those badges are real or not. I've never heard of the Smithsonian—"

Virginia swung around. "It's in Washington, D.C. and it's a really big museum owned by the government. You should go there some time. And, the Central Security Service is a federal police agency. So don't get in our way, bucko, or you'll be facing time in a federal institution where the inhabitants don't like cops much. You'll have a short and miserable life expectancy as Bubba's girlfriend." She turned to Donna, and whispered, "Did that sound convincing?"

Donna looked at the cop. "I think you just pissed him off more. Here he comes."

The officer hurried to them and grabbed Virginia's arm. His eyes widened and his mouth fell open. He expelled a quick breath when she spun around and kneed him in the groin. He staggered back, grabbing himself, as he slowly went down on his knees, then collapsed onto the ground, moaning. Three other officers came running with their tasers out, then stopped when they saw the badges. One walked to the downed officer, the other two approached Virginia, Donna, and Andy. One spoke to her. "Who are you, and what happened?"

Virginia watched the cars slow as they passed the Inn, then turned to the officer. "We're with the Smithsonian Central Security Service and he grabbed me. I don't like that and I stopped him. I know you've never heard of us, but—"

The officer nodded. "Oh, I've heard of the agency. You guys are federal special agents and go after antiquities, historical item thefts, and find or recover stolen art and artifacts." He looked at Virginia and Donna. "If I weren't married, I'd seek a transfer to your agency."

"Thank you." Virginia tilted her head. "How come you know about us and he didn't?"

The officer smiled. "I use to be with the D.C. Metropolitan Police. We had to know all the agencies around town. Trust me, there are plenty. I got married and we moved here, so I'm with the Flagstaff PD now."

Virginia nodded toward the officer still moaning and rolling about on the ground. "I'm sorry about your friend."

"To be honest, he's somewhat of a bully and he's had this coming for some time. I think he's through now. Attacking a federal officer is not a good idea. Anyway, he gives the others a bad name. Most cops are good people just trying to do the job the best we can. We don't need people like him around. He was on his way out before this anyway, so you probably actually helped us."

"I hope he's all right."

"The paramedics are working on him. Looks like they gave him an ice pack. That must have been one hell of a kick."

"I used my knee."

The officer cringed. "Ouch. What brings you to Flagstaff, and why the interest in this case? Oh, here comes Detective Allen. He'll ask the questions now, I guess."

"Okay. Nice talking to you, Sir." Virginia turned to the approaching detective.

Detective Allen, bald, with wire framed glasses and dressed in a dark green polo shirt and tan wool trousers with his service weapon on his left side and badge clipped to his belt stopped in front of Virginia and Donna. He glanced at Andy at his side. "I'm Detective Allen, Flagstaff PD. Since no one arrested you, I take it you have some official reason to be at my crime scene."

"We're with the Smithsonian Central Security Service, and we're working on something that has drawn some international interest. When we saw all the commotion at our hotel we thought it might be of interest to us, especially if the victims are Arabic."

Detective Allen looked at the uniformed officer standing with them. "You ever heard of that agency?"

"Yes." The officer nodded. "They're for real. I knew of them when I worked in Washington."

"Okay, he says you're for real, so I'll go along with him, for now. What does your case have to do with my triple murder?"

"They may be part of a terrorist organization known as The Golden Crescent." Virginia wet her lips. "If so, we think the Saudi intelligence service took them out. If they did, you'll never catch them."

"Well, they're Arabic all right. Come from Yemen, at least that's what their passports say, assuming they aren't fake. The job was nice and neat. Each victim got two small caliber shots to the head. No mess, and very quiet. Executed. The Saudis, you say?"

Andy removed his orange University of Texas baseball cap and wiped his bald head. "That's our best guess."

"Why would they kill other Arabs and why are all these people looking for you?"

"The Saudis don't like competition." Donna stuck her hands in her pockets. "They want the spoils all to themselves. And it seems they aren't the only ones trying to get to us."

"Can I ask what you're working on that causes other countries and terrorists to kill each other for?"

Virginia shook her head. "Not really. Let's just say we all want a certain quilt."

"A quilt?"

"Yep. A special one."

Detective Allen gave her a bewildered look. "Why is it special and why are you looking for it?

"That's classified Secret."

"A quilt that is classified secret by the government?"

Virginia nodded. "Yep."

"This gets weirder by the minute. How am I going to write this one up?"

"Just say you're working on it. Hopefully, there won't be any more killings in your jurisdiction."

Detective Allen looked at his shoes for a minute, then back at Virginia. "You guys have anything to do with that mess on I-40 today?"

Virginia smiled. "Detective, let's just say—don't ask."

"I thought that's what you'd say."

"I think we'd like to go to our rooms now, if you have no objection."

"When are you leaving town?"

"Tomorrow."

"Good. As long as no one else dies tonight, I never saw you, okay?"

"Right. Have a nice rest of the day, Detective." Virginia led Andy and Donna toward the hotel.

They walked down the hall as doors cracked open and people who had been watching the goings-on from their rooms watched them in the hall. They all entered Virginia and Andy's suite.

The room had obviously been searched and things put back as best as someone could hurriedly do. Virginia went to the closet and removed the pillows. "Well, someone looked at the quilt I hid here." She hurried in to the bedroom and pulled down the covers. "The World's Fair Quilt is still here, but that means the guys who killed the Golden Crescent people are probably around yet and know where we are."

Andy sat on the edge of the bed. "So does Washington." He stared at Donna and Virginia for a moment, then jumped up. "I know how the Golden Crescent has known where we are! I'll be right back." He dashed out the door leaving Virginia and Donna sitting and looking at the door, as it swung closed.

Virginia looked at Donna, "Let's go. He shouldn't be doing whatever it is he's doing all alone."

They raced out into the hall, ran to the exit, and pushed the door open. They hurried to the SUV and found Andy on his knees on the asphalt looking under the vehicle.

"Gotcha!" Andy pulled a small box from under the rear passenger side door. He looked up at Virginia and Donna as they approached.

Virginia stooped and looked at the two small metal boxes on the ground next to Andy. "What have you got?"

"Two homing devices. That's why the terrorists always showed up just as we were leaving some place. They were tracking us. I bet someone at the hotel at Disneyland put them there."

Donna picked them up and looked at them. "This one looks like it was home-made, you're probably right about it. But, this one is professional. Could be they got a new one, or someone else put it on the car when they had the chance."

"Who?" Virginia ran her hands through her blonde hair. "We haven't been anywhere near where anyone could have done it besides Disneyland."

"The car was somewhat out of sight in Barstow. Also, someone could have placed it there before the Golden Crescent found us."

Andy climbed back on his feet. "Yeah, or the Highway Patrol Officer we talked to. Any way you cut it; we're being tracked electronically. But I think we can remedy that situation."

Donna handed him the boxes. "How, break them?"

"No. Something even better." He strolled to a car with New Jersey plates and stuck one of the boxes to the undercarriage with its magnet. He then walked to a car with Nevada plates and placed the second one under the rear of the car. "That'll keep our electronic snoops busy for a while." He turned to the girls. "Shall we go to dinner now? I could use a good steak."

Virginia cast an eye toward their SUV. "Are you sure you got them all?"

CHAPTER 27

The next morning, they loaded the SUV and Donna set her computer, cell phones, and weapons bags up within easy reach. Andy pointed to the car with the New Jersey plates he had placed one of the trackers on, pulling out of the driveway. "There goes one of our problems. I wonder where they're going?"

Virginia watched the car, then smiled. "I saw the lady in there at the ice machine last night. They're going to the Grand Canyon, then to their daughter's home in San Diego."

Donna chuckled. "That'll drive the guys following it bananas. I wonder where the one with the Nevada plates is going?"

"I don't know." Andy pulled into the street headed east to get to the freeway on-ramp. "But maybe they're going to the Grand Canyon, too, then either home, or someplace else. Wherever they're going, chances are we're not."

He looked at the car's gauges and fiddled with the mirror. "I'm glad I gassed up last night. Keep an eye out for trouble." He glanced at the satellite phone on the console between the seats. "Did you turn your phone on or are we going to let them guess where we're going? By the way, where are we going?"

Donna chimed in from the back. "Continue east on I-40, your Route 66, Andy, until we get to Albuquerque. We should get there about lunchtime, if all goes well. Then we'll make a course correction."

They continued along I-40 as the terrain turned from pine forests to high desert scrub. Virginia nodded at a sign they whizzed past. "Someday I want to go to the Painted Desert. Maybe next time."

As they passed the New Mexico state line, Andy glanced up at the mirror. "Looks like someone is in a hurry."

Virginia and Donna twisted around. Not seeing anything, Virginia looked at Andy. "Where? I don't see a car."

"Not a car. There was a helicopter coming up the road, dangerously low. He passed over the other cars back there then veered off into the desert. He was really moving. And, it was black."

"Open the sun roof please, Andy." The roof hummed as it slid open. Virginia climbed up and stuck her head out into the wind and heat and looked around. Squinting, she thought she spotted something on their right, over the desert, moving parallel to them. "Hand me the binoculars, please. She put her hand down and felt the glasses. Focusing, she spotted the chopper Andy had seen. A man was in the open side door hooking up some sort of strap. Then someone handed him a rifle. "Oh boy. We've got trouble. I thought we'd handled the electronic trackers pretty well. There must be another someplace."

"What do you see? Donna asked.

"Bad news. That helicopter is getting ready to attack us, I think. But that would be silly on an interstate with traffic." She ducked down into the car.

Andy pointed ahead. "That semi tractor-trailer is slowing. If he makes a sudden move when we pass, he'll run us off into the desert. At these speeds, that alone could do us in, and he could just crush us to death."

Donna looked ahead, then at her computer. "Okay, we have an off ramp coming. Start slowing, but do it so the truck up ahead won't notice it right away. If we time this right he'll pass it just ahead of us, then we swing off the highway. There's a dirt road about a mile up on the right after you get on the frontage road."

Andy looked over his shoulder. "Okay, but then where are we going?"

"You make a right turn and head south, into the Zuni reservation and away from traffic."

"That'll bring us straight for that chopper."

"Right." Donna closed her computer. "You, Virginia, and I should be able to handle one silly airplane."

Virginia turned. "Are you nuts?"

"Nope. We've got our MP5s and the RPGs and I still have a few EMP devices left. These are rechargeable to boot. Shall we get ready?"

Virginia looked over her shoulder. "This getting attacked has gone on long enough. When we get out of this predicament, we'll make some serious changes in Albuquerque."

Donna wet her lips. "What do you have in mind?"

"We change the rules. We go on the offensive and modify what they're after."

"How?"

"I'm working on it."

"I have an idea, but let's get through this situation first." Andy bounced the SUV over potholes in the rough macadam toward an outcropping of rocks. Approaching the boulders, Andy turned off the road, switched into four-wheel drive and plowed up the dirt trail to the mini-mountain of red rock, leaving a rooster tail dust cloud behind. He swung the car behind a pile of stones as high as the car and parked.

They hopped out. Donna handed them an assortment of weapons. Virginia hefted her MP5, slid a bandolier of grenades over her shoulder and across her chest. Her nine-millimeter Beretta, she stuck in her belt. Donna picked up her MP5 machine gun, a nine-millimeter semiautomatic, and an EMP device. Her pistol, she slipped into her belt behind her back. Andy carried the yellow launcher with a red one affixed to his belt; his revolver stuck out of his pants pocket.

Virginia slung the binoculars around her neck and climbed the rock pile, stopping just below the crest, and peered through the glasses. "He's slowed and approaching with considerable caution. I guess he doesn't want to end up like the last chopper that tried to inconvenience us. There is someone in the cockpit looking our way through binoculars and another fellow slung out the side with a weapon strapped to him. You know something? People trying to kill us is getting old."

Andy crouched, biting his lower lip. "I have an idea."

Donna went down on one knee next to him. "What do you have in mind?"

"I'll take the launcher and run out in plain sight toward that other pile of rocks. I should be able to make it before he fires. When they turn to see what I'm doing, you two fire your machine guns at him. They aren't designed for long-range shots, but they do throw a lot of lead. You may hit the chopper or the guy with that rifle. Your shooting at them will cause them some consternation, and they won't want to get hit. They should lose interest in me, temporarily. Then, I'll stop, bring up the launcher, and fire. Maybe I can bring it down."

She looked up at him. "And if you don't?"

"We go to plan B."

"Which is?"

"Keep shooting while I run and hide."

Virginia scampered down the rocks. "I heard most of that. I don't like you being a target, Andy. I like my man in one piece and not full of holes."

"Then, what should we do?"

"Donna goes around to the other side and hides. I'll climb back up on top of this pile of rocks and you move over between the car and the boulders and get ready. When I fire, I'll aim high, at their rotors, Donna you open up from your position and aim at the cockpit. They'll take evasive action, I hope. Probably dive, and as soon as they make their move, Andy, you fire in the direction they are taking. It will be hard for them to recover from the direction they are changing to, and they'll get hit by the rocket, or our gunfire or both, I hope."

"It's the 'I hopes' in there that bother me." Donna turned and looked at the pothole-filled road. "Here comes their back up."

The semi was bouncing down the road. It stopped, and the rear doors swung open. A ramp shot out and a small armored car roared down the ramp and fishtailed causing a large cloud of dust as the armored car raced toward them.

Andy replaced the yellow launcher with the red one. "What's the max range on this?"

Donna swallowed. "I don't know. Maybe a hudred yards. It's small, so probably less."

"We'll let him get closer, then I'll find out how good a shot I am with this thing. Just don't be behind me when I pull the trigger." Andy, bent over, trotted to a spot between the SUV and the rocks. He loaded a rocket-propelled grenade and hefted the launcher to his shoulder and waited.

The armored car slowed, then turned onto the dirt trail and stopped sideways across the road. Andy took aim at the vehicle and pulled the trigger. The rocket whooshed out of the launcher, knocking Andy slightly back. The red bullet-shaped rocket grenade raced down the slight hill and slammed into the armored car, then exploded, raising the vehicle off the ground, and blowing a large hole in the side. A second later, the gas tank went off, sending hot metal flying across the desert floor. The cab of the tractor-trailer, shredded by flying metal, disintegrated behind the armored car. The trailer then fell on its side. The rear doors banged open and four men staggered out into the blazing sun. As they started to emerge, Andy fired another projectile hitting the rear of the trailer. The blast reduced the back end to scrap metal, and three of the men were cut down by sharp, hot, metal shrapnel. The fourth man dove into a small ravine next to the dirt road. Andy turned at the sound of the helicopter revving up and flying faster toward their position.

Virginia rose up and started firing her machine gun at the rotors and top motor. Donna fired at the cockpit. The barrage of bullets struck the chopper, cracking the front window. Sparks flew from the rotor mount housing.

The pilot swung the nose down and to the right, trying to avoid the onslaught from the machine guns that now tracked his maneuver and away from where Andy stood with a reloaded RPG launcher. The man in the open doorway tried to unfasten his harness and duck inside when Andy tracked the helicopter's move and fired. The yellow projectile flew inside the open door of the chopper, hit the cockpit bulkhead, and exploded in a white-hot blast. The chopper blew apart, and scorched metal and burning plastic fell to the desert below.

A bullet struck a rock near Virginia's leg. She lost her footing and fell backward onto the rocks. Her gun fired a short salvo into the air as she went down.

Donna hurried around the side of the rocks and looked for the source of the gunfire.

Andy ducked and watched the edge of the trench where the fourth man from the truck had hidden. Andy loaded another grenade into the yellow launcher and waited, searching the area with the launcher's sight. The man's head stuck up about twenty feet from where he had jumped into the ditch. He raised his automatic weapon when Donna opened fire. Dirt flew as bullets struck the ground and marched up to where the man had been. She stopped and waited. A minute later, the man jumped from the ditch and raced toward the second mound of rocks. As he approached, with Donna's bullets catching up with him from behind, Andy's RPG plowed into the boulders directly in front of the man, sending deadly shards of rock, fragments, and white-hot magnesium and iron in all directions, cutting the man down as he ran.

Donna raced to the man, kicked his weapon away and trained her gun on him.

Andy scampered up the rock pile Virginia was on. He found her lying across a large smooth boulder, unconscious. He set the launcher down and stroked her head. "Virginia! Can you hear me?" His voice cracked. "Virginia, don't move." He put his ear near her nose and his hand on her chest. "Thank God, you're breathing." He examined her for blood. She had some blood in her hair where her head hit the rock. "Okay, I'll check you for broken bones." He felt her arms and legs. "Your arms and legs seem to be okay. I don't know about your head, back or neck. Can you hear me?"

She moaned then opened her eyes. "Good God, it's bright out here." Her hand went to her head. "Man, my head really hurts. Where is the chopper?"

"Burning about a hundred yards to the south."

"The truck?"

"It and the armored car don't exist anymore and all but one of the men in the back are dead. For all I know, the survivor is now dead, too. Donna's checking on him."

"Good God. If he's alive, she'll start blowing parts of him off if he doesn't answer her questions. We'd better get there before she starts to interrogate him. She doesn't usually do that without inflicting a lot of pain."

Virginia started to sit up, then settled back. "The world won't hold still. I think I'll rest here for a while. Go see that she doesn't maim him for no other reason than she's pissed, especially if he tries or says anything stupid."

"I shouldn't leave you."

"I'll be okay. I'm just sore and I really bumped my head. I've got a beaut of a headache, and I'm dizzy. I'll rest here until you're done, then come and get me."

"Okay." Andy reluctantly climbed down and hurried to Donna. He stopped next to her and looked at the man on the ground. "How is he?"

"Not in the best of shape. That explosion you caused with the RPG sent rocks and molten metal and fragmentation into him. He's bleeding and I think he's got a lot of internal injuries." She bent lower. "How you doing, fella?"

He moaned and moved his head to see her standing above him. "I need a doctor."

"You need a hospital. But before we summon help, you're going to answer some questions."

"Like hell."

"Have it your way. I'll just cause you more pain and remove your ability to please the ladies, then re-ask the question. I'm sure you'll be in a more talkative mood." She pulled out her pistol, chambered a round and aimed it at his crotch.

He looked into her frowning eyes. "Wait! Wait! Someone from the Department of Energy hired us."

"You work for the DOE?"

"We are private contractors and were hired by someone way up in it."

Donna lowered her weapon. "Why'd they try to kill us?"

"You took out the other contract mercenaries and they were some of the best. It was decided that you were too dangerous to have the secret hidden in the quilt. We were sent to get it and eliminate you."

Andy stepped closer. "Does the DOD know about your mission?"

"I don't know." He shook his head. "Who else is left besides me?"

Donna fingered the safety back on her weapon and tucked it into her belt. "No one. You're it."

"Good God. All of them?" He flinched as he tried to move. "They were good."

"Maybe. But it was pretty stupid to attack us."

"All of them? They're all dead? Just the three of you took them all out?"

"Yes. We're pretty good ourselves, especially when someone is trying to kill us or steal what we've got. By the way, we're on your side."

He coughed up some blood. "It isn't the government behind this. There are some powerful men in Washington who want what you have." He twisted and grimaced in pain. "They're using what assets they have available to get the quilt. Why I don't know. Do you have it?"

Donna chuckled. "Like I'd tell you. Let's just say it's safe for now."

He closed his eyes and gritted his teeth. "Call 911, please."

Andy tugged on Donna's arm. "Let's go. We can alert the authorities after we're on the road."

He and Donna started to walk toward the rocks where Virginia was now sitting when Donna stopped and turned her head to the man. "Are there any more like you around?"

"I don't know. I have a question." His jaws tensed as he closed his eyes for a second. "I heard there were some Arabs taken out in Flagstaff and in California. Did you take them down as well?"

"No, not the ones in Flagstaff. Someone else did. We took care of the ones in California." She turned and followed Andy back to Virginia.

CHAPTER 28

Virginia's Washington contact, Dr. John Montgomery, looked at the report in the red SECRET folder on his large polished mahogany desk. He pushed his glasses up and rubbed his eyes. *Virginia. Where are you? Do you really have the quilt like everyone seems to think you do?* He flipped the folder closed, rose, and shuffled to his gray secure metal file cabinet. He placed the file into a hanger in the second drawer, closed it, and spun the combination lock. He slowly returned to his desk and sat. He sipped some cold coffee and stared at the picture of the President on the far wall.

His intercom buzzed. "Doctor. The SecDef is here to see you, Sir."

What does the Secretary of Defense want with me? I report to the Secretary of the Army. "Send him in please, Nancy."

The door opened. The Secretary of Defense walked in and closed the door behind him. He was a tall man with black hair with graying temples, wire rim glasses, and a dark blue pinstripe suit. He stepped across the room and Montgomery leaped to his feet.

"Sit down, John. We need to talk." The SecDef unbuttoned his jacket, and sat in a dark leather chair and pulled it close to the desk. "John, we have a problem."

"Sir?"

"That quilt you have agents hunting for, with Einstein's theory in it, seems to have generated a lot of trouble. Looks like we aren't the only ones after it."

"I know that, Sir. There is a terrorist organization trying to get it, and I know the Saudis are looking for it as well."

"Do you know if your people have actually found it yet?"

"Last time I talked to Mrs. Clark, she said she had it, Sir." *I hope.*

"Do you know where she is at this moment?"

"No Sir. She and her fellow agents have had some interference from the other groups, and she's gone off the grid. Virginia said she thinks we have a leak, so she contacts me, not the other way around."

"So you've lost control of your asset."

Dangerous Threads

Montgomery could feel his pulse quicken. "She operates better on her own, Sir. She's had excellent results in the past under worse conditions. I think she's right."

The Secretary removed two cigars from his jacket pocket and handed one to Montgomery. "They're Cuban, so don't tell Homeland Security." They lit the cigars and took a couple of puffs. "Okay, John, here is the problem. I read your report concerning yesterday where she and her gang took out a set of mercenaries using military hardware on I-40 in the desert. I also learned that last night some terrorists were found murdered near her hotel, but she wasn't there for that. Today, she and her merry band took down another helicopter, an armored car, and just about everyone in it along with a tractor-trailer."

"Yes Sir. From what I've learned, her group was attacked by some black ops-type individuals, and she defended herself."

The SecDef took another pull on his cigar. "She's doing a good job of that, but leaving a lot of wreckage behind. Thanks to your quick response to the news, yesterday's fiasco along the interstate we managed to contain, but only slightly. But today's debacle was on an Indian reservation. Before we could get personnel on the scene, Bureau of Indian Affairs Agents, State Police, Sheriff's deputies, Zuni Police, BATF, and FBI agents were all over it like a cheap suit. They were arguing over jurisdiction when our units arrived. That just escalated things even more. We're trying to keep the press confused but she's not making it easy."

"You said Virginia and her team used military hardware? How'd they get it?"

"No. The mercenaries had it. Both times. I've launched an investigation trying to figure out where they got it." The SecDef puffed on the cigar. "I don't know what your people used, but whatever they did, they used it well. I sure as hell wouldn't want to cross that lady and her team."

Montgomery nodded. "She's good at taking care of herself. She even recruited some street gangs to help her here in Washington and L.A."

The SecDef removed his cigar from his mouth and stared. "Are you serious?"

"Yes, Sir." Montgomery took a drag on the cigar and smiled. "She's very resourceful."

"I guess you're right. I see why you have such faith in her and her little group. They've taken on some seriously talented, battle-hardened men who outnumbered her and her team, and come out ahead and she seems pretty good at using the resources at hand. From what I've learned, John, she's right about the leak, too. It's either a leak in our house or there are some well-connected people out there working against the interests of the United States. Your girl and her team are all alone. You need to regain control of her and her team and soon. Can we back her up, somehow?"

"I don't know Sir. I don't even know where she is at this moment. Someplace in New Mexico, I'm guessing, but it's a big state." He puffed on the cigar, then set it on a paperweight. "I'm not sure she'd trust anyone from the government right now."

"You've got a point. How about that street gang? Could they help us?"

"You're not serious, Sir? A gang of young hoods trusting the government?"

"They trusted her."

"Yes, Sir. But I don't know what she did to convince them to do it. They won't talk to us or the police."

The SecDef wrinkled his brow. "Where is she getting the weapons she's using? Not at a sporting goods store, that's for sure."

"I tried to figure that out. The only thing I can surmise is that she and her friend managed to keep some of the weapons the CIA gave her on her last job."

"The CIA? I thought she worked for the Smithsonian? They don't usually use weapons, they display them."

"She does work for the Smithsonian, but the CIA assisted her and her friend in Italy."

"Oh. How nice of them not to tell us. So, what did they give her, exactly?"

"I don't know. But whatever they are, they're obviously very effective, and they know how to use them."

The SecDef rose. "Well, John, you know the score so far. Let's hope she makes it and the body count doesn't go up much further. She works for you so either help her or figure out how to keep her antics under wraps."

"Sir?"

"Yes, John?"

"Will you authorize me to take whatever action is needed to help her and save the quilt and Einstein's theory of everything it may contain?"

The Secretary of Defense stood looking at Montgomery. "Yes, John. She knows you and hopefully trusts you, so effective immediately, I'll authorize you to access special operations staff. Just keep me in the loop and try to keep the body count down." He turned and left.

Virginia watched the road ahead. "Did you see all those emergency vehicles on the other side of the freeway? I wonder if they were going to our battleground?"

Donna chuckled from the back seat. "Honey, they ain't going to a ball game. Now, I've got us two suites at the Best Western next to Old Town in Albuquerque."

Andy shifted in his seat. "I think we should change cars as well."

Dangerous Threads

"One step ahead of you, Andy. I've rented us a new SUV. Let's go get it first, then go to the hotel. That way if this thing is tattling on us, we lose it."

Virginia reached to use the navigation system when Andy pushed her hand away. "Don't do that. There'll be a record of where we went and if one of our adversaries gets a hold of the car, that's one of the first places they'll look. Anyway, we're getting rid of this car and getting a new one. Where is the car rental place?"

"Donna chimed in. "I've got it on MapQuest on my computer. So here are the directions to the rental agency, and I'll log off." Donna gave the driving instructions to Andy who promptly pointed to another Route 66 sign.

They turned in their SUV and hiked away, lugging their bags. Four blocks away, they called a cab and gave him directions to another car rental agency.

An hour later, Virginia and Andy were settling into their suite at the Best Western Rio Grande Inn when Donna called. "We're on the news on the TV."

Virginia frowned. "We're on TV? How do they know about us?"

"They don't exactly. The media is trying to piece the events together. The fact that military hardware was utilized and that ex-military types were involved has them taking to their special advisors and talking heads as to what may have gone on. No one can figure out who we are, though. There's no official statement as to who they were, either. The press is all over it. They're drawing conclusions that we're the same gang who caused the I-40 problem in Arizona. They've guessed the other guys are mercenaries or terrorists. Turn on your TV. Oh yeah, when are we going for lunch? There's a neat Mexican place in Old Town."

"I should have guessed you'd bring up food pretty soon. Let's go in about a half hour. Andy's in the bathroom with a book."

"Gotcha. I'll come over in a half hour."

Virginia watched the news on her TV. *A lot of speculation, talking expert heads, and anonymous tips, but they can't seem to figure out who we are or who our assailants were.*

Virginia switched on her iPhone for a quick look at her e-mail. There was a message from Dillon, her contact with the Washington Street gang. It warned her that the authorities in Washington were looking for her and wanted his gang to help. He said he and his people wouldn't unless they got the okay from her. She smiled and turned off the phone.

Andy emerged from the bathroom carrying his paperback *San Gabriel's Secret*. He glanced at the TV, then stopped. He pointed to the TV. "Look in the background. Do you see what I see?"

Virginia squinted at the TV. "That yellow truck has Department of Energy on it."

"Yeah. All the others are police of some type. Looks like whoever was behind these attacks went to see what happened first-hand." Andy cracked a smile. "Maybe Montgomery really is okay."

"I just thought of something; how many of those RPGs do you have left?"

Andy sat in the chair next to the king size bed. "None. I just have the launchers remaining. Why?"

"Just wondering. We need to bring our adversaries to us and deal with them on our terms. Those things were quite effective."

Andy leaned forward. "Why bring them to us? That could cause a firefight in a populated area, which is never a good idea, especially for a so-called secret mission. I have an idea."

Virginia jumped at the knock on the room door. She grabbed her nine-millimeter and hurried to the door and peered through the peephole. She opened the door and hustled Donna inside.

Donna looked at her with raised eyebrows. "Getting a little jumpy, huh?" She sauntered into the bedroom, smiled at Andy and plopped on the bed. "How are you doing? Nice shooting back there."

Andy beamed. "Fine, thanks But I'm out of bullets for my launchers. You were pretty impressive, too."

"Thank you, Sir. I know we don't have any more RPGs. But they served their purpose."

Virginia stood in the doorway. "If I can break into this mutual admiration, Andy was about to give us his idea of what we should do." She sat back on her chair. "Go ahead, what did you have in mind?"

Andy cleared his throat. "First, I think we should examine the quilt and try to find the wire recordings. If we can find the wires, we go to some shops that may still have these old recorders and see if we can use or purchase one. Then we see what's actually on the wire recordings, if anything is still there, then we make fake ones to place into the quilt. We keep the original wire recordings with us. They'll be easy to hide. We can ship the quilt to Montgomery and let word out that we did. That'll take the heat off of us for a while, at least until they find the recordings in the quilt are fake."

"Wait a minute." Virginia frowned "You just said the recordings may not be readable? Why?"

"They were made on a high nickel steel wire. Over time it can become—and probably has—corroded, and either lost what was on it or corrupted it."

"So, we've been chasing this quilt down and running and getting shot at for nothing?"

"We did find the long-lost 1933 Chicago World's Fair quilt and we still have to get out of this alive. This may give us an edge."

Donna nodded. "I like it."

Virginia rose. "I like it, too."

"It may also bring out who's after us from our own government." Andy sat back. "And it may confuse or delay the Golden Crescent and the Saudis. I'm also dying to find out what is really on that recoding, if anything."

Virginia looked at Donna and Andy, then she grinned. "Let's do it."

CHAPTER 29

Virginia, in her fire-engine red bikini, reclined on a lounge chair next to Donna in a bright blue bikini. Their beach bags with their semiautomatics rested next to them. A couple of men sat at tables trying to read, and a couple of others sunned in loungers across the pool.

Virginia looked at Donna. "How do you think Andy's doing finding a wire recorder to use?"

Donna lifted one shoulder in a semblance of a shrug. "I haven't a clue. But, since he's not here, I assume he's still in your room making calls." She lowered her sunglasses and looked around. "I don't see anyone too threatening, do you?"

"No. Maybe we're safe for a while. We're supposed to be decoys to keep strangers away from him." She looked at the pool gate. Andy was opening it and rushing toward them.

Out of breath, he plopped down on the foot of Virginia's lounger. "I found a recorder I can use. It's at the university. We have to find as much of the wire as possible." He stopped to take a breath. "Getting any action out here?"

Donna chuckled. "A lot of ogling, but not much else. How are we going to find the microscopic wire? Use a magnet?"

Andy took his glasses off and rubbed his eyes. "No. That could wipe everything off the wire. I've collected some bright lights, magnifiers and tweezers, but I'll need your help. That is, if you two can break away from your admirers."

Virginia sat up, grabbed her towel, and bag. "Very funny. Let's get started before anyone knows what we're up to or where we are." She rose and headed for the pool gate with Donna and Andy following.

Fifteen minutes later, Donna and Virginia, dressed in shorts and T-shirts, walked into the living room of Virginia's suite where Andy had set up his equipment and the World's Fair quilt. Donna looked around. "Where did

Dangerous Threads

you get this stuff?"

Andy grinned. "The daytime hotel manager loaned it to me. She's really nice. She told me about some lost mines in the mountains north of here and how her ex-husband used to use this stuff to look at topographical maps and old mining documents. She said I could keep it if I wanted to."

Virginia poked his arm. "Sounds like *you* have an admirer."

He frowned over the top of his glasses. "Let's get to work, shall we?"

Andy sat up, arching his back. He looked at Virginia and Donna. Virginia, with a yellow pencil stucking out of her blonde hair, carefully placed a long strand of wire into a metal can. Her eyes were bloodshot. Donna rubbed her eyes and ran her fingers through her dark brown hair.

He glanced at the small tin boxes with thin steel wires in them. "I hope that's all of it."

Donna looked at him. "You got that right, cowboy. That was tedious."

Virginia climbed out of her chair and stretched. "Yeah. I wish we could have left that part to the government. Now, when can you get a reading on these things?"

He looked at his watch. "It's five o'clock now. I'll see if I can reach my contact at the university and make an appointment for tomorrow morning."

Haddad Abdel A'hsam, the cultural attaché at the Saudi Embassy and the section head of the Saudis, Al Mukhabarat Al A'amah, sat in his high-backed leather chair behind his ornately carved polished wooden desk. His secretary buzzed him on the intercom. "Your call to Dr. Montgomery is ready, Sir."

"Thank you." He picked up the phone receiver. "Hello, John, nice of you to take my call."

Dr. John Montgomery sighed. "To what do I owe the favor of your call today, Haddad?"

"It's about your secret operatives, the Clarks."

"Why doesn't it surprise me that you know about them? Do you have a spy in my organization?"

"Why would I tell you the answer to that question?" Haddad said. "Let's just say some research into other agencies in your government led me to them."

"I've heard about their merry adventures, too, and it seems they're mounting quite a body count. I guess keeping it under tight wraps is getting harder to do. Your government wants what they have, doesn't it?"

"We did, John, we really did. But now, with all the turmoil in the Middle East, we'd feel safer if you had what's in that quilt."

"You're backing off?"

"Yes. But I thought I'd also let you know that The Golden Crescent is not as effective as it was, due to your lady and her team and, I must add, us."

Montgomery frowned. "I'm not sure what you mean."

"Ms. Virginia has managed to evade or eliminate a number of their organization's members. And, my friend, we've been helping her in that area."

Montgomery voice rose. "You know where she is?"

"Not right now. We lost them, as did you. We eliminated Golden Crescent operatives in Flagstaff. The Golden Crescent should no longer be a major threat to her. But, it seems some of your people tried to erase her in the desert."

A'hsam heard Montgomery take a quick inhale. "Yeah, I ahhh, I found out about that. My boss wants to blame it on you and the Crescent for now, while we investigate."

"I'm having our people keep an eye out for her and assist her where we can. This is unofficial, you understand."

Montgomery chuckled. "Sure. What would the State Department think?"

"I wouldn't tell them or anyone else."

"Don't worry. And Haddad, thanks for the update and assistance."

"John, what are the chances you'd let her, her husband, and her friend work for us in the future?"

"You'll have to get in line behind the Mossad."

Haddad's voice sounded guarded. "I know they were interested in what we were doing, like usual. Are they still trying to get her quilt?"

"Who isn't? I don't know what they are trying to do, if anything. I don't think they know exactly what's going on except that the Golden Crescent and you are involved. That always makes them nervous."

"You're right about that." Haddad paused. "Okay, John, thought you'd like to chat. I'm sure your people are having kittens listening to us talk like a couple of old men, but like I said, we will assist you any way we can. Oh, one other thing."

"Yes?"

"Watch out for some very high-ranking officials in your DOE and State Departments."

Montgomery's heart skipped a beat. "Who? Do you have names?"

"No. Just be on your feet, I think that's your saying."

"Yeah, something like that. It's keep on your toes, and thanks, Haddad." They hung up.

The door to John Montgomery's office flew open. Two security men raced in and took the two leather chairs facing his desk. "Doctor Montgom-

Dangerous Threads

ery. That was quite the phone call. We heard it all. Do you think Haddad was telling the truth?" said the shorter of the men.

Montgomery sat back in his chair. "I think so. But you can never be sure. Could be a ruse. We know for sure that some agents of the Golden Crescent were killed near Virginia's hotel in Flagstaff, Arizona and she didn't do it. They could be just eliminating the competition, though. He was right about some American mercenaries trying to steal her quilt and kill her. At this point, I don't trust anyone and the longer she stays off the grid, the safer she is."

At nine-thirty in the evening, Donna called Virginia's room. "I think someone is snooping around."

"What makes you think so?"

"I've been watching out my window at the parking lot every so often. A little while ago, a white caddie slowly cruised through the parking lot under the security lights and a short black guy walked along the cars. He stopped at every SUV and looked inside, then rattled the doors. He could have been a common crook, but why just the SUVs? And there's been a guy standing near the ice machine trying to look like a tourist for the last half hour."

"I'll tell Andy and call you back."

"Okay."

Virginia looked at Andy, stretched out on the couch watching television with his revolver on his stomach. "Andy. That was Donna. It seems we may have some unwelcome visitors."

"Now? Could they be just local hoods?"

"Sure. They probably are locals. But she's nervous. I have a feeling someone is hunting for us and doesn't really know where we are. Like they're casting a net and seeing what they catch."

He slowly rose to a sitting position. "Okay, where are they?"

"Parking lot and by the ice machine."

"We could just lie low and see if they go away."

"And we wouldn't know if it was really our adversaries or local crooks or if they were still watching the hotel later."

Andy nodded. "Okay, call Donna and have her pack up. When we distract the guy by the ice machine, I'll bring all her gear here to our suite. That way we're all together and can operate smoother."

"Okay. How are we going to distract the ice machine fellow? Wait a minute, Donna and I are going to be the distraction, right?"

"Bingo! You two are so good at it. Get her on the phone, and I'll tell you."

Five minutes later, after seeing the man by the ice machine return from the restroom, Donna and Virginia, dressed in thin, braless tank tops and shorts met in the brightly lit hall and wobbled, and talked, like they had been drinking and partying, in loud voices toward the ice machine. The man's eyes enlarged, and he grinned as he watched them approach. While Donna bumped into the man, Virginia unplugged the ice machine. She stuck her ice bucket under the tap and pushed some buttons. Nothing happened.

Donna looked at the empty ice bucket, then leaned against him and said, in a slurred voice, "Hi. Can you give us a hand? It seems there's no ice. We need ice."

Virginia played with the bucket, then stood up straight, pulling the thin shirt tighter, and smiled at him. "Help us and you can join our party."

He swallowed. "Let me see what I can do." He took the bucket, and started working the machine.

Donna turned and motioned down the hall to Andy, then turned back to the man. She stepped next to him, blocking any view of the hall he might have had. "Any luck? It's really warm, you know."

He turned his head, looking right at Donna's breasts then he looked the other way at Virginia. "I'm doing my best. It seems to have completely shut down." He wet his lips. "Maybe we'll have to use a machine on the second floor."

"Good idea." Virginia stepped closer, making his eyes get even bigger. "Let's go upstairs." She stepped around the man and headed for the stairwell. Donna followed, with the man carrying the ice bucket behind her.

As they entered the staircase, Andy slipped out of Donna's room for the second time with more of her bags, computers, and weapons cache then hurried to his suite.

On the second floor they found the ice machine and let the man fill the bucket up. He handed it to Virginia. "Can we go party now?"

Virginia grinned. "Sure, big boy, want to start right here?"

"Huh?" he looked around. "Here?"

"Sure." She and Donna moved him against the back wall of the recess holding the ice machine and snuggled close. He started to speak when Donna jabbed his leg with a small syringe. He looked confused. He tried to speak, but nothing came out of his mouth but a soft sigh. He slipped to the floor.

Donna looked at the sleeping man. "That's the last of our knock-out drugs. I hope he was worth it."

Virginia nodded. "I think so." She looked up and down the hall. "Looks clear, let's go before someone else comes for some ice." She pulled a small flask from her pocket and poured some whisky on him. "Just in case someone calls the cops."

Donna hurried toward the staircase. "The people in the parking lot may still be here. So, when we get to your room, let's change, and call the po-

Dangerous Threads

lice. The caddie'll beat it when the cops approach and the officer's will think our friend here is either a drunk or on drugs. That should be fun."

CHAPTER 30

At ten in the morning, Andy, Virginia, and Donna entered the small and cluttered office of Professor Mike Hawes of the Electrical and Computer Science Department of the University of New Mexico. After introductions, Virginia and Donna went to the bookstore while Andy headed for the lab with Professor Hawes.

After an hour in the bookstore, Virginia grabbed Donna's arm. "Shall we go to the food court and get something to eat or drink? Andy said this could take some time."

"Sure, why not? We can enjoy a day on a college campus as a break from people trying to kill us." They meandered around the university until they found a small restaurant. They went into the air-conditioned building, picked up glasses of iced tea, some snacks and sat at a table against the back wall with a view of the whole room and entrances. As they finished their snack, Virginia's satellite phone rang. She looked wide-eyed at Donna. "I forgot to switch it off. We could be dead meat."

"Maybe it's Andy looking for us. You might as well answer it, keep the talk short, and turn the darn thing off."

Virginia pulled the phone from her backpack and pressed talk. "Hello?"

"Hi. It's me," Andy said. "I'll meet you at the car." He hung up.

She switched off the phone and jumped up. "You were right. It was Andy. He'll meet us at the car. Let's go."

They hurried outside into the heat and tried to walk as quickly as they could without drawing too much attention. Approaching the car, Virginia spotted Andy sitting in the SUV with the engine and air-conditioning running. "I wonder how it went?" she mumbled.

They slid into the vehicle and buckled up. Virginia looked at Andy. "How'd it go? Was the theory of everything really on the wires?"

Andy sighed. "There were a number of places where Dr. Einstein talked about continuity of relativity theory, gravity, and quantum gravity and he would describe the relationship mathematically—"

"That's good, right?"

Dangerous Threads

"Yeah, it is, sort of. The wire is made of a steel alloy and because it was inside a quilt and stored for over sixty years in a wooden box in a basement, some of it is corroded too far for anything to be easily picked up. There is a lot of good data still readable, though. Maybe more sophisticated equipment could possibly get the information out of the corroded section. I don't know, but not what they have here."

Donna perked up in the back. "How about Sandia Labs? They're around here someplace, I think."

Andy turned to her. "I don't think taking this to a DOE lab at this point is a good idea. They've been trying to kill us."

"It's a DOE lab? I thought the Army or the Defense Department owned it."

"They did. But times change."

"Okay, so what's next?"

Virginia looked out at the desert landscape around them. "I have—"

"I found a source for some wire similar to what we found," Andy interrupted. "It's in an antique store near our hotel. I think we should get it, and send it to Dr. Montgomery and send the quilt to the Smithsonian and hightail it to Washington with the original wires."

Virginia sat staring at him. "Not a bad idea, but dangerous. We could send the quilt to the Smithsonian, as you said, send the original wire to my museum in Texas, and take the fake wires with us. We tell Montgomery we're sending the quilt as we planned and bringing the wire recording with us. We don't mention that we switched them. That may lure our enemies, protect the real recordings, and we can get this damn trip over with."

"I like it when a plan comes together," Donna chimed in.

Andy pulled the car out of the visitor lot and headed for the hotel. They picked up the quilt, gear, and checked out, then drove to a UPS Store. They sent the quilt to Virginia's contact at the Smithsonian. Then, Andy packaged the metal can holding the real wire recordings and shipped them to Virginia at her museum in Texas. An hour later they were driving east on I-40.

Virginia used Andy's cell phone to call her boss at the San Gabriel Museum in Texas. "Hi Doctor Doverspike. I need a favor."

"Virginia, Dear, are you all right? I've heard about some really strange things going on across the country and I'm hoping that these things don't involve you."

"Well, keep hoping."

"Oh. I see." Doverspike hesitated. "What can I do for you?"

"I'm UPSing a package to myself at the museum. When it arrives, I need you to put it in the safe and don't tell a living soul it's there. No one is to know, even if government officials in dark suits, sunglasses, and guns question you. If you would, get the files on the Liberty Hill dig from my desk, put them in a brown envelope, and leave them on my desktop. If questioned, you can say the papers are what I sent back. I was working on them when I left and sent them back to the museum."

"Okay. I can do that, but under one condition."

"I know. I give you all the gory details of our adventure when I get back."

"Yes!"

"You're a dear. You've got a deal." She disconnected and tuned to the others. "That end is covered."

Virginia turned on her cell phone and called Dr. Montgomery. "Hello, Sir. This is Virginia Davies-Clark."

"Virginia! Are you okay? I've been getting more reports about your travels and I'm very concerned about you. Can I send help? Do you want to go to a government office where I can have U.S. Marshals protect you? Can—"

"Doctor Montgomery! Slow down. Andy, Donna, and I are fine. I've just shipped the Chicago World's Fair Quilt to the Smithsonian, and we're bringing the wire recording to you. I'll see you in a few days, if all goes well."

"You actually found it? The wire was in it as we heard? That's wonderful."

"Yeah, well, someone else in Washington seems to want to hog it all for themselves. Big surprise there. I think we've got more to worry about from our own government than the Arabs who've been after us."

"You're right. The Saudis have said they are backing off and will assist you, if need be. The Golden Crescent seems to have been minimalized by you and them. Now why don't you let me send you help?"

"We're safer on our own. See you soon, Sir." Virginia disconnected.

Professor Mike Hawes entered his office, closed and locked his door, and went to his desk. He picked up the phone and dialed a number.

"Sandia Labs," said the woman who answered the phone. "How may I direct your call?"

Professor Hawes responded. "Doctor Collmann, please, this is Professor Hawes." He sat back in his chair in his messy, cramped office.

"Just a moment." Elevator music played for a minute. A voice answered. "Doctor Collmann."

"Ed, this is Mike Hawes of the University of New Mexico. I'm calling about that wire recording you asked me to be on the lookout for."

Collmann's voice lowered. "What did you find out?"

"A professor from The University of Texas and two attractive women came here with a number of pieces of wire recordings and wanted to use our old equipment to play them."

"What did you do? Is he still there?"

Hawes leaned back in his chair. "I let him use the old gear and tried to have him leave the wire so I could use our more sophisticated equipment, but he refused and left."

"Did you hear what was on any of it?"

"Yes. Einstein figured it out. He found an abstract way to rethink the theories of relativity and quantum mechanics and combine the laws of gravity, electromagnetism and the weak and strong forces."

"Wonderful. Why didn't you stall him and contact me sooner? Where is he now?"

"I couldn't stall him any longer than I did. I hoped he'd join the ladies for lunch and leave the wires here so I could switch the wires and contact you, but he didn't. And, it may be wonderful and all, but some of the wire was corroded and those recordings we didn't get. As to his whereabouts, he left a short time ago with the two women."

Collmann grunted. "If we could get our hands on that wire, we could use equipment here at the labs to try to extract data from the corroded sections as well as the still-readable parts."

"Well, he isn't here and he didn't leave the wire. I don't think I can help you any more with this."

"Very well. Thank you, Professor. Oh, did he mention where they were going?"

"Yes. To lunch."

Doctor Collmann called a private number in Washington, D.C. A voice answered. "Hello?"

"Collmann here. Mrs. Clark and her group were in Albuquerque and tried to read the wires at the University of New Mexico. The wires have the theory on them, but parts are corroded."

"Good work. Where are they now?"

"I don't know. They told the professor they were going to lunch, so I assume they're still in Albuquerque."

"Assuming anything with them can be fatal. Do they still have the wire?"

"I assum... I think so."

"Okay. Have a team ready and I'll see if we can locate them. Hang on for a second." Collmann listened to more elevator music. "The tracker on their vehicle is stationary. Here are the coordinates. Get people there as quickly as possible and call me back."

"Yes, sir." He hung up then made another call. "Go to these coordinates and get the wire from the Clarks and their friend and leave no witnesses."

He hung up.

Collmann walked around his office sipping cold coffee for an hour and a half. He rushed back to his desk when the phone rang.

The voice on the line said in a raspy, monotone voice, "No luck. The Clarks turned in their vehicle and walked out of the rental agency yesterday. No one saw them get into another car. The rental company agent asked if they needed a ride and they said no, they could walk."

"Oh. Were any other cars rented about that time?"

"Yeah. Eleven. Mostly to business people and one housewife whose car is at the dealers for repair."

Collmann rubbed his chin. "Who were the business people?"

"They won't part with that information."

"Were any of them women?"

"No."

"Any hotels in the area?"

"We looked. No."

"Crap." Collmann sighed. "Okay. Thanks for the information." He hung up. He thought for a minute then buzzed his secretary. "Conference me with Under Secretary Sherman at DOE and Army Under Secretary for Intelligence John Montgomery at the Pentagon." *I'll call my other contact back shortly.*

Fifteen minutes later, alone in his office, he sat back and talked on his speakerphone. "Gentlemen, it seems Mrs. Clark and her merry band have outmaneuvered us yet again. It looks like she has the unified field theory wire recordings from the 1933 Sears World's Fair Quilt, but we've managed to lose her."

Under Secretary of Energy Sherman responded. "She's taken out most of our contract assets as well. Where is she now?"

"I don't know, Sir. I do know that a small part of the recording has been compromised by corrosion and she still has it."

Montgomery spoke. "Virginia and her group were in a hotel near Old Town Albuquerque. One of our agents stumbled upon her, but before he knew what was happening, they drugged him and called the police. By the time we got him released, they were long gone. I didn't think of them going to the university."

"I had the word out among the science community here in case they tried to read the wire recording. That's how I found out they went to the university," Collmann said.

Montgomery continued, "She's sent the quilt to the Smithsonian and is on her way here with the wire recordings, such as they are. As long as the Golden Crescent and Saudis don't interfere, we should still be okay. We have a lot riding on this, so we need to get it when she reaches Virginia or the outskirts of the District of Columba where we still have assets, and before she comes to the Pentagon."

"Does she suspect you?" Sherman asked.

"No. She calls in once and a while, and updates me. But, I don't think she, her husband, and friend really trust anyone at this point."

Collmann cleared his throat. "Okay, what is the plan? What do you want me to do?"

"Nothing. I think your part is done." Montgomery said. "Shut things down out there so all this can't be traced to any of us. We need to get that wire soon. Our customer is getting impatient, and a lot of money is involved. Remember, gentlemen, when we succeed, we can retire in luxury in Greece or Brazil where there is no extradition. So, Dr. Collmann, we'll take it from here. Oh, one more thing; Dr. Collmann, do not go behind our backs again, or you'll never retire in Greece." They disconnected.

Collmann sat back in his chair and looked out the window at the high desert landscape. *I'd better tell the third party the results now, too, then get out of town for a while. I'm not looking forward to that.*

Haddad Abdel A'hsam set the headphones on the workbench in the high security listening post in the basement of the Saudi Embassy. He glanced at his men seated on lab stools and wooden chairs around the room.

"Gentleman, it appears that Allah has again smiled upon us. "Now we know for certain who is behind these attacks on Ms. Virginia. My concern now is insuring Doctor and Mrs. Clark and their friend, Ms. Bolette, make it back to Washington and get that wire recording to someone who can protect it and not these traitorous men." He sighed and shook his head. "But, she has no idea that her DOD benefactor is a traitor and the DOE is involved. We may have to intercept her or get her help from her own government."

The man operating the wiretap spoke, "Do we know who else besides the two men in Washington are involved, and do you know where they are now?"

"No. We need to know who that other party Dr. Collmann talked to is. Get an intercept on his cell phone and a bug on his home and office phones. I'll get people started on finding their customer, but I think I know how to find Ms. Virginia and company if and when they get to Washington. Trust me, they'll need all the help they can get." He nodded to a man sitting before a bank of electronic equipment. "Get Sarah for me."

After a short wait, A'hsam spoke to the woman.

"Sarah, the Clarks and Ms. Bolette are between New Mexico and Washington. My guess is they'll enter Texas near Amarillo pretty soon, assuming they take a direct route. I don't know what they're driving, but have people watch for them on I-40 and have your people keep an eye on I-

10 as well. Also, watch for anyone else interested in them. Then, once you have deployed your people, I want you to report to me here at the embassy as soon as possible."

"Do you want me to have them taken out?"

"No! I want you to still keep them alive and safe until they get to Washington. That is, if your people can find them. I need you here."

"Yes, Sir."

The man operating the wiretap looked up from his equipment. "Any idea what Ms. Virginia will do once she gets close to Washington?"

"Yes." A'hsam smiled. He dialed his secretary. "I need you to get me the Cultural Attaché at the Israeli Embassy. He's head of station for the Mossad."

The morning paper reported that Sandia Laboratory guards making rounds at eleven the previous night found the body of Dr. Collmann electrocuted in an unfortunate accident in his lab. On page six, it also reported that University of New Mexico Professor Mike Hawes was dead on arrival at the hospital after a hit and run accident.

CHAPTER 31

Virginia turned in her seat and glanced at Donna sorting out her remaining cache of weapons. "We still have over fifteen hundred miles to go. What's our armament situation?"

Donna looked up. "Well, if we don't get attacked by the Marines, we should be okay. Those last encounters took a serious toll on my little collection. We've got more than enough ammunition for our side arms and MP-5s to overthrow a small government. I've got two single-use EMPS and one rechargeable unit. We have a dozen tire blowing bouncy balls, a couple flash-bang grenades, and three smoke grenades. I've got six magnesium firebombs that not just go boom but will make Hell look like a meat locker. We also have a radio, radio frequency jammer, some ceramic knives, and six bear strength pepper spray canisters. That's about it."

Andy coughed. "That's it? That sounded like a small armory. We should be in great shape and better yet, why don't we avoid more bad people?"

"Andy, Dear," Virginia patted his leg, "We're trying, remember? We switched cars and got out of Albuquerque as fast as possible. We aren't using our cell phones either."

"Yeah." Donna started stuffing the weapons back into their bags. "But if they have the CIA or military intelligence go looking for what we're driving, they'll find out pretty fast." She watched a Texas State Trooper car slowly pass them. "Andy, I hope you're doing the speed limit." Donna consulted her maps.

Virginia noted a road sign and pointed. "How far to Amarillo?"

Donna consulted the GPS on her business laptop. "About half an hour, why? We've still got lots of time to drive."

"We can gas up, eat, and find a place to stop tonight." Andy flexed his fingers around the steering wheel. "I have an idea. Let's spend the rest of the day in Amarillo and also spend the night."

Donna and Virginia looked at him, then responded together. "Why?"

"Because, the guys searching for us are expecting us to make a beeline to Washington on I-40, or go north to another eastbound route, or go south to I-10 and hurry. They won't be expecting us to stop."

Virginia stared out the window. "I like the idea. This seat is getting a little rough on my behind."

"I could go with a breather," Donna said.

"Donna, book us some real nice rooms in Amarillo, Texas. I could use a nice big Texas steak tonight."

"You've got it." She punched keys on her computer.

Dr. Montgomery paced in his Pentagon office glancing at the clock every few minutes. When the phone rang, he darted across the carpet and grabbed the receiver. "Montgomery."

A young voice answered. "Sir, I think we may have located the package and the route."

"Where?"

"Interstate Forty. They were spotted at a rest stop about an hour ago."

"An hour ago?" Montgomery sat in his desk chair. "Why wasn't I informed before now?"

"We wanted to be absolutely sure, Sir. We projected their path and think we know about where they'll stop tonight. Do you want us to deploy a wet team?"

"Can you intercept them?"

"Sir?"

"Can you intercept them? With them you can't assume anything. We can't wait for tonight. Get them at a rest stop or gas station or fast food joint or something. Go in fast and take them down, grab the package and get out. Don't let the local authorities catch you or leave any witnesses. This concerns national security."

"Yes, Sir. I'll contact the wet team and fly them from their staging point as soon as we re-locate them."

"Re-locate? You lost them?"

Montgomery heard the officer swallow. "Not exactly. We know where they were a short time ago and there isn't much they can do at this point to change direction. Not until they get to Amarillo."

"Fine. Find them and get the package."

"Yes, Sir." The line went dead.

Montgomery sat back and looked at the picture of the President on the far wall, then to a picture of a Greek beach. *Sorry, Virginia. This is very important to me, and the sooner I get what you've got, the better it will be for me.*

Dangerous Threads

Haddad Abdel A'hsam's phone rang. He quickly picked it up and answered. "A'hsam."

"Sir, we have another intercept on the gravity case. The one with Virginia—"

"I know which case it is. What did you pick up?"

"She and her group are approaching Amarillo, Texas, and the Pentagon just dispatched a wet team to intercept her and take the recordings. She's on I-40, and she's in a 2011 white Suburban with New Mexico license plates."

"Send me everything electronically right now and keep up the good work." He dialed another number.

"Operations."

"Do we have any operatives in the Amarillo area?"

"Texas?"

"Yes, Texas! Where do you think it is, on the moon? Do we have any operatives there?"

"Black ops?"

"No, they're going to an ice cream social. Yes, black ops!" *Why does Allah make me work with such idiots?*

"No, Sir."

"Thanks." A'hsam slammed the phone down. He took a couple deep breaths, then buzzed his secretary. When she answered he said, "Get me the Cultural Attaché at the Israeli Embassy. He's head of station for the Mossad."

A couple minutes later the station chief for the Mossad answered. "Haddad Abdel A'hsam, to what do I owe the pleasure of another call so soon? You find the young lady?"

"Sort of. I need your help as we discussed."

"Okay. Now what exactly do you need?"

A'hsam updated the Mossad agent. "This needs to be secret, of course. We can't let on that our two agencies are in bed, as the Americans like to say."

"Send me the details by the scrambler we set up last night and I'll get agents on it. Just keep anyone you have near her away. I'll let you know when we've secured her and her team."

"I'll do that, and thanks." He looked at his computer. The information from the wiretaps was there. He encrypted it and sent it to the Israeli Embassy.

He looked at the monitor. *May Allah, Jehovah, and Jesus protect you, Ms. Virginia, you're going to need it.* He thought for a minute. *At one time I was ready to kill you, Miss Virginia, but not now. You, your husband, and friend have all my respect.*

Approaching the outskirts of Amarillo, Andy motioned toward a huge sign denoting a gas station and store ahead at the next off ramp. "I think we should gas up here and stretch, then go into town. It's probably got a better view of our surroundings and we'll be able to spot trouble easier than in the city."

Virginia nodded. "Good idea."

They exited the I-40 freeway at the off ramp and drove to the big service center and truck stop. Andy found an empty slot at the gas pumps and slid the Suburban into it next to the pump. They got out of the car and scouted the area. Nothing seemed out of the ordinary. Andy started to pump the gas as Virginia and Donna walked into the center.

A couple of minutes after the ladies entered the building, two black SUVs jerked to a stop in front of the building. The doors flew open and men, dressed in black jumped out, their faces covered with black ski masks and carrying MP-5s. Two turned and rushed at Andy. As they ran across the blacktop, Andy released the gas nozzle and reached for his .38 special. As he pulled out his gun, the men seemed to stumble and fell to the pavement. Blood started to pool around them.

He glanced up and watched the other four men disappear into the building. Andy snapped his cell phone off his belt and hit the number for Virginia's cell phone. No answer. He ran to the building, yanking open the doors, and rushed inside. He saw one of the men in black at the front counter looking around as if confused. He kept tapping his earpiece. Andy started to raise his gun when the man went stiff and fell to the floor. People were standing around staring in shock. Andy stepped around the fallen man and sprinted for the restrooms. When he was a few feet away the door opened to the men's room and Virginia and Donna exited. They looked at Andy, then Virginia spoke. "You okay?"

He looked at the marking on the door and gave her a confused look. "Yeah, I'm fine. You won't believe what just happened."

"Yes, we will." Virginia and Donna stepped aside as two olive-skinned men, in coveralls, walked out of the men's room and smiled. "You ladies had things well in hand. Sorry we missed the action. The one who attacked you, Mrs. Clark, is dead." They nodded toward Andy. "Dr. Clark, we'd advise you finish pumping your petrol and leave here as quickly as possible."

"The security cameras, what happened, the police will be here—"

Virginia took his arm. "Stop babbling, Dear, just pump the gas, and let's get out of here. These nice gentlemen will take care of everything else."

"But—" He hesitated, then, with a couple backward glances, followed Virginia and Donna back outside to their SUV. The men in black who had been lying on the pavement were gone, as were their vehicles.

Andy swallowed and finished pumping the gas, then slid into the car.

Dangerous Threads

Virginia and Donna fastened their seatbelts. He started the engine and pulled out heading toward the freeway entrance. He glanced at Virginia, then into the rearview mirror at Donna. "Will one of you please tell me what just happened?"

Virginia gave him a small smile. "Did you see the gold emblem on the leader's necklace?"

"No. I was kind of in shock." He accelerated onto the freeway. "Why, what was it?"

"The Star of David."

CHAPTER 32

Andy accelerated down the freeway. After checking the mirrors he turned to Virginia. "Okay, what just happened back there was spooky. How'd the guys in black know where we were and secondly, how'd the other team know we were there and who the hell were our benefactors?"

"I have no idea. I've got our phones off and…" she turned and looked at Donna. "Did you have your computer on the internet or your cell phone on?"

Donna shook her head. "No and no. But this car has a GPS navigation system. Can it be tracked?"

Andy frowned. "I don't think so, but I'm not an expert on car GPSs. Maybe if the car is on, the GPS is on. We haven't had it turned on. Someone—or a number of someones—are out there looking for us and they spotted us, or they knew we were leaving Albuquerque and going east, so they plotted our path on the map and sent people to look for us."

"Okay, then. We need to throw them off." Donna unfolded a map of Texas. "Now, we are going to Dallas, then east. Take the next off ramp two miles up the road and head south."

"Got it."

Virginia's eyes narrowed, "The men in black, as you called them, were Americans, not Arabic. So they were from our own government. The other guys, I don't know. They're probably not Arabs, especially with the Star of David the one guy had. Why'd he let us see it? Maybe to let us know they were friends? But why would Israel be in the game and helping us?"

Andy shook his head. "I don't know, but we seem to have picked up a guardian angel somewhere along the line. We're going to need that angel when we get near Washington. I wish I knew who was behind this."

Virginia ran her fingers through her blonde hair. "I'm convinced that Montgomery is one of the conspirators. He must have help and I'm guessing it's someone high up in the Department of Energy."

Donna leaned forward. "Why the energy department?"

"Because the DOD and DOE have a big interest in the… what was it you called the thing on the wire recording, Andy?"

"The theory of everything."

"Yeah, that's it. They have a big interest so they would want it, if it exists."

"Okay, I can see that," Donna said. "But we're bringing it to them. Why try and kill us?"

"I think, and this may be just my delusional mind working, that we have some officials who are going to pad their retirements and sell it to the highest bidder, or may have done so already and they need it soon. If they think we have it, and we told them we do, then they want it before we can deliver it to the proper officials."

Andy nodded his head, then turned off the freeway onto the road Donna had told him to take toward Dallas. "I think you're right. So how do we catch them, and stay alive at the same time?"

"We have an angel, as you put it. The question is who? In our last phone call to Montgomery, he said the Golden Crescent has been pretty well decimated by us and the Saudis. I can see the Saudis helping eliminate the Golden Crescent. They're some of the competition. But, what if they discovered that our own people are trying to kill us and they decided to help us instead of being our adversary?"

Donna rubbed her chin. "I'm not sure I fully buy into that. If they've eliminated the competition, then why help us?"

"Because, if they suspect treachery on the part of our officials, they might be concerned if there is another party involved. They might want to know who the buyer is and the Saudis don't want this theory proof getting in the wrong hands. They have a stake in this, too. So, if they help us, then we can get it to someone who can safeguard it."

"I see where you're coming from," Donna sat back in her seat. "But would they call the Israelis?"

"They're on somewhat friendly terms with Israel and may need their help if they don't have the assets to find us and help us."

"I don't know, but it is a theory, a shaky one at best but it does explain some things. Maybe someone is on our side after all."

Andy turned the radio on. "By side-tracking we may be able to stay ahead of anyone trying to kill us."

Virginia nodded. "I hope so. How far to Washington?"

"The way we're going, about four or five days. Three to four if we get back on a freeway," Donna said. "Are we going directly into Washington or stopping in Virginia and staying outside the district?"

Virginia turned her head toward the backseat. "I think we should stay in Warrenton, Virginia. Andy and I stayed there when this started and we were pretty safe. Now, with the untraceable credit cards, we should be doubly safe. We can figure out what to do when we get there. For now, we need to stay off the grid and away from where they might be looking."

"Right. That's a tall order, seeing that they keep finding us."

Four days later they pulled into the Hampton Inn just off U.S. 29 in Warrenton, Virginia. Andy parked and went inside to register. Donna and Virginia got out of the SUV. They walked around the building trying to look like they were stretching their legs while watching the area around the hotel and the adjacent roads for suspicious cars or people. They returned to find Andy had moved their car and was unloading bags from the back.

Andy smiled as they approached. "I got us two adjoining rooms on the second floor. Give me a hand with these, will you? See anything out of the ordinary?"

"No. Looks quiet. Let's hope it stays that way," Virginia said.

Virginia and Donna took their bags, the duffle bags with their remaining arsenal, and followed Andy into the hotel. They took the elevator to the second floor and walked to their rooms.

Virginia plopped onto the king-size bed and laid back, propped up on her arms, and looked at Andy. "We need to draw our nemesis out into the open and take care of them ourselves or find a way to have them arrested."

"Seeing that Montgomery may be one of the bad guys, I wonder how many more there are, and who's at the top." Andy started to unpack. "We're probably dealing with some very high ranking people, so bringing them down won't be easy."

"I agree. We do have the Smithsonian behind us."

"Virginia, Dear, it's a museum and the Smithsonian Central Security Service is mainly set up to go after antiquities and art-type bad guys, not these characters."

"Good point. I think the FBI and Army CID are out as well."

"Who do we have on our side?"

When the pounding began, they jumped toward the connecting door. "Just a second," Andy said as he walked to the door and opened it. He looked at Donna. She grinned.

"Hi. Unpacked yet?" He stepped aside to let her in.

Donna stared at him for a second, then walked into the room. "Yep, and I inventoried our toys as well. What are you two up to at this point?"

"I've started to unpack, and Virginia is contemplating the state of the universe."

"I heard you ask who's on our side a second ago. I have an idea."

Virginia sat up. "Who?"

Donna went to the recliner and eased herself into it. "Well, we know the Israelis have helped us, and the Saudis have been quiet, or at least helping eliminate the Golden Crescent from being a problem and haven't tried to kill us directly or even recently. And, you've met the head shed at the Saudi intelligence service. Maybe we give him a call. We could possibly set up a meeting on neutral ground where we can cover each other and hopefully not get killed."

CHAPTER 33

Virginia stepped to the pay phone in a restaurant in Middleburg, Virginia and dialed the number for the Saudi Embassy in Washington, D.C. After three rings a female voice answered. Virginia cleared her throat. "I'd like to speak to Haddad Abdel A'hsam, the cultural attaché, please. It is rather urgent."

"May I say who is calling?" the voice asked.

"Virginia Davies-Clark."

"Oh! One moment please, Mrs. Davies-Clark."

A few seconds later, A'hsam answered the phone. "Virginia, how are you doing?"

"I'm still alive, and I think I owe some of that to you."

"You guessed?"

"Yes. I don't know why you're helping us though, but I'll take all the help I can get. The reason I called is I have a problem, and I think you can help me if you are in the mood."

"For such a pretty and talented lady, I will make the time. You realize that by now your NSA has picked up your name and that you are talking to me and are tracing your call?"

"Yes, so let's make this quick. I'd like to meet with you at Uno's Pizza in Gainesville, in the Target shopping center, at seven tomorrow night."

"Okay. I know the place. I'll be there at seven as you request. I have some information for you as well."

"You do? I hope it is something that will help end this."

"It is."

"Thank you, Sir."

"Miss Virginia, please call me Haddad. I will be bringing a friend as well, if you don't mind."

"Mossad?"

"You are very perceptive. We'll see you tomorrow night." He disconnected.

Virginia walked back to the car and slid in. "He's meeting us at seven

Dangerous Threads

tomorrow night at Uno's Pizza in Gainesville. He's bringing a friend, someone from Mossad."

Andy looked at her. "Mossad? That explains the Star of David back at that gas station a few days ago. Looks like you were right, they're working together to help us. I wonder why?"

"We'll know tomorrow. In the meantime, I think we should get out of here. I'm sure the NSA has tracked the phone call and someone has their people on their way to kill us."

Donna spoke up from the rear seat. "I've plotted a course back to Warrenton that takes us off the main roads. And, Andy, of course she's right. You should be getting used to that by now."

Andy started the car. "Okay, Donna, where do I go?"

Dr. Montgomery looked up from the papers on his desk as his secretary entered. "Sir, NSA traced a phone call placed by Virginia Davies-Clark. She's in Middleburg, Virginia. Do you want to send a task team?"

"No. She'll be long gone by the time they got there. Who'd she call?

"The Saudi Embassy."

He jerked up in his chair. "Who?"

"The Saudi Embassy, Sir."

"Why?"

She looked at her notebook. "She was setting up a meeting in Gainesville for tomorrow night."

"Where?"

"At a pizza place. The NSA said they lost contact for a few seconds and missed the actual location and time, but how many pizza places can there be in Gainesville?"

"Probably way too many for us. I'll have to think about it. Thanks for the update."

"Yes, Sir." She turned and went back to her desk.

Montgomery leaned back in his chair and stared at the picture on the opposite wall. He sighed and reached for the phone and dialed Undersecretary Sherman at DOE.

Sherman answered on the second ring. "Sherman."

"Bill, this is John Montgomery. Virginia is in Virginia."

"No shit, John. Virginia is always in Virginia."

"Don't get cute. You know what I mean."

"So, where exactly is she in Virginia?" Sherman asked. "It's a big state."

"The NSA picked up a call she made from Middleburg to the Saudi Embassy."

"The Saudi Embassy? Why?"

"To set up a meeting at a pizza place in Gainesville."

Sherman chuckled. "The Saudis like pizza?"

"How the hell should I know?" Montgomery said in a tense voice. "Probably. Everyone else does."

"What's she up to?"

"I don't know, and I don't know which pizza place or the exact time, but it is for tomorrow night."

"I'll have some men follow the embassy guy. Who is her contact there?"

"I don't know that either. Maybe Haddad Abdel A'hsam, the cultural attaché."

"He's their spy station chief. Why him?"

"If I knew I'd tell you. She must be staying in the area, but I don't know where, either."

"John, what do you know exactly?"

Montgomery took a deep breath and let it out. "If we don't stop her, we're toast. She's turned out to be everything we heard about her and more. Smart, crafty, and dangerous. Now that she's got her husband and that Bolette woman with her, she's extremely dangerous."

"No shit, Sherlock. She and her merry band have taken out a number of our well-trained and combat-experienced mercenaries and without a scratch on her. She found something that's been missing for almost seventy years and now has what is worth billions of dollars in her possession and you can't find her. You'd better find that pizza place and stop her. Otherwise, our customer will be very upset with one more setback, to say nothing of what may appear to be a double cross." The DOE secretary hung up.

Montgomery slowly lowered the phone handset into the saddle and wiped his forehead. He buzzed his secretary. "Find out how many pizza places there are in Gainesville and the surrounding area."

In ten minutes she called him back. "It looks like there are eleven or so pizza places in Gainesville, Sir. More if you count the surrounding areas."

"Thanks." He scribbled the number eleven on a pad. *Too many restaurants to send agents to, especially not knowing the time. Now what? Maybe we should follow the Saudi cultural attaché when he leaves tomorrow night and join he and Virginia for dinner.* He picked up the phone and dialed a number to an Army installation, which officially doesn't exist on any map of Virginia.

Virginia sat on the bed in their room facing Andy, with his fingers laced behind his head, in the chair. Donna sat next to Virginia.

Andy wrinkled his nose. "So, the Saudis have been helping us and they sent the Mossad?"

Dangerous Threads

"Appears so. Who would have guessed? A'hsam said he's bringing someone from Mossad to our meeting tomorrow night. Now we need to be ready for a couple things. First, we get there well in advance to see if anyone else shows up who wasn't invited. Second, we have our story straight and we see if they can help us get the leaders of the group who's after us. Third, we'd better have a plan for what we want to do."

Donna looked at her. "What do we want to do?"

"I think we need a sting and set the government people after us up as a double cross to whoever they are selling or working for. I think the Saudis want to help and keep the secret of the theory of everything safe."

Donna grinned. "I like the idea of a sting. Maybe it won't get us killed."

"Me too," Andy said. "What do you have in mind?" He looked at his watch. "What's for lunch?"

Donna rose and stretched. "I like the idea of eating, and I think we should strategize next to the pool."

After lunch they reconvened at a table under an umbrella at the pool. Virginia, wearing her bikini, sat with a pen and notebook. "Okay, I think we need to tell Dr. Montgomery that we have the wire recording and we know he's one of the people who's been trying to have us killed and steal the recording. We want a percent of what he's selling it for, or we sell it to the highest bidder we find on our own. I can tell him we have some interested parties right now. We will ask for a meeting with him and his partners or else."

Donna shifted in her seat. "Then what? You know they'll bring some muscle to take it and kill us."

"They will be careful because of what we did to the others they sent before. But, that's where the Saudis and Mossad come in."

"What if the NSA heard your call and notified the big guns at DOE and the DOD? Would they try and find us at the restaurant or follow Mr. A'hsam and attack us in the restaurant?" Andy asked as he wiped his bald head with a towel.

"Maybe. That's why we're getting there early and watching, and I'm sure Mr. A'hsam didn't get his job because he's stupid. I just hope this isn't an example of the Peter Principal."

"I like it anyway, but we need to refine this a bit," Andy added. "I hope the Saudis and the Israelis go for it."

"Me, too. In the meantime, we need to rest, and think more about this while no one is trying to kill us."

CHAPTER 34

At five-thirty the following evening, Virginia, Andy, and Donna pulled into the parking lot of the large strip mall in Gainesville and parked. Andy slid his .38 special in its holster into his pocket, stashed his canister of bear strength pepper spray, and attached his new walkie-talkie to his belt. Donna placed her 9mm semiautomatic into her purse and her pepper spray into the pocket of her shorts. She checked the EMP device and put it into her purse as well. The walkie-talkie dangled from her belt. Virginia checked the magazine in her 9mm semiautomatic and placed it into the outside pocket of her backpack along with her pepper spray. She also loaded a half dozen of the bouncy tire shredders into her backpack. She clicked on her walkie-talkie and made a sound check with the others.

Virginia tightened her short ponytail and pulled her ball cap on as they all slid out of the car. "Okay, take your location in the mall around Uno Pizza and watch. Call if you see anyone suspicious."

Donna nodded. "Okay, but right about now everyone looks suspicious. What if A'hsam sends his own team to do exactly what we're doing? That could get messy."

"Yes, but we won't take any immediate action, just watch. Try to look inconspicuous." She looked at Donna in her denim shorts and bright red T-shirt. "In your case, try and look like you're shopping or something. Did you really have to wear that outfit?"

"Yeah. I like it. Anyway, I figured I'd try and look like a shopper, and if necessary, draw attention away from you and Andy."

"Good idea. Okay, let's go." Virginia headed for her reconnoiter spot as Andy and Donna made for theirs.

At six, Virginia's walkie-talkie buzzed then Andy's voice came on. "I've spotted three men who are trying to look like shoppers, but are watching the area like we are."

Donna's voice came on next. "I've spotted two. You see any action, Virginia?"

"No one around the restaurant that seems out of place. At six-thirty I'll

Dangerous Threads

go inside. Andy, you and Donna keep watch. When A'hsam and his friend arrive you can come in, but sit at another table watching the exits like planned."

"Roger that," they responded.

At six-thirty, Virginia entered Uno Pizza and asked for a table for three. She told the waiter seating her that her friends would arrive about seven. She sat facing the door and sipped some water. At seven, A'hsam entered with another man. He spotted Virginia and walked quickly to her table.

A'hsam stopped and smiled. "Mrs. Virginia Davies-Clark, I'd like to introduce Mr. David Greenbaum from the Israeli Embassy."

Virginia looked at the short man with black hair and glasses in a rumpled suit and loose tie that looked more like an accountant than a spy and smiled. "Nice to meet you, Sir."

Greenbaum gave a slight bow. "So nice to finally meet you, Mrs. Clark. I've heard a lot about you."

"Please sit down, gentlemen." As they sat, she continued. "I think I owe you a debt of thanks for saving us in Texas a few days ago."

"It was my pleasure, and you do not owe me." Greenbaum nodded toward A'hsam, "He does, big time."

"One of your men displayed the Star of David outside his black shirt. I saw it."

"He was supposed to do that to let you know they were on your side." Greenbaum opened the menu on the table before him. "What's good here? Anything kosher?"

"I doubt it, but my husband is fond of the pizza."

"Sound recommendation." Greenbaum smiled. "I'll bless it when it gets here so it's kosher."

"Me too," said A'hsam with a grin.

Virginia frowned. "Bless it?"

"It's a joke we learned from a Catholic priest friend we play squash with." Greenbaum glanced at Donna and Andy. "Should we order three so your husband and the pretty lady sitting with him can join us?"

Virginia frowned. "They're trying to watch our backs while we're here."

A'hsam nodded. "We figured that. But we have it covered. They can join us. No one will disturb us, that I can promise you."

"I'm sure the NSA knows about our little meeting and had notified whoever is behind all this, so I'm expecting the worst."

"I agree, but you probably have limited resources by now; so David and I took precautions on your behalf."

"Okay." Virginia waved Andy and Donna over to her table. The waiter quickly set more places as Greenbaum ordered three pepperoni pizzas. Once seated, Virginia looked at the two men. "Can you tell me what's going on and why my own government is trying to kill us?"

A'hsam nodded. "You have been betrayed, Virginia. Your Dr. Montgomery and the Undersecretary for Research at the DOE, a Dr. Sherman, are planning on getting the wire recording of Einstein's unified field theory, or theory of everything, as your husband so rightly dubbed it, and selling it to a third party for a couple billion dollars in gold."

"A couple billion dollars? How do you know this?"

A'hsam chuckled. "I'm a spy, remember? So is my esteemed friend sitting next to me. We have our ways. Trust me, neither he nor I want this wire recording falling in the wrong hands. That is why we took precautions to find and protect you."

Andy took a sip of water. "Well, we thank you for that. But may I ask why you're not trying to get it from us?"

Greenbaum spoke. "The turmoil in the Middle East is increasing. Neither of us believes our part of the world would be a safe place for something with its potential for use as a weapon. Our problem is we do not know who the third party is in all this. The Golden Crescent is pretty much out of it in the U.S, thanks to you and A'hsam here. But, someone is willing to corrupt some of your high government officials to get their hands on it, and that worries us. What is worse… we have no idea who it is."

Andy ordered a beer. "Can you help us ferret this third party out?" The others ordered beer as well.

"We came tonight to see that you are safe and how we can help you keep the secret safe," Greenbaum added. "Do you have something in mind?"

"Yes. It's Virginia and Donna's idea, so I'll let them tell you about it."

Virginia waited as the waiter came with their drinks and plates for their pizzas. "Here's what we were thinking of. We'll tell them—that is, Dr. Montgomery—that we had second thoughts when another party approached us to buy the wire recordings for a huge sum, I mean a boatload of money. That should panic him and he'll try to get us and the wire recordings, or try and make a deal. Whoever's behind this, at the top, will not be happy so it will mean he needs to try and make a deal with us and then double cross us. That, or we spread the word we have Einstein's unified field theory wire recording and are looking for a buyer. Either way, the rats will come out of the woodwork."

Greenbaum removed his glasses and rubbed his nose. "Not too bad. But there are things that can go wrong."

"Yes, there are. That's why I need your help."

A'hsam leaned back in his chair. "How about you tell your Dr. Montgomery that we or the Israelis are offering you money and a place in our countries in exchange for the unified field theory recordings? That way you have what appears to be a real customer and not some phantom?"

Dangerous Threads

Donna raised her eyebrow. "I like that. But, how would we sting them? If they came to what was to be the sale, they could say they were acting on behalf of the government. They'll paint us as spies or terrorists or charge us with treason. They'll look like good guys."

"Yes, if they knew where the sale was to take place. But you could tell them you'd prefer to bring it to them, but are getting nervous about your safety because someone from your own government is trying to kill you and take it."

"You think they'd fall for something that simple? We've taken them down a few times on our own already and they know it."

"If they were panicking, yes." A'hsam put his napkin on his lap as the pizzas arrived. "After you tell them that, we could insure the information gets leaked that we and the Israelis are interested in the recording and are looking for you to make a deal. So, you don't have to do anything but stay hidden for a while. Then we'll leak that we found you, are setting up a meeting, where it will take place and when, then let them respond. If we do it right, the third party will get the information and he, or they, will not be happy and take action on their own. You and we will not have to do anything until that happens. We will find out the identity of the third party and you can turn him and the actual recordings over to your proper authorities."

"It may work." Virginia tilted her head and gave them her innocent look. "Actual recordings?"

"We both did a background check on each of you." A'hsam nodded toward Greenbaum. "We found that you and Miss Bolette here are extremely dangerous, cunning, and smart as well as pretty. Coupled with the talents of your husband, you are a force to be reckoned with. I think that's the term your Mr. John Wayne said in a movie I saw. You're too smart to travel with the real recordings, so the ones you have with you are either blank or fictitious and the real ones are someplace safe." He took a bite of the pizza. "This is good. I'm glad you heeded your husband's suggestion for pizza tonight." He turned to Greenbaum. "David, have some, this is good."

"So you figured we had a fake recording with us all along?"

A'hsam smiled. "Yes."

Greenbaum ate a slice and reached for another. "We, at the Mossad, will assist in this as well. It is in our mutual interests that we bring this adventure of yours to a satisfactory and safe conclusion." He bit off some more pizza.

A'hsam's cell phone rang. "A'hsam here. Yes, I understand. Remove them from the area and do it cleanly. They are not to be allowed to intercept Miss Virginia and her party. Let one escape well after she and her group have left the area." He hung up as Greenbaum's phone rang.

Greenbaum answered in Hebrew then disconnected. "My people are assisting yours, Haddad." They looked at Virginia, Andy, and Donna, then

A'hsam spoke. "It appears our tails from our embassies reported where we are and a contract wet team has been dispatched to take you all out and retrieve the wire recordings. Looks like the basis for our trap is already working."

Virginia's eyes widened. "You were followed? They're here?"

"Yes. We knew we were going to be followed and prepared for what was to come. That's what we do. Do not worry. A'hsam and I have the place covered," Greenbaum said. "They are being eliminated as we speak, so there is no rush about finishing our marvelous food. One of them will be allowed to go after we've left so he can report back to whoever sent him. The others will recover sometime tomorrow afternoon from the drugs we're giving them and they can report back then with their tails between their legs. I do like these cute sayings you Americans have." He eyed the pizza. "I'll have another slice for the road."

A'hsam took another slice of pizza, too, then sipped his beer. "I shouldn't be drinking this beer or eating this pizza, but I'm sure Allah understands, and it is good. I'll have to start coming here. When you leave, we will cover your exit and not follow you, so your present location will be safe, but how do you want to communicate? Telephones would not be secure and are traceable."

Donna slid a paper across the table. "Here is a secure e-mail address to me. Use the code name Tom Swift for you gentlemen and Nancy Drew for us. Your e-mail account is already set up in Yahoo. Any questions?"

A'hsam looked at David Greenbaum. 'We'll need our grandchildren to set this up for us."

"I'm sure you and I can do it. Okay, we'll put the plan in operation tonight. Virginia, you place the call to Dr. Montgomery's office at 2100 hours from a remote phone, and make it short so your NSA won't track you in time, then go to wherever you're staying and wait for us to contact you."

"Sounds like a plan. If you gentlemen don't mind, we'll be leaving now. Andy, get the check."

Greenbaum held up his hand. "No. Dr. Clark, it is our treat. This was really good and it was a pleasure meeting you all in person. Now, just be careful, the night has eyes."

CHAPTER 35

At exactly nine that night, Virginia called Dr. Montgomery's office from the Tyson's Corner Marriott using an office phone she and Donna charmed a clerk into letting them use. Virginia listened as the phone rang then went to voice mail. "Dr. Montgomery. This is Virginia Davies-Clark. I'm in Washington, D.C. at a secure location and have the wire recording you wanted. With people from my own government trying to kill me and steal the recording, I'm afraid to come in. My husband, my friend, and I are considering our options and have been approached by others, like the Israelis and the Saudis. I'll contact you later."

She hung up and looked at Donna. "Let's go. Andy's waiting in the car for us, hopefully with the engine on. I'm sure the NSA picked up my name from that call, so time is of the essence."

She and Donna hurried out of the building and walked down the street to where Andy was waiting. They slipped into the SUV as he pulled into traffic and disappeared into the night. As they drove, Andy looked over at Virginia. "Are you going to call Dillon and his gang? They might be able to help us as well."

"I don't know." Virginia sat back into her seat and contemplated the idea for the next few miles. "You know, the Israelis and the Saudis do make for strange bedfellows. They have helped us, but in the beginning they were adversaries. I'm wondering if they still are."

"Why are you wondering now?" Donna asked from the back seat. "They took out the team that came to kill us tonight, saved our asses in Texas, and took out those Golden Crescent fellows in Flagstaff. And, we made the call to Dr. Montgomery's office as planned."

"That's just it. They seemed to have turned from foe to friend somewhere along the line. Maybe they are right and being honest about the turmoil in the Middle East making it dangerous for anyone in that area to have it. Then again, maybe it's a front to get it from us. What if our new friends are following us right now? They said they wouldn't, but should we really trust them right now?" She turned to Andy. "Andy, I think you're right so turn around, and let's go to Dillon's neighborhood in the District. I think we may need him and his gang after all."

Andy changed direction and drove toward the District of Columbia. Forty-five minutes later they pulled into the street where the same cab companies, auto repair shop, and a number of vacant lots with broken chain-link fences with broken appliances scattered about as on their previous visit to the neighborhood. Andy pulled to the curb and waited. Within minutes, three black and one Hispanic youth with baggie pants and oversized shirts hanging from their broad shoulders approached the vehicle. Andy slid the window down and Donna put her 9mm on the seat next to her and Virginia held her Walther PPK .380 semiautomatic on her lap. One of the black men walked up to Andy's side and looked into the car, spotting the guns Virginia and Donna held. He stepped back reaching under his shirt then stopped. He moved close again and took another look, then smiled. "Youse the dinosaur cops, right? The ones Dillon talks about."

Andy stared at him for a second then said. "Yes, we're the dinosaur cops and Dillon's friends. We need to contact him right away. We could use your help."

The youth looked at Virginia. "Youse Miss Virginia, right? The lady who took Hermie down."

Virginia nodded. "Yep, that's me. And, just in case anyone is wondering, my friend in the back seat is even worse than me. She'd just as soon blow off some body parts as to shake your hand."

"Thanks a lot," mumbled Donna.

The young man looked at Donna. "Dangerous and beautiful as well. I like that. You married, honey?"

"Yes." She fingered her 9mm as the man watched her.

"I think Miss Virginia might be right." He straightened and turned to the others. "Dems the dinosaur cops Dillon told you about. Call him and tell him they're visiting again and need our help."

Virginia leaned toward the window. "Please don't use my name. The government is listening."

He looked at the other man pulling out his cell phone. "You heard the dinosaur lady. Just tell Dillon the dinosaur cops are back and need to talk to him." The youth nodded and started talking in the phone.

Within minutes, a lowered, red Honda Civic approached and pulled to the curb across from them. Dillon got out of the passenger side dressed in pressed Dockers slacks and a chambray shirt and hurried across the street. "My friends. How can me and my boys be of assistance?"

"It's a long story," Virginia said.

Dillon pointed to the lowered car. "Come to my office and tell me about it. If we can help you, we will."

Virginia climbed out of the car and put her gun in her waistband. "One

Dangerous Threads

thing you can do now is making sure this area is secure. I don't know if we were followed."

Dillon called over one of the black men and gave him orders while he and Virginia walked to the red Civic.

Virginia got into the car as Dillon had the driver get out and stand guard while he got in and started talking to Virginia. Fifteen minutes later they both exited the vehicle and Dillon escorted Virginia back to her car. Virginia got in and turned to Donna. "Set Dillon up with his new code name and e-mail address and give him our Nancy Drew one. He and his gang are going to help us."

"Okay, if you say so." Donna pulled her laptop out and banged away on the keyboard. She scribbled a note on a piece of paper and handed it through the window to Dillon. "Your code name is the Hardy Boys, and our code name is Nancy Drew. These are the e-mail addresses to use. Do not mention any of us by name in any correspondence."

Dillon took the paper and stuffed it into his shirt pocket. "Okay. Got it." He leaned closer. "Are you really more dangerous than Miss Virginia?"

Donna's eyes narrowed. "She's a pussy cat compared to me."

"Right." Dillon gulped air. "No problem. Miss Virginia told me what she wants us to do and we will do it for her and the doctor dinosaur cop. You a dinosaur cop, too?"

Donna thought for a second. "Yes, I'm one, too."

"If you're a dinosaur cop, like them and you're a friend of theirs, then you're okay with me and you will be welcome here like them."

"Thank you, Mr. Dillon."

"I guess you really are like them, shows respect. You can call me Dillon. You are?"

"I'm Donna."

"Nice to meet you, Miss Donna." Dillon turned to Virginia. "I've got the code names and your instructions. You've got my new cell number too, so I guess we're good to go. Have a nice night." He walked to his car and motioned for the youths standing around to follow him. Andy waited. Dillon motioned for them to go. Andy started the engine and drove out of the area and back into the central part of the District and onto I-66 toward Warrenton, Virginia.

As they drove, Donna leaned forward. "You really trust a local hood? He runs a street gang."

"We know." Virginia nodded. "And yes, I trust him. He's helped us before."

"Wow. What did you do to get his cooperation, take down... wait a minute; didn't that one guy back there ask if you were the lady who took down Hermie? Who's Hermie?"

"Yes. I took out three of their biggest guys and Andy disarmed and scared a couple, including Dillon. Hermie was the biggest and meanest of them. I gave him a big dose of bear strength pepper spray and shot fifty-thousand volts into his balls. He and the other two ended up in the hospital. When we were done in the neighborhood, we gave them back their weapons and didn't have them arrested. We told them we worked for the Smithsonian Central Security Service and were federal officers and didn't have a beef with them so we weren't going to arrest them. We treated Dillon, their leader, with respect, which is a big thing to these macho guys."

"I'll be damned. Okay, what did you and Dillon talk about and what's he going to do for us? What do we have to do for him in exchange?"

Virginia twisted around. "Some of his boys are going to be near our hotel while we're there and follow us as a security patrol or body guards, if you will. If our two new friends from Uno's Pizza do anything, they'll find we have some extra surprise firepower. We probably won't see the boys, but they will be there."

"And what do we have to do in exchange?"

"I promised Dillon we would each write letters of commendation for him and a couple of his homeys to get into the local junior college that has rebuffed their applications. They applied after our initial contact with them. Andy and I will also talk to the admissions dean about letting them in. Andy being a full professor should help."

"That's it? They want to go to college? Did they ever finish high school?"

"They've been doing some things for us and they even went to all the Smithsonian museums and want to learn more. They have also been talking to and taking care of an elderly gentleman who's an acquaintance of ours and have learned a lot from him. They may be hoods and have records, but since we met them and treated them with respect and they got a look at what is out there beyond the confines of their present world. They want a shot at an education and a future. I don't know what majors they'll pick or if they'll ever graduate; but if they want a chance, we'll help them get it."

"Okay by me." Donna settled into her seat. "It's getting late, when will we be back at the hotel?"

Andy looked at the dashboard GPS screen. "In about forty-five minutes, if there are no problems."

At eleven fifteen that evening Dr. Montgomery, settled into his desk chair in his home office. Dressed in his pajamas and robe, he called his Pentagon voice mail to retrieve his messages. He heard Virginia's message. *She's still here? What happened to our team that was to take her out and get the unified field theory? How the hell did she manage to take them out, too? Where is she?* He quickly dialed Dr. Frank Sherman's home number.

Dangerous Threads

He waited through three rings when the phone was answered.

"Hello?"

"Frank, Virginia is in Washington, and our special ops team seems to have failed. She met with the Saudis and Israelis."

"What? How? What happened?"

"I don't know exactly. I haven't heard from the team we sent to that pizza place in Gainesville." Montgomery's heart raced. "Virginia called me tonight after their meeting and left a message on my voice mail. She's upset that someone from her government is trying to kill her so she's reluctant to come in. She's exploring her options."

"What the hell does that mean?"

"Frank, she met with the Saudis and Israelis, for God's sake. I think she's looking to sell the unified field theory on her own."

"That's not good. That's treason. Did the NSA get a fix on her location?"

"I haven't heard from them. I'll call the NSA at Fort Meade and see what they have and call you back. Oh, it isn't treason because we aren't at war."

"John, don't split hairs at a time like this. I'll wait for your call."

Ten minutes later, Dr. Montgomery redialed Frank Sherman. "Frank, I talked to my contact at the NSA. They picked up on Virginia's call, but they were only able to trace it to Tyson's Corner. She wasn't at that restaurant when she called me. I seriously doubt she's still in Tyson's Corner. I've also had some people watching the Washington street gang she recruited early on in all this. I just tried to contact them, but I can't reach them. This is getting scary."

"Well, John, you are right about that. I just got word from our customer that he's extremely unhappy. It seems the word in certain circles tonight is that the Saudis and Israelis are negotiating with her and her team. They want to buy the unified field theory from her and provide a safe haven for her in their countries. We have some serious competition, our customer is royally pissed she's still alive, and even more that she's considering selling it to someone else on her own. This could have serious consequences for us."

"What do you want to do? She, her husband, and friend have taken out all the contract professionals we sent to get the recordings. I don't want to risk any more people and take the chance of increased visibility."

"Our customer wants to meet with her tomorrow to negotiate, then kill her, and get the unified field theory recordings. He wants both of us there when he does."

"I don't like this." Montgomery shifted in his chair. "How does he plan on contacting her?"

"He said he has his own resources and if the others could find her, he can, too."

"Frank, she contacted them, not the other way around."

"Shit. I don't know what he's going to do; but we have a serious problem. You should call her cell phone and leave a message that we will come to her at a time and place of her choosing. Tell her we want to wrap this up and we'll protect her from whoever is after her. Say whatever the hell you think will make her feel comfortable, but do it quick. That'll placate our customer a little as well."

"Okay, I'll call her now." He hung up. Montgomery sat staring at the black, fifties-looking push-button phone on his desk. He swallowed, then with sweaty hands picked up the handset, and dialed Virginia's cell number.

When it went to voice mail, he spoke. "Virginia. This is Dr. Montgomery. I received your message tonight and want to talk to you. I'd like to set up a meeting with you tomorrow at a place and time of your choosing so you'll be safe. We can wrap this project up and get the unified field theory recordings secured. You and your team have done an outstanding job, and we have a bonus for you we'd like to discuss. Give me a call as soon as you get this message." He hung up. *For my sake, that had better work.*

Montgomery slowly rose and started to walk around his desk when his phone rang. *She's calling already? That was quick.* He returned to his chair and sat then answered the phone. "Hello?"

"Shepherd? This is Sheepdog. Can you talk?"

The wet team leader is calling now? "Shepherd here and clear, Sheepdog. Report."

"Roger that, Sir. We arrived at the designated location as planned and deployed. Within minutes, we encountered highly trained operatives who spoke Arabic and Hebrew and overwhelmed us. Sir, we were not briefed there would be resistance of that nature. Our pre-mission briefing indicated we would confront two women, a university professor, and possibly some diplomats only. During the brief confrontation, I was drugged, but recovered. The rest of my team has disappeared. The targets have also vanished. Your instructions?"

"Where are you now, Sheepdog?"

"It appears that my present twenty is in an alley next to the Manassas, Virginia train station. How I got here I'm not sure."

"Sheepdog, are you still armed? Are you carrying any ID?"

"Affirmative, Sir."

"Dispose of your weapons and ID, now."

"Copy that, Sir." There was quiet. "Oh, shit, I'm going down. There are a lot of cops approaching with weapons drawn and dogs. I don't like dogs. Someone must have tipped them where to find me. I'll try and—" Suddenly Montgomery heard gunfire. The line went dead.

Montgomery sat, beads of sweat formed on his brow as he tried to slow his racing heart. The phone rang again. With a shaking hand he answered. "Hello?"

"Dr. John Montgomery?" a female voice asked.

"Yes. Who is this?"

"I'm Jane Welch, a nurse at the Washington Hospital Center Trauma Unit."

Shit, now what? Can this get any worse? He cleared his throat. "How can I help you, Ms. Welch?"

"We have six men here. One of them said they work for you."

"Names?"

Nurse Welch recited the men's names.

"Why are they there? What are their conditions?"

"Five are in emergency surgery for severe knife wounds and the sixth man who gave me your name just expired."

"My God." Montgomery swallowed. "Who brought them in?"

"The paramedics and Washington Metro Police. They were found in a vacant lot. Someone called the police and they found them, then called for paramedics. The cops that came in with them said it seems they trespassed on some gang's turf. They interviewed some young men in the neighborhood, but they claim to have no knowledge of the incident. The officers said your men were armed. Not good in the district unless they have permits. The police want to talk to you, so I'm sure you'll be hearing from them tomorrow."

"Those men work for the DOD and are authorized to carry weapons. Please give the officers my name and ask them to contact me directly at my office tomorrow. I'll send someone for the body of the deceased. Please keep me posted on the condition of the other gentlemen."

"Yes, Sir. Thank you." She hung up.

Good God. This can't get worse. He picked up the phone's handset again and called Frank Sherman. "Frank, I just heard what happened to the team I had watching the street gang and our team we sent to take out Virginia."

"Great, John, what happened? Did the men watching the street gang get any intel?"

"No." Montgomery licked his lips. "The wet team is missing and the leader may have been shot by the Manassas police. They ran into operatives they hadn't anticipated that spoke Arabic and Hebrew. Sounds like our adversaries were expecting them. The six men I had watching the street gang had a similar result. They are in the Washington Hospital Center Trauma Unit. One is in their morgue, and the other five are in surgery."

"Is this Virginia woman a trained agent? What about her husband and her friend? Are they trained spies or do they have military special ops training? This is uncanny. She and her party lead a charmed life. They've taken down trained operatives and mercenaries without a scratch. Did they even break a sweat? I'm beginning to question the sanity of a direct meeting with her."

"John, can you talk our customer out of it?"

"Is the Pope Jewish?"

"I figured that. We're going to need some serious back-up."

"The customer said he'd provide all the security we need. He's confident, but I'm getting nervous."

"You told him about what we've done and the miserable results we've had against her with specially trained and armed mercenaries?"

"Yeah, I told him, but he has an über-big ego. You know, John, from what we know about Mrs. Clark, and our customer's ego, the meeting with her could get us all killed."

CHAPTER 36

Virginia, Donna, and Andy sat in a booth at the IHOP east of Warrenton on U.S. 29. Donna checked e-mail on her iPad. "Looks like Nancy Drew got a message from Tom Swift."

Andy looked at his Mickey Mouse watch. "It's eight-thirty. That was fast. What's he say?"

Virginia swallowed her pancakes. "Which Tom Swift?"

Donna checked the message. "Our kosher friend. He said they leaked the word that we had the unified field theory, were upset with our government for trying to kill us, and we are willing to entertain bids to purchase it. He said they also leaked that both Israel and the Saudis have made initial contact and are negotiating. Cute. This'll either bring out the bad guys and we take them down with some help from our new friends, or we're toast."

"I'll check my voice mail. Maybe Montgomery called back." Virginia looked at Andy. "I'll be quick so the NSA won't be able to track it." She turned on her cell phone and called up her voice mail. Montgomery's message was there. She listened, then turned off the phone. "Montgomery wants a meeting. Looks like things are starting to happen fast."

"I think we need to tell Tom Swift about it." Andy took another bite of his waffle. "Anything from the Hardy Boys?"

"Yeah. Just came in. It seems there were some men hanging around Dillon's neighborhood and after some slight persuasion, they said they worked for the DOD. Last seen, the police found them with some very brutal deep cuts, broken bones, and severely damaged internal organs in a vacant field. The cops and paramedics rushed the men to a hospital. Also, no one has been snooping around our hotel or is anywhere near us for now, except his boys." Donna looked at Virginia and Andy. "These are the guys we're going to help get into college?"

"They're protecting our asses as we speak. You bet we are," Andy said, then sipped some coffee. "Donna, tell Tom Swift what's happened and ask if and when we should set up a meeting with Montgomery and company. Oh, yeah, where and when and we'd better tell them about Dillon's men."

Virginia set her empty orange juice glass down. "I think we should leave out the part about Dillon's people for now. Just in case."

"Okay. I'll get this out to Tom Swift, then I get to finish breakfast before my food gets cold." Donna started to type on the iPad screen's keyboard.

David Greenbaum, Mossad chief, stepped from his office in the Israeli Embassy, and walked down the hall to a steel door. A face, eye, and voice recognition security system clicked the door open and he entered. He walked down the sets of metal stairs into a sub-basement and through another three-foot thick steel door with huge locking bolts. The room was dimly lit. The walls were light tan with large monitors covering two of them. Against another wall were six-foot high worker cubicles with pale green monitors providing most of the light. A little to the front of center and facing the banks of wall hung monitors was a long stainless steel table with chairs arranged so the occupants could watch the monitors. Behind them was a long console like the ones used by NASA to launch the manned space missions. Greenbaum walked around the console and sat at the table next to a young woman with dark hair drawn back in a ponytail. "What have you got?"

"Sir, We received a message from Nancy Drew."

Greenbaum nodded.

"They made the call to Dr. Montgomery last night. After her call, our wiretap on his phone picked up a call he made to Frank Sherman of the DOE. They seem nervous, but called Mrs. Clark's cell phone and left a message requesting a meeting. It is to include Sherman and Montgomery, plus their client. But, the client thinks he's going to provide the security and when he gets the wire recording, he's going to kill Mrs. Clark, her husband, her friend, and if I may add a guess, I think Montgomery and Sherman are expendable as well."

"Good guess. Okay, has Virginia responded yet?"

"No. But she got an e-mail from someone called Hardy Boys. Seems a group of men were watching a neighborhood they shouldn't and paid for it. It also said where she is staying is safe and wherever she is now, she's safe there too."

"The Hardy Boys?"

"Yes, Sir. Sir, who are the Hardy Boys?"

"They're fictional characters in a set of young adult books and are amateur detectives. Who these particular Hardy Boys are, I'm not sure. They could be the street gang she's used, but why use them as body guards?"

"We'll keep monitoring, Sir."

"Thanks." He rose and started for the door when she called him back.

Dangerous Threads

"What is it?"

"Sir, We just got an e-mail from Nancy Drew. She wants to know where and when to set up the meeting with, as she puts it, Dr. Montgomery and his traitorous minions. She does have a way with words."

"I'll contact Haddad Abdel A'hsam and get his take. I'll let you know what we plan on doing as soon as I know. In the meantime, keep up the electronic surveillance."

"Yes, Sir."

Greenbaum returned to his office, settled into his desk chair, and called the Saudi embassy on an encrypted phone. "Haddad Abdel A'hsam, please," he told the woman who answered the phone.

In a minute, A'hsam came on the line. "David, what have you heard from Mrs. Clark?"

"I'm guessing the same as you. She has communicated with Montgomery as we told her to do. Our leak that we had been in contact with her for the recording produced the results we hoped for and now they want a meeting with Miss Virginia and company. This so-called customer of Montgomery's thinks he's going to steal the recording and kill all the others. Oh, there is one more ripple in the pond. Virginia has her own set of bodyguards."

"Yes, as Tom Swift, we've picked up pretty much the same stuff." A'hsam coughed. "I think I know who her bodyguards are and frankly, I wouldn't want to antagonize them. I don't know what she and her husband did, but they are well liked by that street gang and they'll do whatever she asks. So, she wants to set up a meeting with Montgomery, his customer and Sherman, and wants to know where and when?"

"Yes, that's what she asked for. Any bright ideas?"

"As a matter of fact, I do. And I think I know where she hid the real recording. If all goes well, we can eliminate her adversaries in her government, and while doing that, we can have operatives get the real recordings, and you and I will be heroes in our own countries."

"A'hsam, You're not planning on killing Virginia and her team, are you?" asked Greenbaum. "I can't let you do that."

"No, no. When we get through, she'll be a hero and we'll be set for life in our respective countries."

"Okay, what are we going to tell her?"

"Tom Swift is going to tell her to arrange a meeting at the Middleburg Baptist Church Graveyard. It's on West Federal Street, just a block south of US Highway 50, the main street of the town. She can get there by taking South Jay Street or South Hamilton Street off of US 50. Set the meeting time for three this afternoon. It'll be harder for Montgomery's client to do anything too drastic in broad daylight and with short notice. That also gives us time to set up what we need and her time to get her bodyguards there as well. David, are you ready on your end?"

"Yes."

"Good."

Greenbaum chuckled. "This time, are you Tom Swift or me?"

"You do it. I need to arrange for a B&E of her museum in Georgetown, Texas and get the real recording of Einstein's uniform field theory. Let me know what she says."

"Sounds like a plan. I'll call you after I hear from her." Greenbaum hung up.

Virginia sat on a chair in her hotel room and read the e-mail from Tom Swift. She looked at Donna and Andy. "I think doing this is in the day time is a great idea, but I think I need to tell Dillon and his gang to back off. If the Saudis and Israelis have people there, I don't want Dillon or his people caught in the crossfire."

Andy rubbed his bald head then pushed his glasses up on his nose. "They could watch our backs on the way there and when we leave. We could also have them scout it out ahead of time and let us know what they think. Personally, I like the idea of them being close this time."

Donna nodded. "I like that idea. I'm getting nervous about us having to defend ourselves on the fly and our arsenal is getting depleted."

"Okay. Then the plan is, we go there after Dillon and company scout it out and we rely on our new international friends to be there to help us, along with our diminished arsenal, when the shit hits the fan."

Andy sat on the edge of the bed. "When you put it that way, it doesn't sound so good. We should have Dillon and his guys around the cemetery to provide back up if necessary and cover our escape."

Virginia nodded. "Okay Donna, send the instructions to Montgomery and to Dillon. I hope this works."

At two-thirty Andy pulled the SUV up outside the graveyard. The stone grave monuments of various sizes and configurations cast shadows in the afternoon sun. He parked on Federal Street under a large tree. Virginia watched the road as Donna scanned the cemetery with binoculars.

"Someone's arrived early. Maybe Montgomery's mysterious customer." Virginia pointed at two black Chevy SUVs with diplomatic license plates approaching and driving into the graveyard and stopping at the gravesite she specified.

A couple minutes later a black Cadillac limo with government plates drove in and stopped behind the SUVs. "Look who just arrived, and early to boot." Virginia scrutinized the surrounding area. "I don't see any suspicious hit men. I don't even see Dillon's people. He said they're here and didn't see anything out of the ordinary."

She and Andy watched as the doors of the SUVs opened and six men got out of each SUV. Then the rear doors of the limo opened and Dr. Sherman and Dr. Montgomery got out. Two other men exited the vehicle from the front. One held a submachine gun close to his side. Sherman and Montgomery walked to the front SUV and shook hands with a tall, dark-haired man in a gray suit, light blue shirt and bright red tie. "That must be their customer," Virginia said. "Donna, anything?"

"Besides the number of goons out there by the cars with guns not too cleverly hidden under their jackets and one with a submachine gun, no. There are some people trimming some trees and some groundskeepers scattered around, but they don't seem to be paying any attention to this group. There's a couple by a grave behind them paying respects. I don't see Dillon's... wait a minute, yes I do. I recognize one of Dillon's boys. He's walking across the street with a girl. I guess they have our backs after all. What college do they want to get into?"

Virginia looked at her watch. "Okay gang, show time. Andy, try backing into the cemetery in case we have to make the great escape."

"That'll be a little obvious, but under the circumstances, I was thinking about doing just that." He started their SUV, made a U-turn and drove a hundred feet to the entrance and backed into the cemetery and stopped in the middle of the road behind the other vehicles. "We'd better check our weapons."

After verifying their weapons were ready, Andy and Virginia got out and walked to the group standing by the lead car. Donna slid across the back seat and exited the car on the opposite side, and while walking around the car, and out of sight for a couple seconds, dropped a couple of the tire-shredding balls. They popped open near the limos rear end. She tossed the remaining three at the SUVs, rolled a shiny metal ball under the lead SUV, then came around and joined Andy and Virginia.

Virginia stepped toward Montgomery. "Since no one is shooting at us I take it we're safe here."

"Yes." Montgomery wet his lips. "We've brought some security people with us, just in case. Do you have the recording?"

"Yeah. Right here." Virginia pulled a small tin box from her backpack and handed it to Montgomery. "I guess that wraps it up." Her other hand pressed the activate button on the small EMP device, with a range of a hundred yards, in her pocket. The idling cars stopped and the communications devices the guards had in their ears gave off a loud pop then stopped working. The men put their hands to their ears and glanced at each other with bewildered looks. Dr. Sherman checked his Blackberry and frowned.

Montgomery looked at the cars and then at the guards and Sherman. He turned to Virginia. 'What just happened?"

"How the hell should I know? We just got here remember?"

"You are a crafty woman, Virginia. What did you do?"

"Get a life. If you use shoddy equipment and hang out with losers, that's not my problem."

"We'll see about that." Montgomery handed the tin to the man with the red tie.

The man opened the box and looked at the thin wires inside. He cleared his throat. With a slight Middle Eastern accent he asked, "This is all of it?"

Virginia took a deep breath. "You were expecting the Encyclopedia Britannica in leather bindings and gold trim?"

He glared at her. "Don't be condescending with me. You are just a woman. You are only good for breeding and having male children. You should know your place."

Virginia snapped. "You figured out I'm a woman all by yourself or did you need help? And, I am not a baby machine, you idiot! I'll be any way I want and just so you know, I think your government and religion in Iran su—"

The man stiffened. "How'd you know I am from Iran?"

"The way you talk, and who else would pay these losers for that recoding? The Saudis and the Israelis won't give them a dime. I should know; I talked to them. And, every other country over there is screwed up, so that leaves Iran. That and your license plates."

The Iranian adjusted his jacket lapel. "You didn't make a deal with the Saudis or Israelis?"

"Obviously not. By the way, how much are you paying Dr. Sherman and Dr. Montgomery to betray their country?"

The man took a deep breath. "Four billion dollars, U.S."

Donna looked past the Iranian, tilted her head, and furrowed her brows, then straightened and stepped forward. "You, an Iranian diplomat are paying these two U.S. Government officials from the DOD and DOE four billion dollars for the recording of the unified field theory that Einstein, a U.S. citizen, hid in the World's Fair quilt that we recovered? That recording belongs to our government. Their selling it makes them traitors."

"That is no concern of mine."

Montgomery smiled. "Yes, but we don't need to be underpaid bureaucrats any longer. Sherman and I can retire someplace as very rich men. Someplace where they don't have extradition."

"I see." Donna nodded. "What do you plan to do with us? Pay us a nice big finder's fee so we'll be quiet and go away?"

The Iranian motioned to his men. Three pulled semiautomatics and aimed them at Virginia, Andy and Donna. "No. I thought this was an apropos meeting place you selected since it represents where you're going."

Montgomery's man with the submachine gun raised his weapon, but two of the Iranian gunman cut him down before he could take aim. Montgomery's face turned ashen. The other gunmen aimed their weapons at Sherman and Montgomery as well. "You two gentlemen are going to retire very early as well, and save my country four billion dollars."

Virginia's eyes widened and a small grin formed on her lips. She nodded to Donna then pulled her taser out and fired the wires into the Iranian's groin and pulled the trigger sending fifty thousand volts into his crotch, then she dove for the ground knocking the tin box from the shaking and falling Iranian's hands. Andy and Donna pulled their guns and dropped to the earth as Donna pressed the red button on the small box in her pocket. The lead, black SUV buckled and jumped off the ground a few feet as it exploded, sending shards of hot metal flying while an orange ball of fire shot into the air. The two Iranian guards holding pistols were blown apart while pieces of the SUV fell on the second SUV and the front of the limo. Shots rang out as bullets peppered the limo and the remains of the two SUVs. Virginia looked up at the three gunmen who fell against what was left of the second black SUV. They left a bloody trail as they slid to the ground.

A voice boomed. "United States Marshals, drop your weapons and put your hands on your heads." The grounds keepers and tree trimmers ran forward with guns drawn, silver stars within circles bouncing on their chests from chains around their necks. The men near Montgomery and Sherman dropped their weapons and raised their hands as directed.

One of the marshals stopped next to Virginia. "Mrs. Clark. You and your SCSS team can get up. Good work."

Virginia, Andy, and Donna rose; watched the deputy marshals handcuff all the men not dead, including Sherman, Montgomery, and the Iranian in the red tie and read them their rights. Virginia looked at the lead deputy marshal. "Nice timing, but I didn't contact you. How'd you know we'd be here?"

"We got a message from you, or someone purporting to be you, and the Smithsonian Central Security Service and got here about an hour before you did. Oh, we also told some armed young men who claimed they were your private security force it might be better if they stayed over on US 50 in town and didn't come near here for a while. They're waiting for you at the Red Fox Inn. I'm sure the owner isn't real happy having them there, but they're having an early dinner on Uncle Sam. They didn't want to go, made me promise to take real good care of you and your team, or else. I think they really meant it."

"You didn't arrest them?"

"No. For one thing, as a federal marshal, their having firearms isn't my concern at this time. Second, they're guarding someone we want to keep safe. They're really loyal to you. I think they'd make great marshal material."

Virginia chuckled. "Most of them have criminal records."

"They said you and your husband were going to try and help them get into college. If they take the right classes, stay out of trouble, and their convictions weren't for crimes that are too serious, we might be able to pull some strings."

"That would be great. But I'm not sure being cops was number one on their list of potential career paths, though."

"You never can tell. Nice job killing the electronic equipment around you, and shocking and knocking that box from the big guy's hand. That was both an interesting and a dangerous way to do it though. Do you always do things with such a bang?"

"Pretty much. When the Iranian said they were going to kill us, we had to take action. I saw you guys watching, then start heading in our direction and didn't want him to pocket it. I didn't like him anyway. I was hoping you were here to help us, but wasn't sure who you were, so we kind of took things into our own hands… just in case."

"Well, good job. A bit messy, but quite effective." The marshal turned to Donna. "Thanks for helping us by asking those questions. We've got their confessions on record, I guess you spotted our man with the parabolic antenna and recorder at the listening post in that tree over there."

"Yes. I wasn't sure what was going on at first, then I saw that you all were no longer acting as groundskeepers and tree trimmers, so I thought you might be the cops or FBI or something, and you were on our side, but things escalated real fast. I was hoping that listening device was over a hundred yards away and out of range of our EMP device. Looks like we were right. May I ask a question?"

"Sure."

"Why are federal marshals here instead of the FBI?"

"The call for help came directly to the U.S. Marshal's office and then the SCSS called us. A few minutes later we received orders from… shall we say… very high up to take action. The U.S. Marshal Service is the only federal law enforcement agency that can enforce all federal laws. The others have specific areas they are authorized to work by acts of congress. Operating under orders, we mobilized and you know the rest."

"Oh. I didn't know you were the only federal cops who can enforce all federal laws." Donna and the marshal turned toward a commotion nearby.

The Iranian, with the taser wires still sticking in him and cuts on his head and in his coat, struggled with two marshals handcuffing him before turning and yelling, "Do you know who I am? I'm the Cultural Attaché for the Iranian Embassy. I have diplomatic immunity. You can't touch or arrest me or search my vehicle. It is an official embassy car." He glared at Virginia. "That woman attacked me. I insist that she be arrested immediately. Get these wires off of me. Someone needs to find out what happened to my vehicles!"

As a deputy marshal picked up the tin box, the Iranian yelled. "That is mine and the property of my government and embassy. You have no right to seize or search it. I demand you return it to me right now!"

"The wires are attached to you so we can't touch them, diplomatic immunity, remember?" The deputy stepped close to him and with his nose inches from the Iranian's, he said. "In case you didn't notice, the box was in the open, on the ground, in a Virginia cemetery in the United States. I don't need a search warrant and it was not in your possession, so it does not have any diplomatic protection, got it? As for the lady, I didn't see her attack you, and I'm sure none of the other marshals did, either. Anyway, assault is a state crime and we're federal, so we aren't interested. Can't you macho rag heads protect yourselves from a woman? "

He watched the Iranian turn red, then he looked at the wires hanging from the Iranian's clothes and chuckled. "In the meantime, consider yourself a guest of the United States Government until we sort things out. Oh, by the way, we'll be more than happy to tow what's left of your vehicles now that they seem to be..." The deputy turned and looked at the smoldering wreckages then back at the Iranian, "...disabled. If anything happens to be found on the ground around here, or anything falls out while we're towing what's left of them... well, it doesn't have diplomatic immunity either."

Virginia watched as two U.S. Marshals prisoner transport vans approached with their emergency lights flashing. A few seconds later, three Middleburg Police cruisers, fire engines, and a paramedic van, with lights flashing and sirens blaring, came screeching to a stop just outside the graveyard. The police officers ran into the graveyard. The fire engine and paramedics slowly inched toward the group. "Looks like someone should have told the local cops what was going on ahead of time."

"Couldn't. You know, national security and all. Plus, there wasn't a lot of time to waste trying to get them up to speed." The lead deputy US Marshal watched them approach then shook his head and sighed. "I'd better put on my diplomat hat and smooth some feathers. Can you come into our office tomorrow in Washington to make a declaration and sign some papers?"

"We can write up our report tonight at the hotel." Virginia wrinkled her nose. "Can you meet us at the Smithsonian American History Museum quilt exhibit at noon tomorrow? I need to give the Smithsonian Central Security Service a copy as well.'

The deputy leaned close and glanced at Donna. "Is your friend there married?"

"Yes."

"Too bad." He straightened up. "Yeah, considering the circumstances, I can meet at the museum. Any special reason?'

"Yeah. I want to look at a quilt."

"A quilt?" He gave her a bewildered look, then shrugged. "Okay. Noon at the museum. I'll be there."

"Oh, you might want to remove the tire shredders we put behind the cars."

The marshal looked at the car, then back at Virginia. "Shredders?"

"Yeah, Donna put the shredders there in case we needed quick escape and wanted to retard our pursuers."

"Right... I'll tell my men." He walked toward the advancing police officers, mumbling.

As they walked back to their car Andy adjusted his burnt orange University of Texas baseball cap then turned to Virginia. "We didn't contact the Marshal's Service or the Smithsonian. Who did?"

"Probably Mr. Greenbaum or Mr. A'hsam. They were the only ones who knew of this meeting besides Dillon, and I seriously doubt he'd call the police. I'm guessing one or both of them. The thing is, our Middle Eastern friends are in for a big surprise as well."

Virginia's cell phone rang as they turned south off of US 50, the Mosby Parkway, onto US 15. "Hello?"

"Virginia!" Her boss, Dr. Doverspike's voice sounded frantic. "We were robbed! Virginia, the box you shipped to the museum for safekeeping was stolen. I have the police investigating, but they haven't come up with anything. I'm so sorry."

"It's okay. I thought someone might do just that. There wasn't anything of real value in it anyway. Tell the cops to stand down. It isn't important now and they'll never catch who did it." She could hear his heavy breathing and him trying to calm down. "Dr. Doverspike. I'll tell you all about it when I get back. I bet they didn't touch anything else."

"You know who did it? Who? We need to tell the police." Doverspike's voice was still frantic but with less edge. "No, they didn't touch anything else. The police commented on that. There were no finger prints or tool marks or anything they could find."

"Relax and call off the boys in blue. Tell that cute police captain friend of yours the burglars won't be returning to Georgetown, and if I told them who did it, they couldn't arrest them anyway. I'll tell you all about it when I get home. I'll be back in a few days."

"Okay, I guess. I was so worried about it and all."

"Not to worry. Now relax, it's okay."

"If you say so. Have a safe trip home and you must tell me about your adventures when you get here." He hung up.

Andy looked at her with a shocked expression then spoke. "What do you mean there was nothing of importance in that box? That was the original Einstein recording of the Uniform Field Theory and someone stole it? Probably the Saudis and or the Israelis. We need to get it back."

Virginia smiled. "Like I said earlier, it probably was the Saudis, and or the Israelis who notified the US Marshals about the meeting today. But, I figured the recordings wouldn't be safe with us or at my museum. Someone would eventually think to look there, and sure enough, I think our two foreign government friends tried to capitalize on it. So, while you guys were making up the fake box with the blank wire on it we had here and I was getting the World's Fair Quilt ready to ship by UPS to the Smithsonian, I put the real wires back into it. The wires in that box they stole have nothing on them. They were left over from the ones we put in the little tin box I gave to Montgomery."

Andy scowled. 'Why didn't you tell us?"

Donna pouted. "Yeah, why? We're on the same team."

"The fewer people who knew the better. I didn't want you guys to know in case there were problems and you were captured. You couldn't give something away you didn't know."

Donna gave her a half smile. "I guess you're right, but still…"

"Help me write the report tonight for the marshals and the Smithsonian?"

"Okay. After dinner, though."

"I agree," Andy said.

Virginia shook her head. "You two and food. Okay, after dinner."

Donna shrugged. "One needs to keep priorities straight. By the way, do you have anything else on your mind you'd like to share with us?"

"Yeah. In the paper this morning there was an article about the quilt. It said the 1933 Sears Contest winning quilt, *The Unknown Star,* which was displayed at the 1933 Chicago World's Fair and was given to Mrs. Roosevelt, disappeared for almost seventy years. The article said the quilt was located by the Smithsonian recently and is going on exhibit today. So tomorrow we're going to see the quilt and the secret it contains."

Donna poked Virginia from the back seat. "Does anyone, except us, know the secret wire recordings are in the quilt?"

"No. They were pretty well corroded anyway, but they're safe at the Smithsonian, especially since no one knows they're there. We can finally go home, after we do all the paperwork, of course."

At noon the next day, Virginia stood in front of the display case holding the 1933 World's Fair quilt, *The Unknown Star.*

Andy and Donna stood behind her. Andy stepped forward to look at the card next to the quilt. "The history of this quilt is really an interesting story and here it is." Andy read the placard next to the quilt. "This gives some of the history of *The Unknown Star,* and gives credit to you for finding it and giving it to the museum. Not too bad, Virginia, you've got your name on a display at the Smithsonian."

The deputy marshal walked up and stood next to Virginia studying the quilt. "This is the mystery quilt I heard about?'

"Yep. *The Unknown Star.*"

"You really found it after almost seventy years when no one else could?"

Virginia nodded. "Yep."

"You got your report?"

"Yep." Virginia handed the folder with the details of all their investigation in it. "You'd better classify that TOP Secret."

The marshal frowned. "Because it has to do with this quilt and the uniform field theory tapes I heard about?"

"Yep." Virginia looked at the marshal. "What's going to happen to Sherman and Montgomery?"

"That's up to the Attorney General, but I think it's safe to say they won't be getting their government pay or pensions and will be spending the rest of their lives at a large government installation with high walls, bars, guards, and fences."

"The Iranian?"

"His ambassador stripped him of diplomatic immunity last night, and he's presently in jail facing serious federal and state charges as well. Who knows, maybe he'll get to room with the other two. He acted without the proper authority of their government and it's caused an international incident the Iranians would like to see go away. It seems he had a backdoor deal with North Korea for copies of the recordings his government didn't know about, until now. They tossed him to the wolves." The marshal glanced at her. "I hear you make quilts."

"Yes."

"What, no yep?"

"No. I was just having a little fun. I've been making quilts for a number of years now."

"My mother made them. Had a whole room set up to do them in. Quilting's quite an art." He handed her a sealed, manila envelope, with her name on the front. "This is for you. Have a nice time in Washington." He turned and walked away.

Andy stepped close. "What'd he give you?"

"I don't know." Virginia tore open the top of the envelope, pulled out a linen paper with the president's letterhead on it and read at it. "It's from The President of the United States. It's a thank you and official commendation from him and Congress." She looked inside the envelope again and pulled out two documents. "Here they are, one for each of us," she said handing them to Donna and Andy.

"Now," she took Andy's arm, "let's go home. I have quilts to make."

AUTHOR'S NOTES

At the 1933 Century of Progress in Chicago, Sears Roebuck and Co. sponsored a quilt contest. The Grand Prize was to be one thousand dollars. The quilt that won the prize was a pieced one called The Unknown Star by the maker, Margaret Rogers Caden of Kentucky. The quilt, itself, was presented to the wife of the then-President, Mrs. Franklin D. Roosevelt. During President Roosevelt's tenure in office, the quilt disappeared and has not been seen since.

Sears Roebuck and Co. in 1934 issued a quilt pattern booklet of the prize-winning quilts in the contest. The booklet was "Century of Progress in Quilt Making." The prize-winning quilt was offered in both kit form and perforated pattern form. It was re-named "Feathered Star" in this publication.

The prize-winning quilt received reams of publicity during this time. Pictures and articles about it appeared in many newspapers and periodicals throughout the country. Other pattern sources featured it, too. Capper's showed it in May 1934, and called it "Quilt of the Century." A book "Quilting" by Alice Beyer, published in Chicago, displayed this quilt also.

In the late 1940s, Mountain Mist again issued this same quilt pattern. It was called "Star of the Bluegrass," perhaps in reference to Margaret Rogers Caden's home state of Kentucky.

Here we have in very vivid form a prime example of the name changes for a quilt pattern. From "The Unknown Star" to "Feathered Star" to "Quilt of the Century" to "Star of the Bluegrass," with perhaps a few other names in between. This pattern has acquired lasting fame, as this quilt as "Star of the Bluegrass" continued on in its prize-winning ways. In 1952, it again won a Grand Prize of one thousand dollars for the five women of the Middlebury Grange #139, New Haven, Conn., who made it for a National Quilt Contest. This quilt, too, was presented to the wife of the then President, Mrs. Harry S. Truman. This, then is the saga of one quilt pattern.

Sources:
Unknown Star—"Quilting:—Alice Beyer, 1934
Feathered Star—Sears; Century of Progress of Quilt Making, 1934
Quilt of the Century—Cappers May 1934
Quilt of the Century—Kate's Blue Ribbon Quilt, 1971 (Cappers reprint).
Star of the Bluegrass—#100 Mountain Mist Star of the Bluegrass—

Dangerous Threads

McCall's Needlework Spring & Summer 1953

Other references are *Patchwork Souvenirs of the 1933 World's Fair, The Sears National Quilt Contest, and Chicago's Century of Progress Exposition* By Merikay Waldvogel and Barbara Brackman Rutledge Hill Press, Nashville, 1993 Softcover, 123 pages.

The story also involves the uniform or unified field theory. The uniform field theory is a type of field theory that allows all that is usually thought of as fundamental forces and elementary particles to be written in terms of a single field. At this time, there is no accepted uniform field theory, and thus remains an open line of research. Dr. Einstein coined the term uniform field theory. He attempted to unify the general theory of relativity with electromagnetism, hoping to recover an approximation for quantum theory. A "theory of everything" is closely related to unified field theory, and sometimes used to mean the same thing, but differs by not requiring the basis of nature to be fields, and also attempts to explain all physical constants of nature.

The Smithsonian Central Security Service is a figment of the author's imagination and does not really exist.

The weapons and gadgets Virginia, Andy and Donna used in the story are real.

There are over sixteen intelligence agencies in the U.S. Government. The National Security Agency or NSA at Ft. Mead, MD is one. Most of what they do and how they do it is highly classified. The NSA's ability to listen in on phone calls on land lines in real life is classified and to really do so against US citizens involves obtaining a court order. But, they do have the capability of listening to cell and satellite phones. They use key words, names and phrases to trigger the computers to listen in. They can also trace the location of a cell phone.

The U.S. Marshal Service is the only federal law enforcement agency that is authorized by act of congress to enforce all federal laws. The other federal law enforcement agencies have specific laws and areas they are authorized to enforce by federal statute. The marshals work with both the judicial and executive branches of the federal government.

The white granite and classic lines of Union Station mentioned in the book actually did set the mode for Washington's classic monumental architecture for the next forty years through the construction of the Lincoln and Jefferson Memorials, the Federal Triangle, the Supreme Court Building and the National Gallery of Art.

The Red Fox Inn, established in 1728, and used in the book is located in Middleburg, Virginia. The inn is steeped in the lore of both the Revolutionary and the Civil Wars. During the Civil War it was used as a Confederate headquarters and hospital. It is still used as an inn and restaurant. Other locations in historic Middleburg used in this novel are real.

Jack Warner, of Warner Brothers Pictures in Hollywood, was made a Lt. Colonel in the U.S. Army by President Roosevelt for making army training films, military movies and propaganda films for the theaters during World War Two.

Clarkson College of Engineering in Potsdam, NY is now Clarkson University.

Post-it is a registered trademark of 3M Company

Sears Roebuck and Company is a registered trademark of the TALX Corporation

ABOUT THE AUTHOR

Dr. David Ciambrone is a retired aerospace and defense company executive, scientist, professor of engineering, and a business and environmental consultant and is now a best-selling, award-winning author living in Georgetown, Texas with his wife Kathy. He has published twenty-five (25) books: four (4) non-fiction, two (2) textbooks for a California university, and nineteen (19) mysteries and has two (2) new mysteries in work. He is the author of the Virginia Davies Quilt Mysteries.

Dave has been a speaker at writer's groups, schools, colleges, libraries, quilt guilds, writer's conferences, and business/scientific conferences internationally.

Dr. Ciambrone also wrote three newspaper columns and wrote a column for a business journal.

Dave is a member of Sisters in Crime, the San Gabriel Writer's League, the Writer's League of Texas, Mystery Writers of America, the International Thriller Writers Association, The Beacon Society, and DFW Sherlock Homes Society.

Dave was appointed a U.S. Treasury Commissioner and to the management board of the Resolution Trust Corporation (RTC) by President Clinton.

He is a Fellow of the International Oceanographic Foundation.

Visit David at

Author's Website:davidciambrone.com

Facebook:facebook.com/david.ciambrone?fref=ts

Twitter: twitter.com/mysterywriter5

LinkedIn: linkedin.com/pub/david-ciambrone-sc-d-fiof/11/ab5/bb3

Amazon: amazon.com/author/davidciambrone

Progressive Rising Phoenix Press is an independent publisher. We offer wholesale pricing and multiple binding options with no minimum purchases for schools, libraries, book clubs, and retail vendors. We offer substantial discounts on bulk orders and discounts on individual sales through our online store. Please visit our website at:
www.ProgressiveRisingPhoenix.com

If you enjoyed reading this book, please review it on Amazon, B & N, or Goodreads.
Thank you in advance!

Printed in the USA
CPSIA information can be obtained
at www.ICGtesting.com
JSHW011202160124
55278JS00013B/115